CRISTINA GARCÍA

Bordering Fires

Cristina García was born in Havana and grew up in New York City. Her first novel, *Dreaming in Cuban*, was nominated for a National Book Award and has been widely translated. Ms. García has been a Guggenheim Fellow, a Hodder Fellow at Princeton University, and the recipient of a Whiting Writers' Award. She lives in Napa with her daughter and husband.

ALSO BY CRISTINA GARCÍA

Dreaming in Cuban (1992)
The Agüero Sisters (1997)
Monkey Hunting (2003)
¡Cubanísimo! (2003)
A Handbook to Luck (2007)

Bordering Fires

Bordering Fires

THE VINTAGE BOOK OF CONTEMPORARY
MEXICAN AND CHICANO/A LITERATURE

Edited and with an introduction by
CRISTINA GARCÍA

VINTAGE BOOKS

A Division of Random House, Inc.

New York

A VINTAGE BOOKS ORIGINAL, OCTOBER 2006

Copyright © 2006 by Cristina García

All rights reserved. Published in the United States by Vintage Books, a division of
Random House, Inc., New York, and in Canada by Random House of Canada
Limited, Toronto.

Vintage and colophon are registered trademarks of Random House, Inc.

The permissions acknowledgments beginning on page 267
constitute an extension of this copyright page.

Library of Congress Cataloging-in-Publication Data
Bordering fires : the vintage book of contemporary Mexican and Chicano/a
literature /edited and with an introduction by Cristina García.
p.   cm.
I. Mexican literature—20th century—Translations into English.   2. American
literature—Mexican American authors.   3. American literature—20th century.
I. Title.   II. García, Cristina, 1958–
PQ7237.E5 B67 2006
860.8'09720904 22
2006044721

Vintage ISBN-10: 1-4000-7718-4
Vintage ISBN-13: 978-1-4000-7718-2

Book design by Debbie Glasserman

www.vintagebooks.com

Printed in the United States of America
10 9 8 7 6 5 4 3 2 1

For my parents, with love

A big, heartfelt *gracias* to Rafael Pérez-Torres,
Francisco Goldman, Javier Durán, and Thomas Colchie
for their generosity and expertise.

CONTENTS

❊ NEW DEPARTURES

INTRODUCTION

"The history of Mexico is the history of a man seeking his parentage, his origins . . ."
—Octavio Paz

The border that separates Mexico from the United States is more than a geographic divide. It is a charged wire that attracts and repels, an invitation, a threat, a political imposition, a lively ongoing dialogue, a series of perforations. At the border, languages and cultures collide, mingle, explode, redefine themselves. New lexicons are continually born there, identities negotiated, alternate realities built. There is no shortage of misery either, or exploitation, or trip wires of misunderstanding. Yet the border remains, as always, a fertile place for dreaming.

There isn't just one border but many borders on both sides of the Rio Grande. To be Mexican, Mexican-American, or Chicano/a is to be part of grandly diverse and complex communities with multiple allegiances and multiply hyphenated identities. In small towns across the American South and Midwest, for example, growing Mexican neighborhoods are changing the face and rhythms of life in formerly dying communities. The daughters and sons of these immigrants are playing on Little League teams, going bowling, celebrating their *quinceañeras.* Everywhere, in places you might least expect it, the U.S. is acquiring a Spanish accent. And in Mexico, it is rare to find a family without relatives *en el otro lado,* on the other side, whose stories of success and hardships—and whose periodic returns for Christmas and fiestas—fuel their own imaginations and aspirations. It is, most definitely, a two-way cultural migration.

There is no such thing anymore, if there ever was, as a purely Mexican or Chicano/a identity. There are historical commonalities, of course—the ancient cultures of Mesoamerica, the fact of the Conquest, Catholicism, colonialism, the Spanish language, and a host of indigenous ones—but these are the foundations upon which numerous, divergent cultures have survived and flourished. What does a third-generation Chicano artist in Chicago have in common with a newly arrived immigrant to South Central Los Angeles? What do the rituals and language of Tex-Mex culture have to do with the upper-class concerns of Mexico City professionals? What do these different people call themselves, and with whom are they aligned?

For some time, Mexican and Chicano/a writers on all sides of these multifaceted borders have been chronicling their changing, often fractured realities in a literature that is as rich and varied as any in contemporary world letters. There is much cross-pollination, and hybridization. Politics and art go hand in hand with the search for identity, and there is strong resistance in the cultural community to anything or anyone that would reduce the richness of this experience. As activist and performance artist Guillermo Gómez-Peña has written, "The mirrors are always breaking." Chicano/a writers have traditionally looked back to Mexico for their "roots" but, often as not, have found themselves further alienated in their own supposed homeland. Mexican writers, on the other hand, look to their counterparts in *el norte* with a mixture of suspicion, longing, and fear.

They might try to disavow their Chicano/a peers as not "real" Mexicans, yet it is impossible for them to dismiss the power and distinction of their work.

The aim of *Bordering Fires* is simple: to showcase the preoccupations and sensibilities of a wide range of contemporary Mexican and Chicano/a writers all under one roof. It has been a challenging task, given the enormous body of work to consider. By no means an exhaustive collection, this anthology purports to be an introduction to—at best, a rich sampler of—these complex literary traditions. I think of each piece here as a classic in its own right; classic in that it captures something essential about its culture but also classic in its beauty and quality of expression.

Poetry, fiction, and essays are the focus of the collection, but there are a number of superb theater and performance pieces, *corridos*, and other literary and oral forms that would have quadrupled the volume in hand. The work of the youngest generation of Mexican and Chicano/a writers—a very dynamic and productive group—also remains largely uncollected. You may be wondering at this point (if you haven't already), what a Cuban-American writer like me is doing editing this anthology in the first place. All I can say is that I came to these works out of deep passion and respect. In the process, I crossed a few borders of my own. My hope is that in some small way, this anthology will contribute to spreading the word on an extraordinary literature.

The book is organized in keeping with the idea of pliant borders, of moving back and forth across them yet respecting separate traditions, the Mexican one with deep roots in its precolonial and colonial history, side by side with the newer Chicano/a tradition, flourishing for the past fifty years. It was important for me that the pieces, gathered in five intuitive groups, worked individually as well as in relation to the other selections in the book. The prelude, an excerpt from Samuel Ramos's essay "The Use of Thought," begins the collection because he was the first contemporary Mexican writer to seriously reflect on the issue of identity. Highly influential and controversial, Ramos's work, though uneven, made it possible for later writers such as Octavio Paz to explore the subject more profoundly.

EARLY INFLUENCES

This first group represents the work of masters who, each in their own way, left an unmistakable imprint on Mexican literature. While their legacy to subsequent generations of Mexican writers is palpable, their influence has often extended beyond their own borders to most of the Spanish-speaking world. Octavio Paz, in a 1975 interview, spoke of the poet, essayist, critic, and prose writer Alfonso Reyes—who famously cast off the baroque imagery of his predecessors and peers—as "achieving transparency in Spanish at certain times." He went on to recall the Argentine novelist Adolfo Bioy Casares saying that "when he and Borges wanted to know if a paragraph was well written, they would say 'Let's read it in the tone in which Alfonso Reyes would read it.'"

In his story "Major Aranda's Hand," Alfonso Reyes shows himself to be a practitioner of magical realism a decade before it became the hallmark of the Latin American literary boom of the 1960s. The severed right hand of a military man (he lost it in battle, still gripping a sword) goes from a quiet fate in a quilted jewel case to slowly developing a life of its own. "It went freely from one place to another, a monstrous little lap dog, rather crablike. Later it learned to run, with a hop very similar to that of hares, and, sitting back on the fingers, it began to jump in a prodigious manner. One day it was seen spread out on a current of air: it had acquired the ability to fly." Profoundly irreverent, Reyes's story slyly explores the possibilities and costs of subversion.

This anthology might also have begun with the work of Ramón López Velarde, who is considered to be Mexico's first modern poet. Before him, many Mexican poets had borrowed heavily from other cultural traditions. In the wake of the Mexican Revolution (1910–20), which violently threw off the country's longstanding feudal system, López Velarde felt freed to fully employ the imagery of Mexican reality to create highly original, personal poems. "I long to eject every syllable that is not born of the combustion of my bones," López Velarde wrote. Out of everyday and seemingly mundane details, he managed, again and again, to construct startlingly luminous phrases.

> *My godmother invited my cousin*
> *Agueda to spend the day*
> *with us, and my cousin*
> *came with a conflicting*
> *prestige of starch and fearful*
> *ceremonious weeds.*

When it was first published in 1955, the novel *Pedro Páramo* was immediately hailed as a masterpiece and its author, Juan Rulfo, already in his forties and the author of a single collection of short stories, became a celebrity in the Spanish-language literary world. Rulfo never completed another novel, but *Pedro Páramo* remains, in the estimation of many critics, one of the greatest books of the twentieth century. Gabriel García Márquez claimed to have learned the novel by heart after reading it countless times, and credited it, along with Kafka's *Metamorphosis*, with influencing him most when he first began writing. Oscillating mysteriously between the past and the present, *Pedro*

Páramo chronicles the history of the fictitious village of Comala. Rulfo once described the structure of the novel as "made of silences, of hanging threads, of cut scenes, where everything occurs in a simultaneous time which is no-time."

Poet and dramatist Xavier Villaurrutia is best known for only a handful of poems. But these poems, the finest of which were collected in *Nostalgia for Death,* have haunted and fascinated generations of Mexican poets in their wake. As Octavio Paz has written, "These twenty-odd poems count among the best in our language and of his time." Openly homosexual at a time when few writers in Latin America dared to be, Villaurrutia investigates in his work a rich duality of desire and death. In "L.A. Nocturne: The Angels," he writes:

> *If at a given moment, everyone would say*
> *with one word what he is thinking,*
> *the six letters of DESIRE would form an enormous luminous scar,*
> *a constellation more ancient, more dazzling than any other.*

CHICANO/A VOICES I

Gloria Anzaldúa's groundbreaking essay, "How to Tame a Wild Tongue," opens this section of the anthology. Anzaldúa powerfully confronts the machismo of her culture and argues for the legitimization of Chicano Spanish. This language, she wrote, grew naturally out of the Chicanos' need to have a linguistic space of their own. "A language which they can connect their identity to, one capable of communicating the realities and values true to themselves—a language with terms that are neither *español ni inglés,* but both."

In contrast, the essayist and journalist Richard Rodriguez has inspired much controversy in the Chicano/a community for his stand against bilingual education as well as his intricate examinations of cultural identity. The intensity and lyricism of his prose and the persuasiveness of his arguments, whose twists and turns astonish readers with their unexpected illuminations, make him one of America's keenest observers of the frequently misapplied and misunderstood term "multiculturalism." In "India," the piece included here, Rodriguez probes the multifarious implications of what it means to be Indian.

The poet Jimmy Santiago Baca suffered terrible privation in his early life and survived to become a passionate witness to what fellow poet Gary Soto deemed "a culture of poverty." In his two connected epic poems, *Martín & Meditations on the South Valley*, Santiago Baca has given us a story of mythic proportions, steeped in details of the Chicano Southwest, with all the brutality and tenderness of love itself.

> *Eddie blew his head off*
> *playing chicken*
> *with his brother. Para proof*
> *he was a man,*
> *he blew his head off.*

Rudolfo Anaya has been called the godfather of Chicano literature, and with good reason. Over many prolific years, Anaya has produced several novels, including the classic, *Bless Me, Ultima*, as well as plays, short stories, essays, and poems. His territory is largely New Mexico, and he exquisitely captures the spirit of place—as well as the dilemmas of living between cultures. "We are a border people," Anaya has said, "half in love with Mexico and half suspicious, half in love with the United States and half wondering if we belong." In the short story "B. Traven Is Alive and Well in Cuernavaca," Anaya playfully describes one writer's return to Mexico, and the confusion and adventures that ensue.

CONTEMPORARY MEXICAN VOICES

The third section of this anthology features Mexican writers who, while deeply influenced by their predecessors, took on the modern world and Mexico's place in it. Writers such as Octavio Paz and Carlos Fuentes became key figures in Latin American literary circles, and their works played a role in reshaping the canon of contemporary world literature. The other two writers included here, Elena Poniatowska and Rosario Castellanos, are considered pillars of Mexican literature—and feminism—who have written brilliantly about the dispossessed, among other subjects.

The Death of Artemio Cruz, first published in 1962, put the young writer Carlos Fuentes at the forefront of Mexican literature. The novel captures, with a virtuoso style, the history of modern Mexico as seen through the life of one man. Fuentes begins the story on the deathbed of his protagonist, amid the jumble of his perceptions and disoriented thoughts: "I don't want to talk. My mouth is stuffed with old pennies, with that taste. But I open my eyes a little more, and between my eyelashes I can make out the two women, the doctor who smells of aseptic things: his sweaty hands, stinking of alcohol, are now tapping my chest under my shirt. I try to push that hand away."

Although born in Paris, Elena Poniatowska has been very much a part of Mexican literary debates on politics, identity, and place. She is probably best known for *Massacre in Mexico*, an extraordinary account of the 1968 killing of students in Mexico City by the national army. Poniatowska artfully mixes fact and fiction, in the style of Tom Wolfe's New Journalism, into powerful, memorable narratives. She is represented by an excerpt from *Here's to You, Jesusa!*, the hardscrabble story of one Mexican peasant woman.

What can be said about the late poet and essayist Octavio

Paz that might do his immense talents justice? He is considered by many to be Mexico's foremost man of letters. His seminal work, *The Labyrinth of Solitude*, published in 1950, is a profound analysis of Mexican culture and the Mexican psyche. It is still widely read and quoted to this day. In "The Day of the Dead," Paz studies his countrymen's entrancement by and cohabitation with death. "If we do not die as we lived, it is because the life we lived was not really ours: it did not belong to us, just as the bad death that kills us does not belong to us. Tell me how you die and I will tell you who you are."

Paz's many volumes of poetry and critical works, formally brilliant and often experimental, have tackled an enormous array of subjects and won him the Nobel Prize in 1990. But it is to poetry that he returned again and again for the greatest clarity of vision. "Poetry makes things more transparent and clearer and teaches us to respect men and nature," he once said. In "I Speak of the City," Paz attempts to make sense of the simultaneity of urban experiences that is Mexico City.

> the city that dreams us all, that all of us build and unbuild and rebuild as we dream,
> the city we all dream, that restlessly changes while we dream it,

Rosario Castellanos grew up in the southern Mexican state of Chiapas, the only daughter of an aristocratic landholding family. As a child, she witnessed firsthand the lives of the poor Mayans who were her parents' servants and slaves. Her life and her literary preoccupations (she wrote novels, essays, poems, and plays) have largely revolved around these early, traumatic experiences. Her feminist inquiries into Mexican culture challenged the status quo and were the first such texts published in Mexico. "It is thanks to her that those of us who now attempt to do so are able to write," Poniatowska said. In her remarkable novel *The*

Book of Lamentations, Castellanos took as inspiration a nineteenth-century Mayan rebellion that culminated with the crucifixion of a child and transposed it to 1930s Mexico.

CHICANO/A VOICES 2

The next group of voices from the Chicano/a tradition begins with the work of Ana Castillo—poet, novelist, short story writer, essayist, activist, and feminist. In her many books and especially in her collection of essays, *Massacre of the Dreamers*, Castillo questions and deconstructs rigid notions of what it means to be female, intelligent, sexual, and brown-skinned. The poem included here, "Daddy with Chesterfields in a Rolled Up Sleeve," deftly sorts through machismo, racism, oppression, and conflicting family allegiances.

> Men try to catch my eye. i talk to them
> of politics, religion, the ghosts i've seen,
> the king of timbales, México and Chicago.
> And they go away.
> But women stay. Women like stories. . . .

Sandra Cisneros is probably the best-known Chicano/a writer of her generation. Her sparse, delicately wrought stories, the humor and heartbreak of her poems, and the lyricism of her novel *Caramelo* have attracted many fans. Cisneros is particularly adept at capturing the clear-eyed innocence of young girls struggling to find themselves in cultures that do not value their contribution, except in very traditional, circumscribed ways. In her short story "Never Marry a Mexican," the protagonist rationalizes her avoidance of wedding bells and details the life of a dangerous romantic obsession: "Never marry a Mexican, my ma said once and always. She said this because of my father. She said this though she was Mexican too. But she was born here in the U.S., and he was born there, and it's *not* the same, you know."

Dagoberto Gilb writes from the other side of the gender divide. His stories, many about macho Southwestern men with easily-skewered hearts, capture the upheavals of cultural displacement and changing sex roles, often to hilarious, poignant effect. In "Maria de Covina," taken from the short story collection *Woodcuts of Women*, Gilb details the life and fantasy-fueled loves of one young Chicano, a department store clerk in Los Angeles.

The journalist Rubén Martínez brings a critical eye to border issues and the dangers that beset the thousands of Mexicans who come to the United States illegally each year. In his superbly reported book, *Crossing Over: A Mexican Family on the Migrant Trail*, excerpted here, Martínez chronicles the lives of one such family profoundly affected by the exodus of its children. With his taut, unsparing language and his compassion and understanding for the people he writes about, Martínez gives insistent life to headlines that are often easy to ignore.

NEW DEPARTURES

There is an unprecedented explosion of literary production in Mexico today. Novelists, short story writers, essayists, poets, playwrights, and cross-genre writers are publishing in the country's newspapers and magazines, in its literary journals and small-edition presses as well as with its major houses. Many writers have crossed the border into foreign-language publication and are generating international interest. The four writers here are a scant sampling of Mexico's many excellent new voices.

Not a single piece in Ignacio Padilla's collection of short stories *Antipodes* is set in Mexico or features Mexican characters.

Rather, its fictional worlds are populated by a variety of settings and nationalities: a Scottish engineer in the Gobi Desert, a cross-dressing pilot who climbs Mount Everest, a disillusioned monk who retreats to a remote Libyan cave to conjure the devil. (This last story, "Hagiography of the Apostate," is included here.) Padilla is one of a growing number of Mexican writers who are less concerned with identity politics and issues of Mexican culture than they are with creating work that is more personal, conceptual, existential, and internationalist.

Ángeles Mastretta's first novel, *Arráncame la vida,* was published in 1985 and became an international bestseller. In her short story collection, *Women with Big Eyes,* also a popular and critical success, Mastretta writes about the *tías,* or aunts, of Mexico— beloved fixtures in every family. Each tale explores, often in a few economical pages, the central passion and obsession of each of these "aunts" and, in aggregate, gives us a generous, sympathetic portrayal of Mexican womanhood.

One of the most prolific and respected writers of his generation, Carlos Monsiváis has worked as a journalist, essayist, critic, and translator. He is particularly appreciated for his *crónicas,* an essayistic form in which he uses vernacular Spanish to explore the cultures of Mexico—high, low, pop, and everything in between. In his essay "Identity Hour or, What Photos Would You Take of the Endless City?" Monsiváis takes verbal snapshots of the urban, postapocalyptic sprawl that is Mexico City. He describes the city as a place "where almost everything is possible, because everything works thanks only to what we call a 'miracle'—which is no more than the meeting-place of work, technology and chance."

The closing poem is "Fish of Fleeting Skin" by Coral Bracho, a well-known poet. With dazzling imagery and deft juxtapositions, Bracho talks about borders and elusive spaces, of slippery places owned only, and temporarily, by the imagination.

On the border an abyss of tones, of sharp clarity, of forms. One should enter lightly, darkly that instant of dance.

And it is here, in "that instant of dance," in the interstices of culture and identity, and along their many lively borders, that the voices and *voces* of the Mexican and Chicano/a peoples are heard.

—Cristina García
June 2006

For some time I have wanted to show that the only legitimate course in Mexico is to think as Mexicans. This must seem like a trivial and platitudinous affirmation; but in our country it is a necessary one, because we often talk as if we were foreigners, far removed from our spiritual and physical surroundings. All thought must be based on the assumption that we are Mexicans and have to see the world in our perspective, as the logical consequences of geographic destiny. It naturally follows that the object or objects of our thought should be those right around us. Seeking knowledge in the world at large, we shall have to see it through the particular circumstances of our little Mexican world. It would be a mistake to interpret these ideas as the mere result of narrow-minded nationalism. It is rather a question of ideas which have a philosophical motivation. Only the man who can see the world about him in his perspective has vital thought.

—From "The Use of Thought" by Samuel Ramos

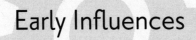

Early Influences

Major Aranda's Hand

Major Aranda suffered the loss of a hand in battle, and, unfortunately for him, it was his right hand. Other people make collections of hands of bronze, of ivory, of glass and of wood; at times they come from religious statues or images; at times they are antique door knockers. And surgeons keep worse things in jars of alcohol. Why not preserve this severed hand, testimony to a glorious deed? Are we sure that the hand is of less value than the brain or the heart?

Let us meditate about it. Aranda did not meditate, but was impelled by a secret instinct. Theological man has been shaped in clay, like a doll, by the hand of God. Biological man evolves thanks to the service of his hand, and his hand has endowed the world with a new natural kingdom, the kingdom of the industries and the arts. If the strong walls of Thebes rose to the music of Amphion's lyre, it was his brother Zethus, the mason, who raised the stones with his hand. Manual laborers appear therefore in archaic mythologies, enveloped in magic vapor: they are the wonder-workers. They are "The Hands Delivering the

3

Fire" that Orozco has painted. In Diego Rivera's mural the hand grasps the cosmic globe that contains the powers of creation and destruction; and in Chapingo the proletarian hands are ready to reclaim the patrimony of the earth.

The other senses remain passive, but the manual sense experiments and adds and, from the spoils of the earth, constructs a human order, the son of man. It models both the jar and the planet; it moves the potter's wheel and opens the Suez Canal.

A delicate and powerful instrument, it possesses the most fortunate physical resources: hinges, pincers, tongs, hooks, bony little chains, nerves, ligaments, canals, cushions, valleys and hillocks. It is soft and hard, aggressive and loving.

A marvelous flower with five petals that open and close like the sensitive plant, at the slightest provocation! Is five an essential number in the universal harmonies? Does the hand belong to the order of the dog rose, the forget-me-not, the scarlet pimpernel? Palmists perhaps are right in substance although not in their interpretations. And if the physiognomists of long ago had gone on from the face to the hand, completing their vague observations, undoubtedly they would have figured out correctly that the face mirrors and expresses but that the hand acts.

There is no doubt about it, the hand deserves unusual respect, and it could indeed occupy the favorite position among the household gods of Major Aranda.

The hand was carefully deposited in a quilted jewel case. The folds of white satin seemed a diminutive Alpine landscape. From time to time intimate friends were granted the privilege of looking at it for a few minutes. It was a pleasing, robust, intelligent hand, still in a rather tense position from grasping the hilt of the sword. It was perfectly preserved.

Gradually this mysterious object, this hidden talisman, became familiar. And then it emigrated from the treasure chest to the showcase in the living room, and a place was made for it among the campaign and high military decorations.

Its nails began to grow, revealing a slow, silent, surreptitious life. At one moment this growth seemed something brought on by inertia, at another it was evident that it was a natural virtue. With some repugnance at first, the manicurist of the family consented to take care of those nails each week. The hand was always polished and well cared for.

Without the family knowing how it happened—that's how man is, he converts the statue of the god into a small art object—the hand descended in rank; it suffered a *manus diminutio;* it ceased to be a relic and entered into domestic circulation. After six months it acted as a paperweight or served to hold the leaves of the manuscripts—the major was writing his memoirs now with his left hand; for the severed hand was flexible and plastic and the docile fingers maintained the position imposed upon them.

In spite of its repulsive coldness, the children of the house ended up by losing respect for it. At the end of a year, they were already scratching themselves with it or amused themselves by folding its fingers in the form of various obscene gestures of international folklore.

The hand thus recalled many things that it had completely forgotten. Its personality was becoming noticeable. It acquired its own consciousness and character. It began to put out feelers. Then it moved like a tarantula. Everything seemed an occasion for play. And one day, when it was evident that it had put on a glove all by itself and had adjusted a bracelet on the severed wrist, it did not attract the attention of anyone.

It went freely from one place to another, a monstrous little lap dog, rather crablike. Later it learned to run, with a hop very similar to that of hares, and, sitting back on the fingers, it began to jump in a prodigious manner. One day it was seen spread out on a current of air: it had acquired the ability to fly.

But in doing all these things, how did it orient itself, how did it see? Ah! Certain sages say that there is a faint light, imperceptible to the retina, perhaps perceptible to other organs, particularly if they are trained by education and exercise. Should not the hand see also? Of course it complements its vision with its sense of touch; it almost has eyes in its fingers, and the palm is able to find its bearings through the gust of air like the membranes of a bat. Nanook, the Eskimo, on his cloudy polar steppes, raises and waves the weather vanes to orient himself in an apparently uniform environment. The hand captures a thousand fleeting things and penetrates the translucent currents that escape the eye and the muscles, those currents that are not visible and that barely offer any resistance.

The fact is that the hand, as soon as it got around by itself, became ungovernable, became temperamental. We can say that it was then that it really "got out of hand." It came and went as it pleased. It disappeared when it felt like it; returned when it took a fancy to do so. It constructed castles of improbable balance out of bottles and wineglasses. It is said that it even became intoxicated; in any case, it stayed up all night.

It did not obey anyone. It was prankish and mischievous. It pinched the noses of callers, it slapped collectors at the door. It remained motionless, playing dead, allowing itself to be contemplated by those who were not acquainted with it, and then suddenly it would make an obscene gesture. It took singular pleasure in chucking its former owner under the chin, and it got into the habit of scaring the flies away from him. He would regard it with tenderness, his eyes brimming with tears, as he would regard a son who had proved to be a black sheep.

It upset everything. Sometimes it took a notion to sweep and tidy the house; other times it would mix up the shoes of the family with a true arithmetical genius for permutations, combinations and changes; it would break the window panes by throwing rocks, or it would hide the balls of the boys who were playing in the street.

The major observed it and suffered in silence. His wife hated it, and of course was its preferred victim. The hand, while it was going on to other exercises, humiliated her by giving her lessons in needlework or cooking.

The truth is that the family became demoralized. The one-handed man was depressed and melancholy, in great contrast to his former happiness. His wife became distrustful and easily frightened, almost paranoid. The children became negligent, abandoned their studies, and forgot their good manners. Everything was sudden frights, useless drudgery, voices, doors slamming, as if an evil spirit had entered the house. The meals were served late, sometimes in the parlor, sometimes in a bedroom because, to the consternation of the major, to the frantic protest of his wife, and to the furtive delight of the children, the hand had taken possession of the dining room for its gymnastic exercises, locking itself inside, and receiving those who tried to expel it by throwing plates at their heads. One just had to yield, to surrender with weapons and baggage, as Aranda said.

The old servants, even the nurse who had reared the lady of the house, were put to flight. The new servants could not endure the bewitched house for a single day. Friends and relatives deserted the family. The police began to be disturbed by the constant complaints of the neighbors. The last silver grate that remained in the National Palace disappeared as if by magic. An epidemic of robberies took place, for which the mysterious hand was blamed, though it was often innocent.

The most cruel aspect of the case was that people did not blame the hand, did not believe that there was such a hand animated by its own life, but attributed everything to the wicked devices of the poor one-handed man, whose severed member was now threatening to cost us what Santa Anna's leg cost us. Undoubtedly Aranda was a wizard who had made a pact with Satan. People made the sign of the cross.

In the meantime the hand, indifferent to the harm done to others, acquired an athletic musculature, became robust, steadily got into better shape, and learned how to do more and more things. Did it not try to continue the major's memoirs for him? The night when it decided to get some fresh air in the automobile, the Aranda family, incapable of restraining it, believed that the world was collapsing; but there was not a single accident, nor fines nor bribes to pay the police. The major said that at least the car, which had been getting rusty after the flight of the chauffeur, would be kept in good condition that way.

Left to its own nature, the hand gradually came to embody the Platonic idea that gave it being, the idea of seizing, the eagerness to acquire control. When it was seen how hens perished with their necks twisted or how art objects belonging to other people arrived at the house—which Aranda went to all kinds of trouble to return to their owners, with stammerings and incomprehensible excuses—it was evident that the hand was an animal of prey and a thief.

People now began to doubt Aranda's sanity. They spoke of hallucinations, of "raps" or noises of spirits, and of other things of a like nature. The twenty or thirty persons who really had seen the hand did not appear trustworthy when they were of the servant class, easily swayed by superstitions; and when they were people of moderate culture, they remained silent and answered with evasive remarks for fear of compromising themselves or being subject to ridicule. A round table of the Faculty of Philosophy and Literature devoted itself to discussing a certain anthropological thesis concerning the origin of myths.

There is, however, something tender and terrible in this story. Aranda awoke one night at midnight with shrieks of terror: in strange nuptials the severed hand, the right one, had come to link itself with the left hand, its companion of other days, as if longing to be close to it. It was impossible to detach it. It passed the remainder of the night there, and there it resolved to spend the nights from then on. Custom makes monsters familiar. The major ended by paying no attention to the hand. It even seemed to him that the strange contact made the mutilation more bearable and in some manner comforted his only hand.

The poor left hand, the female, needed the kiss and company of the right hand, the male. Let us not belittle it; in its slowness it tenaciously preserves as a precious ballast the prehistoric virtues: slowness, the inertia of centuries in which our species has developed. It corrects the crazy audacities, the ambitions of the right hand. It has been said that it is fortunate that we do not have two right hands, for in that case we would become lost among the pure subtleties and complexities of virtuosity; we would not be real men; no, we would be sleight-of-hand performers. Gauguin knows well what he is doing when, to restrain his refined sensitivity, he teaches the right hand to paint again with the candor of the left hand.

One night, however, the hand pushed open the library door and became deeply absorbed in reading. It came upon a story by de Maupassant about a severed hand that ends by strangling its enemy. It came upon a beautiful fantasy by Nerval in which an enchanted hand travels the world, creating beauty and casting evil spells. It came upon some notes by the philosopher Gaos about the phenomenology of the hand. . . . Good heavens! What will be the result of this fearful incursion into the alphabet?

The result is sad and serene. The haughty independent hand that believed it was a person, an autonomous entity, an inventor of its own conduct, became convinced that it was only a literary theme, a matter of fantasy already very much worked over by the pen of writers. With sorrow and difficulty—and, I might almost say, shedding abundant tears—it made its way to the showcase in the living room, settled down in its jewel case, which it first placed carefully among the campaign and high military

decorations; and, disillusioned and sorrowful, it committed suicide in its fashion: it let itself die.

The sun was rising when the major, who had spent a sleep-
less night tossing about, upset by the prolonged absence of his
hand, discovered it inert in the jewel case, somewhat darkened,
with signs of asphyxiation. He could not believe his eyes. When
he understood the situation, he nervously crumpled the paper
on which he was about to submit his resignation from active
service. He straightened up to his full height, reassumed his
military haughtiness, and, startling his household, shouted at
the top of his voice: "Attention! Fall in! All to their posts!
Bugler, sound the bugle call of victory!"

My Cousin Agueda

My godmother invited my cousin
Agueda to spend the day
with us, and my cousin
came with a conflicting
prestige of starch and fearful
ceremonious weeds.

Agueda appeared, sonorous
with starch, and her green eyes
and ruddy cheeks protected
me against the fearsome
weeds.

I was a small boy,
knew O was the round one,
and Agueda knitting,
mild and persevering,
in the echoing gallery,

gave me unknown shivers.
(I think I even owe her the heroically
morbid habit of soliloquy.)

At dinner-time in the quiet
shadowy dining-room,
I was spellbound by the brittle
intermittent noise of dishes
and the caressing timbre
of my cousin's voice.

        Agueda was
(weeds, green pupils, ruddy cheeks)
a polychromatic basket of
apples and grapes
in the ebony of an ancient cupboard.

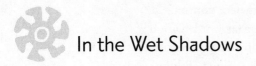

In the Wet Shadows

On the dark wings of the cutting blast
you bring me at the same time pain and joy;
something like a soft breast's frozen virtue,
something that combines the cordial cool
and icy forlornness of a virgin's bed.

And lo, in the mute city's unlooked for gloom,
you are a light before the murky fauces
of my hunger; lo, in the rain's wet shadow
you exude candour like new-washed linen
and, like it, spread an odour of chastity;
lo, in the darkness you distil the essence
of some good fiancée's tearful handkerchief.

I huddle in the thick obscurity
and think for you these lines whose hidden rhyme
you must with rapid divination mark;
for they are petals of night that bring you tidings
of singular thrill; and plunged within my self
in the wet shadows, I send confusedly
these fragile syllables, like a gust of mystery,
to the threshold of your vigilant spirit.

You are all shed upon me like white frost,
and the translucent meteor continues
out of time; and your far words within
me sound with the dreamlike intensity
of a disordered clock striking all hours
in a disordered room. . . .

Excerpt from *Pedro Páramo*

I came to Comala because I had been told that my father, a man named Pedro Páramo, lived there. It was my mother who told me. And I had promised her that after she died I would go see him. I squeezed her hands as a sign I would do it. She was near death, and I would have promised her anything. "Don't fail to go see him," she had insisted. "Some call him one thing, some another. I'm sure he will want to know you." At the time all I could do was tell her I would do what she asked, and from promising so often I kept repeating the promise even after I had pulled my hands free of her death grip.

Still earlier she had told me:

"Don't ask him for anything. Just what's ours. What he should have given me but never did. . . . Make him pay, son, for all those years he put us out of his mind."

"I will, Mother."

I never meant to keep my promise. But before I knew it my head began to swim with dreams and my imagination took flight. Little by little I began to build a world around a hope centered on the man called Pedro Páramo, the man who had been my mother's husband. That was why I had come to Comala.

It was during the dog days, the season when the August wind blows hot, venomous with the rotten stench of saponaria blossoms.

The road rose and fell. *It rises or falls depending on whether you're coming or going. If you are leaving, it's uphill; but* as *you arrive it's downhill.*

"What did you say that town down there is called?"

"Comala, señor."

"You're sure that's Comala?"

"I'm sure, señor."

"It's a sorry-looking place, what happened to it?"

"It's the times, señor."

I had expected to see the town of my mother's memories, of her nostalgia—nostalgia laced with sighs. She had lived her life-time sighing about Comala, about going back. But she never had. Now I had come in her place. I was seeing things through her eyes, as she had seen them. She had given me her eyes to see. *Just as you pass the gate of Los Colimotes there's a beautiful view of a green plain tinged with the yellow of ripe corn. From there you can see Comala, turning the earth white, and lighting it at night.* Her voice was secret, muffled, as if she were talking to herself. . . . Mother.

"And why are you going to Comala, if you don't mind my asking?" I heard the man say.

"I've come to see my father," I replied.

"Umh!" he said.

And again silence.

We were making our way down the hill to the clip-clop of the burros' hooves. Their sleepy eyes were bulging from the August heat.

"You're going to get some welcome." Again I heard the voice of the man walking at my side. "They'll be happy to see someone after all the years no one's come this way."

After a while he added: "Whoever you are, they'll be glad to see you."

In the shimmering sunlight the plain was a transparent lake dissolving in mists that veiled a gray horizon. Farther in the distance, a range of mountains. And farther still, faint remoteness.

"And what does your father look like, if you don't mind my asking?"

"I never knew him," I told the man. "I only know his name is Pedro Páramo."

"Umh! That so?"

"Yes. At least that was the name I was told."

Yet again I heard the burro driver's "Umh!"

I had run into him at the crossroads called Los Encuentros. I had been waiting there, and finally this man had appeared.

"Where are you going?" I asked.

"Down that way, señor."

"Do you know a place called Comala?"

"That's the very way I'm going."

So I followed him. I walked along behind, trying to keep up with him, until he seemed to remember I was following and slowed down a little. After that, we walked side by side, so close our shoulders were nearly touching.

"Pedro Páramo's my father, too," he said.

A flock of crows swept across the empty sky, shrilling "caw, caw, caw."

Up- and downhill we went, but always descending. We had left the hot wind behind and were sinking into pure, airless heat. The stillness seemed to be waiting for something.

"It's hot here," I said.

"You might say. But this is nothing," my companion replied.

"Try to take it easy. You'll feel it even more when we get to Comala. That town sits on the coals of the earth, at the very mouth of hell. They say that when people from there die and go to hell, they come back for a blanket."

"Do you know Pedro Páramo?" I asked.

I felt I could ask because I had seen a glimmer of goodwill in his eyes.

"Who is he?" I pressed him.

"Living bile," was his reply.

And he lowered his stick against the burros for no reason at all, because they had been far ahead of us, guided by the descending trail.

The picture of my mother I was carrying in my pocket felt hot against my heart, as if she herself were sweating. It was an old photograph, worn around the edges, but it was the only one I had ever seen of her. I had found it in the kitchen safe, inside a clay pot filled with herbs: dried lemon balm, castilla blossoms, sprigs of rue. I had kept it with me ever since. It was all I had. My mother always hated having her picture taken. She said photographs were a tool of witchcraft. And that may have been so, because hers was riddled with pinpricks, and at the location of the heart there was a hole you could stick your middle finger through.

I had brought the photograph with me, thinking it might help my father recognize who I was.

"Take a look," the burro driver said, stopping. "You see that rounded hill that looks like a hog bladder? Well, the Media Luna lies right behind there. Now turn that way. You see the brow of that hill? Look hard. And now back this way. You see that ridge? The one so far you can't hardly see it? Well, all that's the Media Luna. From end to end. Like they say, as far as the eye can see. He owns ever' bit of that land. We're Pedro Páramo's sons, all right, but, for all that, our mothers brought us into the world on straw mats. And the real joke of it is that he's the one carried us to be baptized. That's how it was with you, wasn't it?"

"I don't remember."

"The hell you say!"

"What did you say?"

"I said, we're getting there, señor."

"Yes. I see it now. . . . What could it have been?"

"That was a *correcaminos*, señor. A roadrunner. That's what they call those birds around here."

"No. I meant I wonder what could have happened to the town? It looks so deserted, abandoned really. In fact, it looks like no one lives here at all."

"It doesn't just *look* like no one lives here. No one *does* live here."

"And Pedro Páramo?"

"Pedro Páramo died years ago."

It was the hour of the day when in every little village children come out to play in the streets, filling the afternoon with their cries. The time when dark walls still reflect pale yellow sunlight.

At least that was what I had seen in Sayula, just yesterday at this hour. I'd seen the still air shattered by the flight of doves flapping their wings as if pulling themselves free of the day. They swooped and plummeted above the tile rooftops, while the children's screams whirled and seemed to turn blue in the dusk sky.

Now here I was in this hushed town. I could hear my footsteps on the cobbled paving stones. Hollow footsteps, echoing against walls stained red by the setting sun.

This was the hour I found myself walking down the main street. Nothing but abandoned houses, their empty doorways overgrown with weeds. What had the stranger told me they were called? "*La gobernadora,* señor. Creosote bush. A plague that takes over a person's house the minute he leaves. You'll see."

As I passed a street corner, I saw a woman wrapped in her rebozo; she disappeared as if she had never existed. I started forward again, peering into the doorless houses. Again the woman in the rebozo crossed in front of me.

"Evening," she said.

I looked after her. I shouted: "Where will I find doña Eduviges?"

She pointed: "There. The house beside the bridge."

I took note that her voice had human overtones, that her mouth was filled with teeth and a tongue that worked as she spoke, and that her eyes were the eyes of people who inhabit the earth.

By now it was dark.

She turned to call good night. And though there were no children playing, no doves, no blue-shadowed roof tiles, I felt that the town was alive. And that if I heard only silence, it was because I was not yet accustomed to silence—maybe because my head was still filled with sounds and voices.

Yes, voices. And here, where the air was so rare, I heard them even stronger. They lay heavy inside me. I remembered what my mother had said: *"You will hear me better there. I will be closer to you. You will hear the voice of my memories stronger than the voice of my death— that is, if death ever had a voice."* Mother . . . So alive.

How I wished she were here, so I could say, "You were mistaken about the house. You told me the wrong place. You sent me 'south of nowhere,' to an abandoned village. Looking for someone who's no longer alive."

I found the house by the bridge by following the sound of the river. I lifted my hand to knock, but there was nothing there. My hand met only empty space, as if the wind had blown open the door. A woman stood there. She said, "Come in." And I went in.

. . .

So I stayed in Comala. The man with the burros had gone on his way. Before leaving, he'd said:

"I still have a way to go, yonder where you see that band of hills. My house is there. If you want to come, you will be welcome. For now, if you want to stay here, then stay. You got nothing to lose by taking a look around, you may find someone who's still among the living."

I stayed. That was why I had come.

"Where can I find lodging?" I called, almost shouting now.

"Look up doña Eduviges, if she's still alive. Tell her I sent you."

"And what's your name?"

"Abundio," he called back. But he was too far for me to hear his last name.

"I am Eduviges Dyada. Come in."

It was as if she had been waiting for me. Everything was ready, she said, motioning for me to follow her through a long series of dark, seemingly empty, rooms. But no. As soon as my eyes grew used to the darkness and the thin thread of light following us, I saw shadows looming on either side, and sensed that we were walking down a narrow passageway opened between bulky shapes.

"What do you have here?" I asked.

"Odds and ends," she said. "My house is chock full of other people's things. As people went away, they chose my house to store their belongings, but not one of them has ever come back to claim them. The room I kept for you is here at the back. I keep it cleaned out in case anyone comes. So you're her son?"

"Whose son?" I asked.

"Doloritas's boy"

"Yes. But how did you know?"

"She told me you would be coming. Today, in fact. That you would be coming today."

"Who told you? My mother?"

"Yes. Your mother."

I did not know what to think. But Eduviges left me no time for thinking.

"This is your room," she said.

The room had no doors, except for the one we had entered. She lighted the candle, and I could see the room was completely empty.

"There's no place to sleep," I said.

"Don't worry about that. You must be tired from your journey, and weariness makes a good mattress. I'll fix you up a bed first thing in the morning. You can't expect me to have things ready on the spur of the moment. A person needs some warning, and I didn't get word from your mother until just now."

"My mother?" I said. "My mother is dead."

"So that was why her voice sounded so weak, like it had to travel a long distance to get here. Now I understand. And when did she die?"

"A week ago."

"Poor woman. She must've thought I'd forsaken her. We made each other a promise we'd die together. That we would go hand in hand, to lend each other courage on our last journey—in case we had need for something, or ran into trouble. We were the best of friends. Didn't she ever talk about me?"

"No, never."

"That's strange. Of course, we were just girls then. She was barely married. But we loved each other very much. Your mother was so pretty, so, well, *sweet*, that it made a person happy to love her. You *wanted* to love her. So, she got a head start on me, eh?

Well, you can be sure I'll catch up with her. No one knows better than I do how far heaven is, but I also know all the shortcuts. The secret is to die, God willing, when you want to, and not when He proposes. Or else to force Him to take you before your time. Forgive me for going on like this, talking to you as if we were old friends, but I do it because you're like my own son. Yes, I said it a thousand times: 'Dolores's boy should have been my son.' I'll tell you why sometime. All I want to say now is that I'll catch up with your mother along one of the roads to eternity."

I wondered if she were crazy. But by now I wasn't thinking at all. I felt I was in a faraway world and let myself be pulled along by the current. My body, which felt weaker and weaker, surrendered completely; it had slipped its ties and anyone who wanted could have wrung me out like a rag.

"I'm tired," I said.

"Come eat something before you sleep. A bite. Anything there is."

"I will. I'll come later."

Water dripping from the roof tiles was forming a hole in the sand of the patio. Plink! plink! and then another plink! as drops struck a bobbing, dancing laurel leaf caught in a crack between the adobe bricks. The storm had passed. Now an intermittent breeze shook the branches of the pomegranate tree, loosing showers of heavy rain, spattering the ground with gleaming drops that dulled as they sank into the earth. The hens, still huddled on their roost, suddenly flapped their wings and strutted out to the patio, heads bobbing, pecking worms unearthed by the rain. As the clouds retreated the sun flashed on the rocks, spread an iridescent sheen, sucked water from the soil, shone on sparkling leaves stirred by the breeze.

"What's taking you so long in the privy, son?"

"Nothing, mamá."

"If you stay in there much longer, a snake will come and bite you."

"Yes, mamá."

I was thinking of you, Susana. Of the green hills. Of when we used to fly kites in the windy season. We could hear the sounds of life from the town below; we were high above on the hill, playing out string to the wind. "Help me, Susana." And soft hands would tighten on mine. "Let out more string."

The wind made us laugh; our eyes followed the string running through our fingers after the wind until with a faint pop! it broke, as if it had been snapped by the wings of a bird. And high overhead, the paper bird would tumble and somersault, trailing its rag tail, until it disappeared into the green earth.

Your lips were moist, as if kissed by the dew.

"I told you, son, come out of the privy now."

"Yes, mamá. I'm coming."

I was thinking of you. Of the times you were there looking at me with your aquamarine eyes.

He looked up and saw his mother in the doorway.

"What's taking you so long? What are you doing in there?"

"I'm thinking."

"Can't you do it somewhere else? It's not good for you to stay in the privy so long. Besides, you should be doing something. Why don't you go help your grandmother shell corn?"

"I'm going, mamá. I'm going."

"Grandmother, I've come to help you shell corn."

"We're through with that, but we still have to grind the chocolate. Where have you been? We were looking for you all during the storm."

"I was in the back patio."

"And what were you doing? Praying?"

"No, Grandmother. I was just watching it rain."

His grandmother looked at him with those yellow-gray eyes that seemed to see right through a person.

"Run clean the mill, then."

Hundreds of meters above the clouds, far, far above everything, you are hiding, Susana. Hiding in God's immensity, behind His Divine Providence where I cannot touch you or see you, and where my words cannot reach you.

"Grandmother, the mill's no good. The grinder's broken."

"That Micaela must have run corn through it. I can't break her of that habit, but it's too late now."

"Why don't we buy a new one? This one's so old it isn't any good anyway."

"That's the Lord's truth. But with all the money we spent to bury your grandfather, and the tithes we've paid to the church, we don't have anything left. Oh, well, we'll do without something else and buy a new one. Why don't you run see doña Inés Villalpando and ask her to carry us on her books until October. We'll pay her at harvest time."

"All right, Grandmother."

"And while you're at it, to kill two birds with one stone, ask her to lend us a sifter and some clippers. The way those weeds are growing, we'll soon have them coming out our ears. If I had my big house with all my stock pens, I wouldn't be complaining. But your grandfather took care of that when he moved here. Well, it must be God's will. Things seldom work out the way you want. Tell doña Inés that after harvest time we'll pay her everything we owe her."

"Yes, Grandmother."

Hummingbirds. It was the season. He heard the whirring of their wings in blossom-heavy jasmine.

He stopped by the shelf where the picture of the Sacred Heart stood, and found twenty-four centavos. He left the four single coins and took the veinte.

As he was leaving, his mother stopped him:

"Where are you going?"

"Down to doña Inés Villalpando's, to buy a new mill. Ours broke."

"Ask her to give you a meter of black taffeta, like this," and she handed him a piece. "And to put it on our account."

"All right, mamá."

"And on the way back, buy me some aspirin. You'll find some money in the flowerpot in the hall."

He found a peso. He left the veinte and took the larger coin. "Now I have enough money for anything that comes along," he thought.

"Pedro!" people called to him. "Hey, Pedro!"

But he did not hear. He was far, far away.

During the night it began to rain again. For a long time, he lay listening to the gurgling of the water; then he must have slept, because when he awoke, he heard only a quiet drizzle. The windowpanes were misted over and raindrops were threading down like tears. . . . I watched the trickles glinting in the lightning flashes, and every breath I breathed, I sighed. And every thought I thought was of you, Susana.

The rain turned to wind. He heard ". . . the forgiveness of sins and the resurrection of the flesh. Amen." That was deeper in the house, where women were telling the last of their beads. They got up from their prayers, they penned up the chickens, they bolted the door, they turned out the light.

Now there was only the light of night, and rain hissing like the murmur of crickets.

"Why didn't you come say your Rosary? We were making a novena for your grandfather."

His mother was standing in the doorway, candle in hand. Her long, crooked shadow stretched toward the ceiling. The roof beams repeated it, in fragments.

"I feel sad," he said.

Then she turned away. She snuffed out the candle. As she closed the door, her sobs began; he could hear them for a long time, mixed with the sound of the rain.

The church clock tolled the hours, hour after hour, hour after hour, as if time had been telescoped.

"Oh, yes. I was nearly your mother. She never told you anything about it?"

"No. She only told me good things. I heard about you from the man with the train of burros. The man who led me here, the one named Abundio."

"He's a good man, Abundio. So, he still remembers me? I used to give him a little something for every traveler he sent to my house. It was a good deal for both of us. Now, sad to say, times have changed, and since the town has fallen on bad times, no one brings us any news. So he told you to come see me?"

"Yes, he said to look for you."

"I'm grateful to him for that. He was a good man, one you could trust. It was him that brought the mail, and he kept right on even after he went deaf. I remember the black day it happened. Everyone felt bad about it, because we all liked him. He brought letters to us and took ours away. He always told us how things were going on the other side of the world, and doubtless he told them how we were making out. He was a big talker. Well, not afterward. He stopped talking then. He said there wasn't much point in saying things he couldn't hear, things that evaporated in the air, things he couldn't get the taste of. It all happened when one of those big rockets we use to scare away water snakes went off too close to his head. From that day on, he never spoke, though he wasn't struck dumb. But one thing I tell you, it didn't make him any less a good person."

"The man I'm talking about heard fine."

"Then it can't have been him. Besides, Abundio died. I'm sure he's dead. So you see? It couldn't have been him."

"I guess you're right."

"Well, getting back to your mother. As I was telling you . . ."

As I listened to her drone on, I studied the woman before me. I thought she must have gone through some bad times. Her face was transparent, as if the blood had drained from it, and her hands were all shriveled, nothing but wrinkled claws. Her eyes were sunk out of sight. She was wearing an old-fashioned white dress with rows of ruffles, and around her neck, strung on a cord, she wore a medal of the María Santísima del Refugio with the words "Refuge of Sinners."

". . . This man I'm telling you about broke horses over at the Media Luna ranch; he said his name was Inocencio Osorio. Everyone knew him, though, by his nickname 'Cockleburr'; he could stick to a horse like a burr to a blanket. My compadre Pedro used to say that the man was born to break colts. The fact is, though, that he had another calling: conjuring. He conjured up dreams. That was who he really was. And he put it over on your mother, like he did so many others. Including me. Once when I was feeling bad, he showed up and said, 'I've come to give you a treatment so's you'll feel better.' And what that meant was he would start out kneading and rubbing you: first your fingertips, then he'd stroke your hands, then your arms. First thing you knew he'd be working on your legs, rubbing hard, and soon you'd be feeling warm all over. And all the time he was rubbing and stroking he'd be telling you your fortune. He would fall into a trance and roll his eyes and conjure and curse, with spittle flying everywhere—you'd of thought he was a gypsy. Sometimes he would end up stark naked; he said we wanted it that way. And sometimes what he said came true. He shot at so many targets that once in a while he was bound to hit one.

"So what happened was that when your mother went to see this Osorio, he told her that she shouldn't lie with a man that night because the moon was wrong.

"Dolores came and told me everything, in a quandary about what to do. She said there was no two ways about it, she couldn't go to bed with Pedro Páramo that night. Her wedding night. And there I was, trying to convince her she shouldn't put any stock in that Osorio, who was nothing but a swindler and a liar.

" 'I *can't*,' she told me. 'You go for me. He'll never catch on.'

"Of course I was a lot younger than she was. And not quite as dark-skinned. But you can't tell that in the dark.

" 'It'll never work, Dolores. You have to go.'

"Do me this one favor, and I'll pay you back a hundred times over.'

"In those days your mother had the shyest eyes. If there was something pretty about your mother, it was those eyes. They could really win you over.

" 'You go in my place,' she kept saying.

"So I went.

"I took courage from the darkness, and from something else your mother didn't know, and that was that she wasn't the only one who liked Pedro Páramo.

"I crawled in bed with him. I was happy to; I wanted to. I cuddled right up against him, but all the celebrating had worn him out and he spent the whole night snoring. All he did was wedge his legs between mine.

"Before dawn, I got up and went to Dolores. I said to her: 'You go now. It's a new day.'

" 'What did he do to you?' she asked me.

" 'I'm still not sure,' I told her.

"You were born the next year, but I wasn't your mother, though you came within a hair of being mine.

"Maybe your mother was ashamed to tell you about it."

Green pastures. Watching the horizon rise and fall as the wind swirled through the wheat, an afternoon rippling with curling lines of rain. The color of the earth, the smell of alfalfa and bread. A town that smelled like spilled honey . . .

"She always hated Pedro Páramo. 'Doloritas! Did you tell them to get my breakfast?' Your mother was up every morning before dawn. She would start the fire from the coals, and with the smell of the tinder the cats would wake up. Back and forth through the house, followed by her guard of cats. 'Doña Doloritas!'

"I wonder how many times your mother heard that call? 'Doña Doloritas, this is cold. It won't do.' How many times? And even though she was used to the worst of times, those shy eyes of hers grew hard."

Not to know any taste but the savor of orange blossoms in the warmth of summer.

"Then she began her sighing.

" 'Why are you sighing so, Doloritas?'

"I had gone with them that afternoon. We were in the middle of a field, watching the bevies of young thrushes. One solitary buzzard rocked lazily in the sky.

" 'Why are you sighing, Doloritas?'

" 'I wish I were a buzzard so I could fly to where my sister lives.'

" 'That's the last straw, doña Doloritas!' You'll see your sister, all right. Right now. We're going back to the house and you're going to pack your suitcases. That was the last straw!'

"And your mother went. 'I'll see you soon, don Pedro.'

" 'Good-*bye*, Doloritas!'

"And she never came back to the Media Luna. Some months later, I asked Pedro Páramo about her.

" 'She loved her sister more than she did me. I guess she's happy there. Besides, I was getting fed up with her. I have no intention of asking about her, if that's what's worrying you.'

" 'But how will they get along?'

" 'Let God look after them.' "

. . . *Make him pay, Son, for all those years he put us out of his mind.*

"And that's how it was until she advised me that you were coming to see me. We never heard from her again."

"A lot has happened since then," I told Eduviges. "We lived in Colima. We were taken in by my aunt Gertrudis, who threw it in our faces every day that we were a burden. She used to ask my mother, 'Why don't you go back to your husband?'

" 'Oh? Has he sent for me? I'm not going back unless he asks me to. I came because I wanted to see you. Because I loved you. That's why I came.'

" 'I know that. But it's time now for you to leave.'

" 'If it was up to me . . . ' "

I thought that Eduviges was listening to me. I noticed, though, that her head was tilted as if she were listening to some faraway sound. Then she said:

"When will you rest?"

L.A. Nocturne: The Angels

for Agustín J. Fink

You might say the streets flow sweetly through the night.
The lights are dim so the secret will be kept,
the secret known by the men who come and go,
for they're all in on the secret
and why break it up in a thousand pieces
when it's so sweet to hold it close,
and share it only with the one chosen person.

If, at a given moment, everyone would say
with one word what he is thinking,
the six letters of DESIRE would form an enormous luminous scar,
a constellation more ancient, more dazzling than any other.
And that constellation would be like a burning sex
in the deep body of night,
like the Gemini, for the first time in their lives,
looking each other in the eyes and embracing forever.

Suddenly the river of the street is filled with thirsty creatures;
they walk, they pause, they move on.

They exchange glances, they dare to smile,
they form unpredictable couples . . .

There are nooks and benches in the shadows,
riverbanks of dense indefinable shapes,
sudden empty spaces of blinding light
and doors that open at the slightest touch.

For a moment, the river of the street is deserted.
Then it seems to replenish itself,
eager to start again.
It is a paralyzed, mute, gasping moment,
like a heart between two spasms.

But a new throbbing, a new pulsebeat
launches new thirsty creatures on the river of the street.
They cross, crisscross, fly up.
They glide along the ground.
They swim standing up, so miraculously
no one would ever say they're not really walking.

They are angels.
They have come down to earth
on invisible ladders.
They come from the sea that is the mirror of the sky
on ships of smoke and shadow,
they come to fuse and be confused with men,
to surrender their foreheads to the thighs of women,
to let other hands anxiously touch their bodies
and let other bodies search for their bodies till they're found,
like the closing lips of a single mouth,
they come to exhaust their mouths, so long inactive,
to set free their tongues of fire,
to sing the songs, to swear, to say all the bad words

in which men have concentrated the ancient mysteries
of flesh, blood and desire.

They have assumed names that are divinely simple.
They call themselves *Dick* or *John, Marvin* or *Louis.*
Only by their beauty are they distinguishable from men.
They walk, they pause, they move on.
They exchange glances, they dare to smile.
They form unpredictable couples.

They smile maliciously going up in the elevators of hotels,
where leisurely vertical flight is still practiced.
There are celestial marks on their naked bodies:
blue signs, blue stars and letters.
They let themselves fall into beds, they sink into pillows
that make them think they're still in the clouds.
But they close their eyes to surrender to the pleasures of their
    mysterious incarnation,
and when they sleep, they dream not of angels but of men.

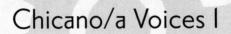

Chicano/a Voices I

GLORIA ANZALDÚA

How to Tame a Wild Tongue

"We're going to have to control your tongue," the dentist says, pulling out all the metal from my mouth. Silver bits plop and tinkle into the basin. My mouth is a motherlode.

The dentist is cleaning out my roots. I get a whiff of the stench when I gasp. "I can't cap that tooth yet, you're still draining," he says.

"We're going to have to do something about your tongue," I hear the anger rising in his voice. My tongue keeps pushing out the wads of cotton, pushing back the drills, the long thin needles. "I've never seen anything as strong or as stubborn," he says. And I think, how do you tame a wild tongue, train it to be quiet, how do you bridle and saddle it? How do you make it lie down?

> Who is to say that robbing a people of
> its language is less violent than war?
>
> —Ray Gwyn Smith

I remember being caught speaking Spanish at recess—that was good for three licks on the knuckles with a sharp ruler. I remember being sent to the corner of the classroom for "talking back" to the Anglo teacher when all I was trying to do was tell her how to pronounce my name. "If you want to be American, speak 'American.' If you don't like it, go back to Mexico where you belong."

"I want you to speak English. *Pa' hallar buen trabajo tienes que saber hablar el inglés bien. Qué vale toda tu educación si todavía hablas inglés con un 'accent,'*" my mother would say, mortified that I spoke English like a Mexican. At Pan American University, I, and all Chicano students, were required to take two speech classes. Their purpose: to get rid of our accents.

Attacks on one's form of expression with the intent to censor are a violation of the First Amendment. *El Anglo con cara de inocente nos arrancó la lengua.* Wild tongues can't be tamed, they can only be cut out.

OVERCOMING THE TRADITION OF SILENCE

> *Ahogadas, escupimos el oscuro.*
> *Peleando con nuestra propia sombra*
> *el silencio nos sepulta.*

En boca cerrada no entran moscas. "Flies don't enter a closed mouth" is a saying I kept hearing when I was a child. *Ser habladora* was to be a gossip and a liar, to talk too much. *Muchachitas bien criadas,* well-bred girls don't answer back. *Es una falta de respeto* to talk back to one's mother or father. I remember one of the sins I'd recite to the priest in the confession box the few times I went to confession: talking back to my mother, *hablar pa' 'trás, repelar. Hocicona, repelona, chismosa,* having a big mouth, questioning, carrying tales are all signs of being *mal criada.* In my culture they are all words that are derogatory if applied to women—I've never heard them applied to men.

The first time I heard two women, a Puerto Rican and a Cuban, say the word *"nosotras,"* I was shocked. I had not known the word existed. Chicanas use *nosotros* whether we're male or female. We are robbed of our female being by the masculine plural. Language is a male discourse.

> And our tongues have become
> dry   the wilderness has
> dried out our tongues   and
> we have forgotten speech.
> —IRENA KLEPFISZ

Even our own people, other Spanish speakers *nos quieren poner can-dados en la boca.* They would hold us back with their bag of *reglas de academia.*

OYE COMO LADRA: EL LENGUAJE DE LA FRONTERA

> *Quien tiene boca se equivoca.*
> —MEXICAN SAYING

"Pocho, cultural traitor, you're speaking the oppressor's language by speaking English, you're ruining the Spanish language," I have been accused by various Latinos and Latinas. Chicano Spanish is considered by the purist and by most Latinos deficient, a mutilation of Spanish.

But Chicano Spanish is a border tongue which developed naturally. Change, *evolución, enriquecimiento de palabras nuevas por invención o adopción* have created variants of Chicano Spanish, *un nuevo lenguaje. Un lenguaje que corresponde a un modo de vivir.* Chicano Spanish is not incorrect, it is a living language.

For a people who are neither Spanish nor live in a country in which Spanish is the first language; for a people who live in a country in which English is the reigning tongue but who are not Anglo; for a people who cannot entirely identify with either standard (formal, Castillian) Spanish nor standard English, what recourse is left to them but to create their own language? A language which they can connect their identity to, one capable of communicating the realities and values true to themselves—a language with terms that are neither *español ni inglés*, but both. We speak a patois, a forked tongue, a variation of two languages.

Chicano Spanish sprang out of the Chicanos' need to identify ourselves as a distinct people. We needed a language with which we could communicate with ourselves, a secret language. For some of us, language is a homeland closer than the Southwest—for many Chicanos today live in the Midwest and the East. And because we are a complex, heterogeneous people, we speak many languages. Some of the languages we speak are:

1. Standard English
2. Working class and slang English
3. Standard Spanish
4. Standard Mexican Spanish
5. North Mexican Spanish dialect
6. Chicano Spanish (Texas, New Mexico, Arizona, and California have regional variations)
7. Tex-Mex
8. *Pachuco* (called *caló*)

My "home" tongues are the languages I speak with my sister and brothers, with my friends. They are the last five listed, with

6 and 7 being closest to my heart. From school, the media, and job situations, I've picked up standard and working class English. From Mamagrande Locha and from reading Spanish and Mexican literature, I've picked up Standard Spanish and Standard Mexican Spanish. From *los recién llegados*, Mexican immigrants, and *braceros*, I learned the North Mexican dialect. With Mexicans I'll try to speak either Standard Mexican Spanish or the North Mexican dialect. From my parents and Chicanos living in the Valley, I picked up Chicano Texas Spanish, and I speak it with my mom, younger brother (who married a Mexican and who rarely mixes Spanish with English), aunts, and older relatives.

With Chicanas from *Nuevo México* or *Arizona* I will speak Chicano Spanish a little, but often they don't understand what I'm saying. With most California Chicanas I speak entirely in English (unless I forget). When I first moved to San Francisco, I'd rattle off something in Spanish, unintentionally embarrassing them. Often it is only with another Chicana *tejana* that I can talk freely.

Words distorted by English are known as anglicisms or *pochismos*. The *pocho* is an anglicized Mexican or American of Mexican origin who speaks Spanish with an accent characteristic of North Americans and who distorts and reconstructs the language according to the influence of English. Tex-Mex, or Spanglish, comes most naturally to me. I may switch back and forth from English to Spanish in the same sentence or in the same word. With my sister and my brother Nune and with Chicano *tejano* contemporaries I speak in Tex-Mex.

From kids and people my own age I picked up *Pachuco*. *Pachuco* (the language of the zoot suiters) is a language of rebellion, both against Standard Spanish and Standard English. It is a secret language. Adults of the culture and outsiders cannot understand it. It is made up of slang words from both English and Spanish. *Ruca* means girl or woman, *vato* means guy or dude, *chale* means no, *simón* means yes, *churo* is sure, talk is *periquiar*, *pigionear* means petting, *que gacho* means how nerdy, *ponte águila* means watch out, death is called *la pelona*. Through lack of practice and not having others who can speak it, I've lost most of the *Pachuco* tongue.

CHICANO SPANISH

Chicanos, after 250 years of Spanish/Anglo colonization have developed significant differences in the Spanish we speak. We collapse two adjacent vowels into a single syllable and sometimes shift the stress in certain words such as *maíz/maiz, cohete/cuete*. We leave out certain consonants when they appear between vowels: *lado/lao, mojado/mojao*. Chicanos from South Texas pronounced *f* as *j* as in *jue (fue)*. Chicanos use "archaisms," words that are no longer in the Spanish language, words that have been evolved out. We say *semos, truje, haiga, ansina*, and *naiden*. We retain the "archaic" *j*, as in *jalar*, that derives from an earlier *h* (the French *halar* or the Germanic *halon* which was lost to Standard Spanish in the sixteenth century), but which is still found in several regional dialects such as the one spoken in South Texas. (Due to geography, Chicanos from the Valley of South Texas were cut off linguistically from other Spanish speakers. We tend to use words that the Spaniards brought over from Medieval Spain. The majority of the Spanish colonizers in Mexico and the Southwest came from Extremadura—Hernán Cortés was one of them—and Andalucía. Andalucians pronounce *ll* like a *y*, and their *d*'s tend to be absorbed by adjacent vowels: *tirado* becomes *tirao*. They brought *el lenguaje popular, dialectos y regionalismos*.)

Chicanos and other Spanish speakers also shift *ll* to *y* and *z* to *s*. We leave out initial syllables, saying *tar* for *estar*, *toy* for *estoy*, *hora* for *ahora* (*cubanos* and *puertorriqueños* also leave out initial letters of some words). We also leave out the final syllable such as *pa* for *para*. The intervocalic *y*, the *ll* as in *tortilla, ella, botella*, gets replaced by *tortia* or *tortiya, ea, botea*. We add an additional syllable at the beginning of certain words: *atocar* for *tocar, agastar* for *gastar*. Sometimes we'll say *lavaste las vacijas*, other times *lavates* (substituting the *ates* verb endings for the *aste*).

We use anglicisms, words borrowed from English: *bola* from ball, *carpeta* from carpet, *máchina de lavar* (instead of *lavadora*) from washing machine. Tex-Mex argot, created by adding a Spanish sound at the beginning or end of an English word such as *cookiar* for cook, *watchar* for watch, *parkiar* for park, and *rapiar* for rape, is the result of the pressures on Spanish speakers to adapt to English.

We don't use the word *vosotros/as* or its accompanying verb form. We don't say *claro* (to mean yes), *imagínate*, or *me emociona* unless we picked up Spanish from Latinas, out of a book, or in a classroom. Other Spanish-speaking groups are going through the same, or similar, development in their Spanish.

LINGUISTIC TERRORISM

> *Deslenguadas. Somos los del español deficiente.* We are your linguistic nightmare, your linguistic aberration, your linguistic *mestizaje*, the subject of your *burla*. Because we speak with tongues of fire we are culturally crucified. Racially, culturally, and linguistically *somos huérfanos*—we speak an orphan tongue.

Chicanas who grew up speaking Chicano Spanish have internalized the belief that we speak poor Spanish. It is illegitimate, a bastard language. And because we internalize how our language has been used against us by the dominant culture, we use our language differences against each other.

Chicana feminists often skirt around each other with suspicion and hesitation. For the longest time I couldn't figure it out. Then it dawned on me. To be close to another Chicana is like looking into the mirror. We are afraid of what we'll see there. *Pena.* Shame. Low estimation of self. In childhood we are told that our language is wrong. Repeated attacks on our native tongue diminish our sense of self. The attacks continue throughout our lives.

Chicanas feel uncomfortable talking in Spanish to Latinas, afraid of their censure. Their language was not outlawed in their countries. They had a whole lifetime of being immersed in their native tongue; generations, centuries in which Spanish was a first language, taught in school, heard on radio and TV, and read in the newspaper.

If a person, Chicana or Latina, has a low estimation of my native tongue, she also has a low estimation of me. Often with *mexicanas y latinas* we'll speak English as a neutral language. Even among Chicanas we tend to speak English at parties or conferences. Yet, at the same time, we're afraid the other will think we're *agringadas* because we don't speak Chicano Spanish. We oppress each other trying to out-Chicano each other, vying to be the "real" Chicanas, to speak like Chicanos. There is no one Chicano language just as there is no one Chicano experience. A monolingual Chicana whose first language is English or Spanish is just as much a Chicana as one who speaks several variants of Spanish. A Chicana from Michigan or Chicago or Detroit is just as much a Chicana as one from the Southwest. Chicano Spanish is as diverse linguistically as it is regionally.

By the end of this century, Spanish speakers will comprise the biggest minority group in the U.S., a country where students in high schools and colleges are encouraged to take French classes because French is considered more "cultured." But for a language to remain alive it must be used. By the end of this century English, and not Spanish, will be the mother tongue of most Chicanos and Latinos.

So, if you want to really hurt me, talk badly about my language. Ethnic identity is twin skin to linguistic identity—I am my language. Until I can take pride in my language, I cannot take pride in myself. Until I can accept as legitimate Chicano Texas Spanish, Tex-Mex, and all the other languages I speak, I cannot accept the legitimacy of myself. Until I am free to write bilingually and to switch codes without having always to translate, while I still have to speak English or Spanish when I would rather speak Spanglish, and as long as I have to accommodate the English speakers rather than having them accommodate me, my tongue will be illegitimate.

I will no longer be made to feel ashamed of existing. I will have my voice: Indian, Spanish, white. I will have my serpent's tongue—my woman's voice, my sexual voice, my poet's voice. I will overcome the tradition of silence.

> My fingers
> move sly against your palm
> Like women everywhere, we speak in code. . .
> —Melanie Kaye/Kantrowitz

"VISTAS," CORRIDOS Y COMIDA: MY NATIVE TONGUE

In the 1960s, I read my first Chicano novel. It was *City of Night* by John Rechy, a gay Texan, son of a Scottish father and a Mexican mother. For days I walked around in stunned amazement that a Chicano could write and could get published. When I

read *I Am Joaquín* I was surprised to see a bilingual book by a
Chicano in print. When I saw poetry written in Tex-Mex for the
first time, a feeling of pure joy flashed through me. I felt like we
really existed as a people. In 1971, when I started teaching High
School English to Chicano students, I tried to supplement the
required texts with works by Chicanos, only to be reprimanded
and forbidden to do so by the principal. He claimed that I was
supposed to teach "American" and English literature. At the risk
of being fired, I swore my students to secrecy and slipped in
Chicano short stories, poems, a play. In graduate school, while
working toward a Ph.D., I had to "argue" with one advisor after
the other, semester after semester, before I was allowed to make
Chicano literature an area of focus.

Even before I read books by Chicanos or Mexicans, it was the
Mexican movies I saw at the drive-in—the Thursday night special of $1.00 a carload—that gave me a sense of belonging.
"Vámonos a las vistas," my mother would call out and we'd all—
grandmother, brothers, sister, and cousins—squeeze into the
car. We'd wolf down cheese and bologna white bread sandwiches
while watching Pedro Infante in melodramatic tear-jerkers like
Nosotros los pobres, the first "real" Mexican movie (that was not an
imitation of European movies). I remember seeing *Cuando los
hijos se van* and surmising that all Mexican movies played up
the love a mother has for her children and what ungrateful
sons and daughters suffer when they are not devoted to their
mothers. I remember the singing-type "westerns" of Jorge
Negrete and Miguel Aceves Mejía. When watching Mexican
movies, I felt a sense of homecoming as well as alienation. People who were to amount to something didn't go to Mexican
movies or *bailes* or tune their radios to *bolero, rancherita,* and *corrido*
music.

· · ·

The whole time I was growing up, there was *norteño* music, some-times called North Mexican border music, or Tex-Mex music, or Chicano music, or *cantina* (bar) music. I grew up listening to *conjuntos*, three- or four-piece bands made up of folk musicians playing guitar, *bajo sexto*, drums, and button accordion, which Chicanos had borrowed from the German immigrants who had come to Central Texas and Mexico to farm and build breweries. In the Rio Grande Valley, Steve Jordan and Little Joe Hernán-dez were popular, and Flaco Jiménez was the accordion king. The rhythms of Tex-Mex music are those of the polka, also adapted from the Germans, who in turn had borrowed the polka from the Czechs and Bohemians.

I remember the hot, sultry evenings when *corridos*—songs of love and death on the Texas-Mexican borderlands—reverberated out of cheap amplifiers from the local *cantinas* and wafted in through my bedroom window.

Corridos first became widely used along the South Texas/ Mexican border during the early conflict between Chicanos and Anglos. The *corridos* are usually about Mexican heroes who do valiant deeds against the Anglo oppressors. Pancho Villa's song, *"La cucaracha,"* is the most famous one. *Corridos* of John F. Kennedy and his death are still very popular in the Valley. Older Chicanos remember Lydia Mendoza, one of the great border *corrido* singers who was called *la Gloria de Tejas.* Her *"El tango negro,"* sung during the Great Depression, made her a singer of the people. The everpresent *corridos* narrated one hundred years of border history, bringing news of events as well as entertain-ing. These folk musicians and folk songs are our chief cultural mythmakers, and they made our hard lives seem bearable.

I grew up feeling ambivalent about our music. Country west-ern and rock-and-roll had more status. In the 50s and 60s, for the slightly educated and *agringado* Chicanos, there existed a sense of shame at being caught listening to our music. Yet I couldn't stop my feet from thumping to the music, could not stop humming the words, nor hide from myself the exhilaration I felt when I heard it.

There are more subtle ways that we internalize identification, especially in the forms of images and emotions. For me food and certain smells are tied to my identity, to my homeland. Woodsmoke curling up to an immense blue sky; woodsmoke perfuming my grandmother's clothes, her skin. The stench of cow manure and the yellow patches on the ground; the crack of a .22 rifle and the reek of cordite. Homemade white cheese sizzling in a pan, melting inside a folded *tortilla*. My sister Hilda's hot, spicy *menudo, chile colorado* making it deep red, pieces of *panza* and hominy floating on top. My brother Carito barbecuing *fajitas* in the backyard. Even now and 3,000 miles away, I can see my mother spicing the ground beef, pork, and venison with *chile*. My mouth salivates at the thought of the hot steaming *tamales* I would be eating if I were home.

SI LE PREGUNTAS A MI MAMÁ, "¿QUÉ ERES?"

Identity is the essential core of who we are as individuals, the conscious experience of the self inside.

—KAUFMAN

Nosotros los Chicanos straddle the borderlands. On one side of us, we are constantly exposed to the Spanish of the Mexicans, on the other side we hear the Anglos' incessant clamoring so that we forget our language. Among ourselves we don't say *nosotros los americanos, o nosotros los españoles, o nosotros los hispanos.* We say *nosotros los mexicanos* (by *mexicanos* we do not mean citizens of Mexico; we do not mean a national identity, but a racial one). We distinguish between *mexicanos del otro lado* and *mexicanos de este lado*. Deep in our hearts we believe that being Mexican has nothing to do with which country one lives in. Being Mexican is a state of soul—not one of mind, not one of citizenship. Neither eagle nor serpent, but both. And like the ocean, neither animal respects borders.

> *Dime con quien andas y te diré quien eres.*
> (Tell me who your friends are and I'll tell you who you are.)
> —MEXICAN SAYING

Si le preguntas a mi mamá, "¿Qué eres?" te dirá, "Soy mexicana." My brothers and sister say the same. I sometimes will answer *"soy mexicana"* and at others will say *"soy Chicana" o "soy tejana."* But I identified as *"Raza"* before I ever identified as *"mexicana"* or "Chicana."

As a culture, we call ourselves Spanish when referring to ourselves as a linguistic group and when copping out. It is then that we forget our predominant Indian genes. We are 70 percent to 80 percent Indian. We call ourselves Hispanic or Spanish-American or Latin American or Latin when linking ourselves to other Spanish-speaking peoples of the Western hemisphere when copping out. We call ourselves Mexican-American to signify we are neither Mexican nor American, but more the noun "American" than the adjective "Mexican" (and when copping out).

Chicanos and other people of color suffer economically for not acculturating. This voluntary (yet forced) alienation makes for psychological conflict, a kind of dual identity—we don't identify with the Anglo-American cultural values and we don't totally identify with the Mexican cultural values. We are a synergy of two cultures with various degrees of Mexicanness or Angloness. I have so internalized the borderland conflict that sometimes I feel like one cancels out the other and we are zero, nothing, no one. *A veces no soy nada ni nadie. Pero hasta cuando no lo soy, lo soy.*

When not copping out, when we know we are more than nothing, we call ourselves Mexican, referring to race and ancestry; *mestizo* when affirming both our Indian and Spanish (but we hardly ever own our Black) ancestry; Chicano when referring to a politically aware people born and/or raised in the U.S.; *Raza* when referring to Chicanos; *tejanos* when we are Chicanos from Texas.

Chicanos did not know we were a people until 1965 when Cesar Chavez and the farmworkers united and *I Am Joaquín* was published and *la Raza Unida* party was formed in Texas. With that recognition, we became a distinct people. Something momentous happened to the Chicano soul—we became aware of our reality and acquired a name and a language (Chicano Spanish) that reflected that reality. Now that we had a name, some of the fragmented pieces began to fall together—who we were, what we were, how we had evolved. We began to get glimpses of what we might eventually become.

Yet the struggle of identities continues, the struggle of borders is our reality still. One day the inner struggle will cease and a true integration take place. In the meantime, *tenemos que hacer la lucha. ¿Quién está protegiendo los ranchos de mi gente? ¿Quién está tratando de cerrar la fisura entre la india y el blanco en nuestra sangre? El Chicano, sí, el Chicano que anda como un ladrón en su propia casa.*

Los Chicanos, how patient we seem, how very patient. There is the quiet of the Indian about us. We know how to survive. When other races have given up their tongue, we've kept ours. We know what it is to live under the hammer blow of the dominant *norteamericano* culture. But more than we count the blows, we count the days the weeks the years the centuries the eons until the white laws and commerce and customs will rot in the deserts they've created, lie bleached. *Humildes* yet proud, *quietos* yet wild, *nosotros los mexicanos*-Chicanos will walk by the crumbling ashes as we go about our business. Stubborn, persevering, impenetrable as stone, yet possessing a malleability that renders us unbreakable, we, the *mestizas* and *mestizos,* will remain.

India

At sunrise the next day, the time the Indians appointed, they came according to their promise, and brought us a large quantity of fish with certain roots. . . . They sent their women and children to look at us. . . .

—Álvar Núñez Cabeza de Vaca

I used to stare at the Indian in the mirror. The wide nostrils, the thick lips. Starring Paul Muni as Benito Juárez. Such a long face—such a long nose—sculpted by indifferent, blunt thumbs, and of such common clay. No one in my family had a face as dark or as Indian as mine. My face could not portray the ambition I brought to it. What could the United States of America say to me? I remember reading the ponderous conclusion of the Kerner Report in the sixties: two Americas, one white, one black—the prophecy of an eclipse too simple to account for the complexity of my face.

Mestizo in Mexican Spanish means mixed, confused. Clotted with Indian, thinned by Spanish spume.

What could Mexico say to me?

Mexican philosophers powwow in their tony journals about Indian "fatalism" and "Whither Mexico?" *El fatalismo del indio* is an important Mexican philosophical theme; the phrase is trusted to conjure the quality of Indian passivity as well as to initiate debate about Mexico's reluctant progress toward modernization. Mexicans imagine their Indian part as dead-weight: the Indian stunned by modernity; so overwhelmed by the loss of what is genuine to him—his language, his religion—that he sits weeping like a medieval lady at the crossroads; or else he resorts to occult powers and superstitions, choosing to consort with death because the purpose of the world has passed him by.

One night in Mexico City I ventured from my hotel to a distant *colonia* to visit my aunt, my father's only sister. But she was not there. She had moved. For the past several years she has moved, this woman of eighty-odd years, from one of her children to another. She takes with her only her papers and books—she is a poetess—and an upright piano painted blue. My aunt writes love poems to her dead husband, Juan—keeping Juan up to date, while rewatering her loss. Last year she sent me her *obras completas*, an inch-thick block of bound onionskin. And with her poems she sent me a list of names, a genealogy braiding two centuries, two continents, to a common origin: eighteenth-century Salamanca. No explanation is attached to the list. Its implication is nonetheless clear. We are—my father's family is (despite the evidence of my face)—of Europe. We are not Indian.

On the other hand, a Berkeley undergraduate approached me one day, creeping up as if I were a stone totem to say, "God, it must be cool to be related to Aztecs."

I sat down next to the journalist from Pakistan—the guest of honor. He had been making a tour of the United States under the auspices of the U.S. State Department. Nearing the end of his journey now, he was having dinner with several of us, American journalists, at a Chinese restaurant in San Francisco. He said he'd seen pretty much all he wanted to see in America. His wife, however, had asked him to bring back some American Indian handicrafts. Blankets. Beaded stuff. He'd looked everywhere.

The table was momentarily captured by the novelty of his dilemma. You can't touch the stuff nowadays, somebody said. So rare, so expensive. Somebody else knew of a shop up on Sacramento Street that sells authentic Santa Fe. Several others remembered a store in Chinatown where moccasins, belts—"the works"—were to be found. All manufactured in Taiwan.

The Pakistani journalist looked incredulous. His dream of America had been shaped by American export-Westerns. Cowboys and Indians are yin and yang of America. He had seen men dressed like cowboys on this trip. But (turning to me): Where are the Indians?

(Two Indians staring at one another. One asks where are all the Indians, the other shrugs.)

I grew up in Sacramento thinking of Indians as people who had disappeared. I was a Mexican in California; I would no more have thought of myself as an Aztec in California than you might imagine yourself a Viking or a Bantu. Mrs. Ferrucci up the block used to call my family "Spanish." We knew she intended to ennoble us by that designation. We also knew she was ignorant.

I was ignorant.

In America the Indian is relegated to the obligatory first chapter—the "Once Great Nation" chapter—after which the Indian is cleared away as easily as brush, using a very sharp rhetorical tool called an "alas." Thereafter, the Indian reappears only as a stunned remnant—Ishi, or the hundred-year-old hag blowing out her birthday candle at a rest home in Tucson; or the teenager drunk on his ass in Plaza Park.

Here they come down Broadway in the Fourth of July

parades of my childhood—middle-aged men wearing glasses, beating their tom-toms; Hey-ya-ya-yah; Hey-ya-ya-yah. They wore Bermuda shorts under their loincloths. High-school kids could never refrain from the answering Woo-woo-woo, stopping their mouths with the palms of their hands.

In the 1960s, Indians began to name themselves Native Americans, recalling themselves to life. That self-designation underestimated the ruthless idea Puritans had superimposed upon the landscape. America is an idea to which natives are inimical. The Indian represented permanence and continuity to Americans who were determined to call this country new. Indians must be ghosts.

I collected conflicting evidence concerning Mexico, it's true, but I never felt myself the remnant of anything. Mexican magazines arrived in our mailbox from Mexico City; showed pedestrians strolling wide ocher boulevards beneath trees with lime-green leaves. My past was at least this coherent: Mexico was a real place with plenty of people walking around in it. My parents had come from somewhere that went on without them.

When I was a graduate student at Berkeley, teaching remedial English, there were a few American Indians in my classroom. They were unlike any other "minority students" in the classes I taught. The Indians drifted in and out. When I summoned them to my office, they came and sat while I did all the talking.

I remember one tall man particularly, a near-somnambulist, beautiful in an off-putting way, but interesting, too, because I never saw him without the current issue of *The New York Review of Books* under his arm, which I took as an advertisement of ambition. He eschewed my class for weeks at a time. Then one morning I saw him in a café on Telegraph Avenue, across from Cody's. I did not fancy myself Sidney Poitier, but I was interested in this moody brave's lack of interest in me, for one, and then *The New York Review.*

Do you mind if I sit here?

Nothing.

Blah, Blah, Blah . . . *N. Y.R.B. ?*—entirely on my part—until, when I got up to leave:

"You're not Indian, you're Mexican," he said. "You wouldn't understand."

He meant I was cut. Diluted.

Understand what?

He meant I was not an Indian in America. He meant he was an enemy of the history that had otherwise created me. And he was right, I didn't understand. I took his diffidence for chauvinism. I read his chauvinism as arrogance. He didn't see the Indian in my face? I saw his face—his refusal to consort with the living—as the face of a dead man.

As the landscape goes, so goes the Indian? In the public-service TV commercial, the Indian sheds a tear at the sight of an America polluted beyond his recognition. Indian memory has become the measure against which America gauges corrupting history when it suits us. Gitchigoomeism—the habit of placing the Indian outside history—is a white sentimentality that relegates the Indian to death.

An obituary from *The New York Times* (September 1989—dateline Alaska): An oil freighter has spilled its load along the Alaskan coast. There is a billion-dollar cleanup, bringing jobs and dollars to Indian villages.

> The modern world has been closing in on English Bay . . .
> with glacial slowness. The oil spill and the resulting sea of
> money have accelerated the process, so that English Bay now
> seems caught on the cusp of history.

The omniscient reporter from *The New York Times* takes it upon himself to regret history on behalf of the Indians.

Instead of hanging salmon to dry this month, as Aleut
natives have done for centuries . . . John Kvasnikoff was put-
ting up a three thousand dollar television satellite dish on the
bluff next to his home above the sea.

The reporter from *The New York Times* knows the price modernity will exact from an Indian who wants to plug himself in.
Mind you, the reporter is confident of his own role in history,
his freedom to lug a word processor to some remote Alaskan village. About the reporter's journey, *The New York Times* is not cen-
sorious. But let the Indian drop one bead from custom, or let
his son straddle a snowmobile—as he does in the photo accompanying the article—and *The New York Times* cries Boo-hoo-hoo
yah-yah-yah.

Thus does the Indian become the mascot of an international
ecology movement. The industrial countries of the world
romanticize the Indian who no longer exists, ignoring the Indian
who does—the Indian who is poised to chop down his rain forest, for example. Or the Indian who reads *The New York Times*.

Once more in San Francisco: I flattered myself that the
woman staring at me all evening "knew my work." I considered
myself an active agent, in other words. But, after several passes
around the buffet, the woman cornered me to say she recognized
me as an "ancient soul."

Do I lure or am I just minding my own business?

Is it the nature of Indians—not verifiable in nature, of
course, but in the European description of Indians—that we
wait around to be "discovered"?

Europe discovers. India beckons. Isn't that so? India sits atop
her lily pad through centuries, lost in contemplation of the
horizon. And, from time to time, India is discovered.

In the fifteenth century, sailing Spaniards were acting according to scientific conjecture as to the nature and as to the

shape of the world. Most thinking men in Europe at the time
of Columbus believed the world to be round. The voyage of
Columbus was the test of a theory believed to be true. Brave,
yes, but pedantic therefore.

The Indian is forever implicated in the roundness of the
world. America was the false India, the mistaken India, and yet
veritable India, for all that—India—the clasp, the coupling
mystery at the end of quest.

This is as true today as of yore. Where do the Beatles go
when the world is too much with them? Where does Jerry Brown
seek the fat farm of his soul? India, man, India!

India waits.

India has all the answers beneath her passive face or behind
her veil or between her legs. The European has only questions,
questions that are assertions turned inside out, questions that
can only be answered by sailing toward the abysmal horizon.

The lusty Europeans wanted the shortest answers. They knew
what they wanted. They wanted spices, pagodas, gold.

Had the world been flat, had the European sought the
unknown, then the European would have been as great a victor
over history as he has portrayed himself to be. The European
would have outdistanced history—even theology—if he could
have arrived at the shore of some prelapsarian state. If the world
had been flat, then the European could have traveled outward
toward innocence.

But the world was round. The entrance into the Indies was
a reunion of peoples. The Indian awaited the long-separated
European, the inevitable European, as the approaching horizon.

Though perhaps, too, there was some demiurge felt by the
human race of the fifteenth century to heal itself, to make itself
whole? Certainly, in retrospect, there was some inevitability to
the Catholic venture. If the world was round, continuous, then
so, too, were peoples?

According to the European version—the stag version—of the pageant of the New World, the Indian must play a passive role. Europe has been accustomed to play the swaggart in history—Europe striding through the Americas, overturning temples, spilling language, spilling seed, spilling blood.

And wasn't the Indian the female, the passive, the waiting aspect to the theorem—lewd and promiscuous in her embrace as she is indolent betimes?

Charles Macomb Flandrau, a native of St. Paul, Minnesota, wrote a book called *Viva Mexico!* in 1908, wherein he described the Mexican Indian as "incorrigibly plump. One never ceases to marvel at the superhuman strength existing beneath the pretty and effeminate modeling of their arms and legs and backs. . . . The legs of an American 'strong man' look usually like an anatomical chart, but the legs of the most powerful Totonac Indian—and the power of many of them is beyond belief— would serve admirably as one of those idealized extremities on which women's hosiery is displayed in shop windows."

In Western Civilization histories, the little honeymoon joke Europe tells on itself is of mistaking America for the extremities of India. But India was perhaps not so much a misnomer as was "discoverer" or "conquistador."

Earliest snapshots of Indians brought back to Europe were of naked little woodcuts, arms akimbo, resembling Erasmus, or of grandees in capes and feathered tiaras, courtiers of an Egyptified palace of nature. In European museums, she is idle, recumbent at the base of a silver pineapple tree or the pedestal of the Dresden urn or the Sèvres tureen—the muse of European adventure, at once wanderlust and bounty.

Many tribes of Indians were prescient enough, preserved memory enough, or were lonesome enough to predict the coming of a pale stranger from across the sea, a messianic twin of completing memory or skill.

None of this could the watery Europeans have known as they marveled at the sight of approaching land. Filled with the arrogance of discovery, the Europeans were not predisposed to imagine that they were being watched, awaited.

That friend of mine at Oxford loses patience whenever I describe my face as mestizo. Look at my face. What do you see?

An Indian, he says.

Mestizo, I correct.

Mestizo, mestizo, he says.

Listen, he says. I went back to my mother's village in Mexico last summer and there was nothing mestizo about it. Dust, dogs, and Indians. People there don't even speak Spanish.

So I ask my friend at Oxford what it means to him to be an Indian.

He hesitates. My friend has recently been taken up as amusing by a bunch of rich Pakistanis in London. But, facing me, he is vexed and in earnest. He describes a lonely search among his family for evidence of Indian-ness. He thinks he has found it in his mother; watching his mother in her garden.

Does she plant corn by the light of the moon?

She seems to have some relationship with the earth, he says quietly.

So there it is. The mystical tie to nature. How else to think of the Indian except in terms of some druidical green thumb? No one says of an English matron in her rose garden that she is behaving like a Celt. Because the Indian has no history—that is, because history books are the province of the descendants of Europeans—the Indian seems only to belong to the party of the first part, the first chapter. So that is where the son expects to find his mother, Daughter of the Moon.

Let's talk about something else. Let's talk about London. The last time I was in London, I was walking toward an early evening at the Queen's Theatre when I passed that Christopher Wren church near Fortnum & Mason. The church was lit; I decided to stop, to savor the spectacle of what I expected would be a few Pymish men and women rolled into balls of fur at evensong. Imagine my surprise that the congregation was young—dressed in army fatigues and Laura Ashley. Within the chancel, cross-legged on a dais, was a South American shaman.

Now, who is the truer Indian in this picture? Me . . . me on my way to the Queen's Theatre? Or that guy on the altar with a Ph.D. in death?

We have hurled—like starlings, like Goths—through the castle of European memory. Our reflections have glanced upon the golden coach that carried the Emperor Maximilian through the streets of Mexico City, thence onward through the sludge of a hundred varnished paintings.

I have come at last to Mexico, the country of my parents' birth. I do not expect to find anything that pertains to me.

We have strained the rouge cordon at the thresholds of imperial apartments; seen chairs low enough for dwarfs, commodious enough for angels.

We have imagined the Empress Carlota standing in the shadows of an afternoon; we have followed her gaze down the Paseo de la Reforma toward the distant city. The Paseo was a nostalgic allusion to the Champs-Elysées, we learn, which Maximilian recreated for his tempestuous, crowlike bride.

Come this way, please. . . .

European memory is not to be the point of our excursion. Señor Fuentes, our tour director, is already beginning to descend the hill from Chapultepec Castle. What the American credit-card company calls our "orientation tour" of Mexico City had started late and so Señor Fuentes has been forced, regrettably,

". . . This way, please . . ."

to rush. Señor Fuentes is consumed with contrition for time wasted this morning. He intends to uphold his schedule, as a way of upholding Mexico, against our expectation.

We had gathered at the appointed time at the limousine entrance to our hotel, beneath the banner welcoming contestants to the Señorita Mexico pageant. We—Japanese, Germans, Americans—were waiting promptly at nine. There was no bus. And as we waited, the Señorita Mexico contestants arrived. Drivers leaned into their cabs to pull out long-legged señoritas. The drivers then balanced the señoritas onto stiletto heels (the driveway was cobbled) before they passed the señoritas, *en pointe*, to the waiting arms of officials.

Mexican men, meanwhile—doormen, bellhops, window washers, hotel guests—stopped dead in their tracks, wounded by the scent and spectacle of so many blond señoritas. The Mexican men assumed fierce expressions, nostrils flared, brows knit. Such expressions are masks—the men intend to convey their adoration of prey—as thoroughly ritualized as the smiles of beauty queens.

By now we can see the point of our excursion beyond the parched trees of Chapultepec Park—the Museo Nacional de Antropología—which is an air-conditioned repository for the artifacts of the Indian civilizations of Meso-America, the finest anthropological museum in the world.

"There will not be time to see everything," Señor Fuentes warns as he ushers us into the grand salon, our first experience of the suffocating debris of The Ancients. Señor Fuentes wants us in and out of here by noon.

Whereas the United States traditionally has rejoiced at the

delivery of its landscape from "savagery," Mexico has taken its national identity only from the Indian, the mother. Mexico measures all cultural bastardy against the Indian; equates civilization with India—Indian kingdoms of a golden age; cities as fabulous as Alexandria or Benares or Constantinople; a court as hairless, as subtle as the Pekingese. Mexico equates barbarism with Europe—beardedness—with Spain.

It is curious, therefore, that both modern nations should similarly apostrophize the Indian, relegate the Indian to the past.

Come this way, please. Mrs. . . . Ah . . . this way, please.

Señor Fuentes wears an avocado-green sports coat with gold buttons. He is short. He is rather elegant, with a fine small head, small hands, small feet; with his two rows of fine small teeth like a nutcracker's teeth, with which he curtails consonants as cleanly as bitten thread. Señor Fuentes is brittle, he is watchful, he is ironic, he is metropolitan; his wit is quotational, literary, wasted on Mrs. Ah.

He is not our equal. His demeanor says he is not our equal. We mistake his condescension for humility. He will not eat when we eat. He will not spend when we shop. He will not have done with Mexico when we have done with Mexico.

Señor Fuentes is impatient with us, for we have paused momentarily outside the museum to consider the misfortune of an adolescent mother who holds her crying baby out to us. Several of us confer among ourselves in an attempt to place a peso value on the woman's situation. We do not ask for the advice of Señor Fuentes.

For we, in turn, are impatient with Señor Fuentes. We are in a bad mood. The air conditioning on our "fully air-conditioned coach" is nonexistent. We have a headache. Nor is the city air any relief, but it is brown, fungal, farted.

Señor Fuentes is a mystery to us, for there is no American

equivalent to him; for there is no American equivalent to the subtleties he is paid to describe to us.

Mexico will not raise a public monument to Hernán Cortés, for example, the father of Mexico—the rapist. In the Diego Rivera murals in the presidential palace, the Aztec city of Tenochtitlán is rendered—its blood temples and blood canals—as haughty as Troy, as vulnerable as Pompeii. Any suggestion of the complicity of other tribes of Indians in overthrowing the Aztec empire is painted over. Spaniards appear on the horizons of Arcadia as syphilitic brigands and demon-eyed priests.

The Spaniard entered the Indian by entering her city—the floating city—first as a suitor, ceremoniously; later by force. How should Mexico honor the rape?

In New England the European and the Indian drew apart to regard each other with suspicion over centuries. Miscegenation was a sin against Protestant individualism. In Mexico the European and the Indian consorted. The ravishment of fabulous Tenochtitlán ended in a marriage of blood—a "cosmic race," the Mexican philosopher José Vasconcelos has called it.

Mexico's tragedy is that she has no political idea of herself as rich as her blood.

The rhetoric of Señor Fuentes, like the murals of Diego Rivera, resorts often to the dream of India—to Tenochtitlán, the capital of the world before conquest. "Preconquest" in the Mexican political lexicon is tantamount to "prelapsarian" in the Judeo-Christian scheme, and hearkens to a time Mexico feels herself to have been whole, a time before the Indian was separated from India by the serpent Spain.

Three centuries after Cortés, Mexico declared herself independent of Spain. If Mexico would have no yoke, then Mexico would have no crown, then Mexico would have no father. The denial of Spain has persisted into our century.

The priest and the landowner yet serve Señor Fuentes as symbols of the hated Spanish order. Though, in private, Mexico is Catholic; Mexican mothers may wish for light-skinned children. Touch blond hair and good luck will be yours.

In private, in Mexican Spanish, *indio* is a seller of Chiclets, a sidewalk squatter. *Indio* means backward or lazy or lower-class. In the eyes of the world, Mexico raises a magnificent museum of anthropology—the finest in the world—to honor the Indian mother.

In the nave of the National Cathedral, we notice the floor slopes dramatically. "The cathedral is sinking," Señor Fuentes explains as a hooded figure approaches our group from behind a column. She is an Indian woman; she wears a blue stole; her hands are cupped, beseeching; tear marks ream her cheeks. In Spanish, Señor Fuentes forbids this apparition: "Go ask *padrecito* to pry some gold off the altar for you."

"Mexico City is built upon swamp," Señor Fuentes resumes in English. "Therefore, the cathedral is sinking." But it is clear that Señor Fuentes believes the sinkage is due to the oppressive weight of Spanish Catholicism, its masses of gold, its volumes of deluded suspiration.

Mexican political life can only seem Panglossian when you consider an anti-Catholic government of an overwhelmingly Catholic population. Mexico is famous for politicians descended from Masonic fathers and Catholic mothers. Señor Fuentes himself is less a Spaniard, less an Indian, perhaps, than an embittered eighteenth-century man, clinging to the witty knees of Voltaire against the chaos of twentieth-century Mexico.

Mexico blamed the ruin of the nineteenth century on the foreigner, and with reason. Once emptied of Spain, the palace of Mexico became the dollhouse of France. Mexico was overrun by imperial armies. The greed of Europe met the Manifest Destiny of the United States in Mexico. Austria sent an archduke to marry Mexico with full panoply of candles and bishops. The U.S. reached under Mexico's skirt every chance he got.

"Poor Mexico, so far from God, so close to the United States."

Señor Fuentes dutifully attributes the mot to Porfirio Díaz, the Mexican president who sold more of Mexico to foreign interests than any other president. It was against the regime of Porfirio Díaz that Mexicans rebelled in the early decades of this century. Mexico prefers to call its civil war a "revolution."

Mexico for Mexicans!

The Revolution did not accomplish a union of Mexicans. The Revolution did not accomplish a restoration of Mexicans to their landscape. The dust of the Revolution parted to reveal—not India—but Marx *ex machina*, the Institutional Revolutionary Party, the PRI—a political machine appropriate to the age of steam. The Institutional Revolutionary Party, as its name implies, was designed to reconcile institutional pragmatism with revolutionary rhetoric. And the PRI worked for a time, because it gave Mexico what Mexico most needed, the stability of compromise.

The PRI appears everywhere in Mexico—a slogan on the wall, the politician impersonating a journalist on the evening news, the professor at his podium. The PRI is in its way as much a Mexican institution as the Virgin of Guadalupe.

Now Mexicans speak of the government as something imposed upon them, and they are the victims of it. But the political failure of Mexico must be counted a failure of Mexicans. Whom now shall Señor Fuentes blame for a twentieth century that has become synonymous with corruption?

Well, as long as you stay out of the way of the police no one will bother you, is conventional Mexican wisdom, and Mexico continues to live her daily life. In the capital, the air is the color of the buildings of Siena. Telephone connections are an aspect of the will of God. Mexicans drive on the sidewalks. A man on the street corner seizes the opportunity of stalled traffic to earn his living as a fire-eater. His ten children pass among the cars and among the honking horns to collect small coins.

Thank you. Thank you very much. A pleasure, Mrs. . . . Ah. Thank you very much.

Señor Fuentes bids each farewell. He accepts tips within a handshake. He bows slightly. We have no complaint with Señor Fuentes, after all. The bus was not his fault. Mexico City is not his fault. And Señor Fuentes will return to his unimaginable Mexico and we will return to our rooms to take aspirin and to initiate long-distance telephone calls. Señor Fuentes will remove his avocado-green coat and, having divested, Señor Fuentes will in some fashion partake of what he has successfully kept from us all day, which is the life and the drinking water of Mexico.

The Virgin of Guadalupe symbolizes the entire coherence of Mexico, body and soul. You will not find the story of the Virgin within hidebound secular histories of Mexico—nor indeed within the credulous repertoire of Señor Fuentes—and the omission renders the history of Mexico incomprehensible.

One recent afternoon, within the winy bell jar of a very late lunch, I told the story of the Virgin of Guadalupe to Lynn, a sophisticated twentieth-century woman. The history of Mexico, I promised her, is neither mundane nor masculine, but it is a miracle play with trapdoors and sequins and jokes on the living.

In the sixteenth century, when Indians were demoralized by the routing of their gods, when millions of Indians were dying from the plague of Europe, the Virgin Mary appeared pacing on a hillside to an Indian peasant named Juan Diego—his Christian name, for Juan was a convert. It was December 1531.

On his way to mass, Juan passed the hill called Tepayac . . .

> *Just as the East was beginning to kindle*
> *To dawn. He heard there a cloud*
> *Of birdsong bursting overhead*
> *Of whistles and flutes and beating wings*
> *—Now here, now there—*
> *A mantle of chuckles and berries and rain*
> *That rocked through the sky like the great Spanish bell*
> *In Mexico City;*
> *At the top of the hill there shone a light*
> *And the light called out a name to him*
> *With a lady's voice.*
> *Juan, Juan,*
> *The Lady-light called.*
> *Juan crossed himself, he fell to his knees,*
> *He covered his eyes and prepared to be blinded.*
>
> *He could see through his hands that covered his face*
> *As the sun rose up from behind her cape,*
> *That the poor light of day*
> *Was no match for this Lady, but broke upon her*
> *Like a waterfall,*
> *A rain of rings.*
> *She wore a gown the color of dawn.*
> *Her hair was braided with ribbons and flowers*
> *And tiny tinkling silver bells. Her mantle was sheer*
> *And bright as rain and embroidered with thousands*
> *of twinkling stars.*
> *A clap before curtains, like waking from sleep;*
> *Then a human face,*

A mother's smile;
Her complexion as red as cinnamon bark;
Cheeks as brown as persimmon.

Her eyes were her voice,
As modest and shy as a pair of doves
In the eaves of her brow. Her voice was
Like listening. This lady spoke
In soft Nahuatl, the Aztec tongue
(As different from Spanish
As some other season of weather,
As doves in the boughs of a summer tree
Are different from crows in a wheeling wind,
Who scatter destruction and
Caw caw caw caw)—
Nahuatl like rain, like water flowing, like drips in a
cavern,
Or glistening thaw,
Like breath through a flute,
With many stops and plops and sighs . . .

Peering through the grille of her cigarette smoke, Lynn heard and she seemed to approve the story.

At the Virgin's behest, this Prufrock Indian must go several times to the bishop of Mexico City. He must ask that a chapel be built on Tepayac where his discovered Lady may share in the sorrows of her people. Juan Diego's visits to the Spanish bishop parody the conversion of the Indians by the Spaniards. The bishop is skeptical.

The bishop wants proof.

The Virgin tells Juan Diego to climb the hill and gather a sheaf of roses as proof for the bishop—Castilian roses—impossible in Mexico in December of 1531. Juan carries the roses in the folds of his cloak, a pregnant messenger. Upon entering the bishop's presence, Juan parts his cloak, the roses tumble; the bishop falls to his knees.

In the end—with crumpled napkins, torn carbons, the bitter dregs of coffee—Lynn gave the story over to the Spaniards.

The legend concludes with a concession to humanity—proof more durable than roses—the imprint of the Virgin's image upon the cloak of Juan Diego . . .

A Spanish trick, Lynn said. A recruitment poster for the new religion, no more, she said (though sadly). An itinerant diva with a costume trunk. Birgit Nilsson as Aïda.

Why do we assume Spain made up the story?

The importance of the story is that Indians believed it. The jokes, the vaudeville, the relegation of the Spanish bishop to the role of comic adversary, the Virgin's chosen cavalier, and especially the brown-faced Mary—all elements spoke directly to Indians.

The result of the apparition and of the miraculous image of the Lady remaining upon the cloak of Juan Diego was a mass conversion of Indians to Catholicism.

The image of Our Lady of Guadalupe (privately, affectionately, Mexicans call her La Morenita—Little Darkling) has become the unofficial, the private flag of Mexicans. Unique possession of her image is a more wonderful election to Mexicans than any political call to nationhood. Perhaps Mexico's tragedy in our century, perhaps Mexico's abiding grace thus far, is that she has no political idea of herself as compelling as her icon.

The Virgin appears everywhere in Mexico. On dashboards and on calendars, on playing cards, on lampshades and cigar boxes; within the loneliness and tattooed upon the very skins of Mexicans.

Nor is the image of Guadalupe a diminishing mirage of the

sixteenth century, but she has become more vivid with time, developing in her replication from earthy shades of melon and musk to bubble-gum pink, Windex blue, to achieve the hard, literal focus of holy cards or baseball cards; of Krishna or St. Jude or the Atlanta Braves.

Mexico City stands as the last living medieval capital of the world. Mexico is the creation of a Spanish Catholicism that attempted to draw continents together as one flesh. The success of Spanish Catholicism in Mexico resulted in a kind of proof—a profound concession to humanity: the *mestizaje.*

What joke on the living? Lynn said.

The joke is that Spain arrived with missionary zeal at the shores of contemplation. But Spain had no idea of the absorbent strength of Indian spirituality.

By the waters of baptism, the active European was entirely absorbed within the contemplation of the Indian. The faith that Europe imposed in the sixteenth century was, by virtue of the Guadalupe, embraced by the Indian. Catholicism has become an Indian religion. By the twenty-first century, the locus of the Catholic Church, by virtue of numbers, will be Latin America, by which time Catholicism itself will have assumed the aspect of the Virgin of Guadalupe.

Brown skin.

Time magazine dropped through the chute of my mailbox a few years ago with a cover story on Mexico entitled "The Population Curse." From the vantage point of Sixth Avenue, the editors of Time-Life peer down into the basin of Mexico City—like peering down into the skull of a pumpkin—to contemplate the nightmare of fecundity, the tangled mass of slime and hair and seed.

America sees death in all that life; sees rot. Life—not illness and poverty, not death—life becomes the curse of Mexico City in the opinion of *Time* magazine.

For a long time I had my own fear of Mexico, an American fear. Mexico's history was death. Her stature was tragedy. A race of people that looked like me had disappeared.

I had a dream about Mexico City, a conquistador's dream. I was lost and late and twisted in my sheet. I dreamed streets narrower than they actually are—narrow as old Jerusalem. I dreamed sheets, entanglements, bunting, hanging larvaelike from open windows, distended from balconies and from lines thrown over the streets. These streets were not empty streets. I was among a crowd. The crowd was not a carnival crowd. This crowd was purposeful and ordinary, welling up from subways, ascending from stairwells. And then the dream followed the course of all my dreams. I must find the airport—the American solution—I must somehow escape, fly over.

Each face looked like mine. But no one looked at me.

I have come at last to Mexico, to the place of my parents' birth. I have come under the protection of an American credit-card company. I have canceled this trip three times.

As the plane descends into the basin of Mexico City, I brace myself for some confrontation with death, with India, with confusion of purpose that I do not know how to master.

Do you speak Spanish? the driver asks in English.

Andrés, the driver employed by my hotel, is in his forties. He lives in the Colonia Roma, near the airport. There is nothing about the city he does not know. This is his city and he is its memory.

Andrés's car is a dark-blue Buick—about 1975. Windows slide up and down at the touch of his finger. There is the smell of disinfectant in Andrés's car, as there is in every bus or limousine or taxi I've ridden in Mexico—the smell of the glycerine crystals in urinals. Dangling from Andrés's rearview mirror is the other appliance common to all public conveyance in Mexico—a rosary.

Andrés is a man of the world, a man, like other working-class Mexican men, eager for the world. He speaks two languages. He knows several cities. He has been to the United States. His brother lives there still.

In the annals of the famous European discoverers there is invariably an Indian guide, a translator—willing or not—to facilitate, to preserve Europe's stride. These seem to have become fluent in pallor before Europe learned anything of them. How is that possible?

The most famous guide in Mexican history is also the most reviled by Mexican histories—the villainess Marina—"La Malinche." Marina became the lover of Cortés. So, of course, Mexicans say she betrayed India for Europe. In the end, she was herself betrayed, left behind when Cortés repaired to his Spanish wife.

Nonetheless, Marina's treachery anticipates the epic marriage of Mexico. La Malinche prefigures, as well, the other, the beloved female aspect of Mexico, the Virgin of Guadalupe.

Because Marina was the seducer of Spain, she challenges the boast Europe has always told about India.

I assure you Mexico has an Indian point of view as well, a female point of view:

I opened my little eye and the Spaniard disappeared.

Imagine a dark pool; the Spaniard dissolved; the surface triumphantly smooth.

My eye!

The spectacle of the Spaniard on the horizon, vainglorious—the shiny surfaces, clanks of metal; the horses, the muskets, the jingling bits.

Cannot you imagine me curious? Didn't I draw near?

European vocabularies do not have a silence rich enough to describe the force within Indian contemplation. Only Shake-

speare understood that Indians have eyes. Shakespeare saw Cali-
ban eyeing his master's books—well, why not his master as well?
The same dumb lust.

WHAT DAT? is a question philosophers ask. And Indians.

Shakespeare's comedy, of course, resolves itself to the European's applause. The play that Shakespeare did not write is Mexico City.

Now the great city swells under the moon; seems, now, to
breathe of itself—the largest city in the world—a Globe, kind
Will, not of your devising, not under your control.

The superstition persists in European travel literature that
Indian Christianity is the thinnest veneer covering an ulterior
altar. But there is a possibility still more frightening to the European imagination, so frightening that in five hundred years such
a possibility has scarcely found utterance.

What if the Indian were converted?

The Indian eye becomes a portal through which the entire
pageant of European civilization has already passed; turned
inside out. Then the baroque is an Indian conceit. The colonial
arcade is an Indian detail.

Look once more at the city from La Malinche's point of view.
Mexico is littered with the shells and skulls of Spain, cathedrals,
poems, and the limbs of orange trees. But everywhere you look
in this great museum of Spain you see living Indians.

Where are the *conquistadores*?

Postcolonial Europe expresses pity or guilt behind its sleeve,
pities the Indian the loss of her gods or her tongue. But let
the Indian speak for herself. Spanish is now an Indian language. Mexico City has become the metropolitan see of the
Spanish-speaking world. In something like the way New York
won English from London after World War I, Mexico City has
captured Spanish.

The Indian stands in the same relationship to modernity as
she did to Spain—willing to marry, to breed, to disappear in

order to ensure her inclusion in time; refusing to absent herself from the future. The Indian has chosen to survive, to consort with the living, to live in the city, to crawl on her hands and knees, if need be, to Mexico City or L.A.

I take it as an Indian achievement that I am alive, that I am Catholic, that I speak English, that I am an American. My life began, it did not end, in the sixteenth century.

The idea occurs to me on a weekday morning, at a crowded intersection in Mexico City: Europe's lie. Here I am in the capital of death. Life surges about me; wells up from subways, wave upon wave; descends from stairwells. Everywhere I look. Babies. Traffic. Food. Beggars. Life. Life coming upon me like sunstroke.

Each face looks like mine. No one looks at me.

Where, then, is the famous conquistador?

We have eaten him, the crowd tells me, *we have eaten him with our eyes.*

I run to the mirror to see if this is true.

It is true.

In the distance, at its depths, Mexico City stands as the prophetic example. Mexico City is modern in ways that "multi-racial," ethnically "diverse" New York City is not yet. Mexico City is centuries more modern than racially "pure," provincial Tokyo. Nothing to do with computers or skyscrapers.

Mexico City is the capital of modernity, for in the sixteenth century, under the tutelage of a curious Indian whore, under the patronage of the Queen of Heaven, Mexico initiated the task of the twenty-first century—the renewal of the old, the known world, through miscegenation. Mexico carries the idea of a round world to its biological conclusion.

For a time when he was young, Andrés, my driver, worked in Alpine County in northern California.

And then he worked at a Lake Tahoe resort. He remembers

the snow. He remembers the weekends when blond California girls would arrive in their ski suits and sunglasses. Andrés worked at the top of a ski lift. His job was to reach out over a little precipice to help the California girls out of their lift chairs. He would maintain his grasp until they were balanced upon the snow. And then he would release them, watch them descend the winter slope—how they laughed!—oblivious of his admiration, until they disappeared.

Meditations on the South Valley:
Poem IX

Eddie blew his head off
playing chicken
with his brother. Para proof
he was a man,
he blew his head off.
Don't toll the bell brother,
'cuz he was not religious.
The gray donkey he liked to talk to
at Dead-Man's Corner
grazes sadly. Eddie's gone, its black-lashed dark eyes
mourn. His tío Manuel shatters a bottle
of La Copita wine against the adobe wall
where he and his compas drink every afternoon,
and Manuel weeps for Eddie.

                "He was the kids without a coat
                during winter. 'Member he stole
                those gloves from SEARS, you 'member,

he stole those gloves? Nice gloves.
He gave 'em to me ese."

Blew his head off.
The explosion of the gun
was the golden flash of his voice
telling us *no more, no more, no more.*
His last bloody words
water the dried weeds
where his jefa threw the stucco fragments
out. Sparrows peck his brains outside
by the fence posts.

> Flaco said, "Don't give him no eulogy!
> He was for brothers and sisters
> in struggle. You know I saw him
> in court one day, when they handcuffed
> his older brother to take his brother
> to prison, you know Eddie jumped the
> benches, and grabbed his brother's
> handcuffs, yelling, don't take my brother
> he is not a bad man!"

Everybody in Southside knew Eddie,
little Eddie, bad little Eddie.
He treated everybody with respect and honor.
With black-board classroom attention
he saw injustice, hanging out en las calles,
sunrise 'til sunset, with the bros and sisters.

Don't ring the bell, brother.
Let it lie dead.
Let the heavy metal rust.

Let the rope fray and swing mutely
in the afternoon dust and wind.

How many times they beat you Eddie?
How many police clubs
are smeared with your blood,
Switch blade en bolsa,
manos de piedra,
en la línea con sus carnales,
to absorb the tire-jack beatings from other locotes,
     billy-club beatings de la jura—
your blood Eddie spotted
sidewalks,
smeared shovel handles,
coated knife blades,
blurred your eyes and painted your body
in a tribal-barrio dance
to set yourself free,
to know what was beyond the boundaries
you were born into,
          in your own way,
          in your own sweet way, taking care
          of grandma, her room giving off the aura
          of a saintly relic,
          old wood floors and walls
          smoothed by the continual passing of her body,
          burnished to an altar of sorts,
          in which she was your saint,
          you cared for,
eating with her each evening,
sharing the foodstamps she had,
walking her to la tiendita,
whose walls were scribbled with black paint

your handwriting and initials,
your boundary marker, deadly symbol to other chavos
entering your barrio—the severe, dark stitches of letters
on the walls
healed your wound at being illiterate—
the white adobe wall with your cholo symbols
introduced you to the world,
                          as Eddie
who leaned on haunches in the sun,
back against a wall,
talking to 11, 13, 15, 17 year old vatos
sniffing airplane glue
from a paper bag,
breathing in typing correction fluid,
smoking basucón, what Whites call crack,
smoking pelo rojo sinsemilla:

                          you listened to their words,
                          chale
                          simón
                          wacha bro
                          me importa madre
                          ni miedo de la muerta
                          ni de la pinta
                          ni de la placa,

and you cried out
hijo de la chingada madre,
cansao
de retablos de calles
pintaos con sangre de tu gente,

                          you cried out
to stop it!
Quit giving the wind our grief stricken voices
at cemeteries,

quit letting the sun soak up our blood,
quit dropping out of high school,
                    in the center of the storm,
you absorbing the feeling of worthlessness,
caught in your brown skin
and tongue that could not properly pronounce English words,
caught like a seed unable to plant itself,
                    you picked up God's blue metal face
and scattered the seed of your heart
across the afternoon air,
among the spiked petals of a cactus,
and elm leaves,
                    your voice whispered
                    in the dust and weeds,
a terrible silence,
not to forget your death.

B. Traven Is Alive and Well
in Cuernavaca

I didn't go to Mexico to find B. Traven. Why should I? I have enough to do writing my own fiction, so I go to Mexico to write, not to search out writers. B. Traven? you ask. Don't you remember *The Treasure of the Sierra Madre?* A real classic. They made a movie from the novel. I remember seeing it when I was a kid. It was set in Mexico, and it had all the elements of a real adventure story. B. Traven was an adventurous man, traveled all over the world, then disappeared into Mexico and cut himself off from society. He gave no interviews and allowed few photographs. While he lived he remained unapproachable, anonymous to his public, a writer shrouded in mystery.

He's dead now, or they say he's dead. I think he's alive and well. At any rate, he has become something of an institution in Mexico, a man honored for his work. The cantineros and taxi drivers in Mexico City know about him as well as the cantineros of Spain knew Hemingway, or they claim to. I never mention I'm a writer when I'm in a cantina, because inevitably some aficionado will ask, "Do you know the work of B. Traven?" And from some dusty niche will appear a yellowed, thumb-worn novel by Traven. Then if the cantinero knows his business, and they all do in Mexico, he is apt to say, "Did you know that B. Traven used to drink here?" If you show the slightest interest, he will follow with, "Sure, he used to sit right over here. In this corner . . . And if you don't leave right then you will wind up hearing many stories about the mysterious B. Traven while buying many drinks for the local patrons.

Everybody reads his novels, on the buses, on street corners, and if you look closely you'll spot one of his titles. One turned up for me, and that's how this story started. I was sitting in the train station in Juárez, waiting for the train to Cuernavaca, which would be an exciting title for this story except that there is no train to Cuernavaca. I was drinking beer to kill time, the erotic and sensitive Mexican time which is so different from the clean-packaged, well-kept time of the Americanos. Time in Mexico is at times cruel and punishing, but it is never indifferent. It permeates everything, it changes reality. Einstein would have loved Mexico because there time and space are one. I stare more often into empty space when I'm in Mexico. The past seems to infuse the present, and in the brown, wrinkled faces of the old people one sees the presence of the past. In Mexico I like to walk the narrow streets of the cities and the smaller pueblos, wandering aimlessly, feeling the sunlight which is so distinctively Mexican, listening to the voices which call in the streets, peering into the dark eyes which are so secretive and so proud. The Mexican people guard a secret. But in the end, one is never really lost in Mexico. All streets lead to a good cantina. All good stories start in a cantina.

At the train station, after I let the kids who hustle the tourists know that I didn't want chewing gum or cigarettes, and I didn't want my shoes shined, and I didn't want a woman at the moment, I was left alone to drink my beer. Luke-cold Dos

Equis. I don't remember how long I had been there or how many Dos Equis I had finished when I glanced at the seat next to me and saw a book which turned out to be a B. Traven novel, old and used and obviously much read, but a novel nevertheless. What's so strange about finding a B. Traven novel in that dingy little corner of a bar in the Juárez train station? Nothing, unless you know that in Mexico one never finds anything. It is a country that doesn't waste anything, everything is recycled. Chevrolets run with patched-up Ford engines and Chrysler transmissions, buses are kept together, and kept running, with baling wire and homemade parts, yesterday's Traven novel is the pulp on which tomorrow's Fuentes story will appear. Time recycles in Mexico. Time returns to the past, and, the Christian finds himself dreaming of ancient Aztec rituals. He who does not believe that Quetzalcóatl will return to save Mexico has little faith.

So the novel was the first clue. Later there was Justino. "Who is Justino?" you want to know. Justino was the jardinero who cared for the garden of my friend, the friend who had invited me to stay at his home in Cuernavaca while I continued to write. The day after I arrived I was sitting in the sun, letting the fatigue of the long journey ooze away, thinking nothing, when Justino appeared on the scene. He had finished cleaning the swimming pool and was taking his morning break, so he sat in the shade of the orange tree and introduced himself. Right away I could tell that he would rather be a movie actor or an adventurer, a real free spirit. But things didn't work out for him. He got married, children appeared, he took a couple of mistresses, more children appeared, so he had to work to support his family. "A man is like a rooster," he said after we talked awhile, "the more chickens he has the happier he is." Then he asked me what I was going to do about a woman while I was there, and I told him I hadn't thought that far ahead, that I would be happy if I could just get a damned story going.

This puzzled Justino, and I think for a few days it worried him. So on Saturday night he took me out for a few drinks and we wound up in some of the bordellos of Cuernavaca in the company of some of the most beautiful women in the world. Justino knew them all. They loved him, and he loved them.

I learned something more of the nature of this jardinero a few nights later when the heat and an irritating mosquito wouldn't let me sleep. I heard music from a radio, so I put on my pants and walked out into the Cuernavacan night, an oppressive, warm night heavy with the sweet perfume of the dama de la noche bushes which lined the wall of my friend's villa. From time to time I heard a dog cry in the distance, and I remembered that in Mexico many people die of rabies. Perhaps that is why the walls of the wealthy are always so high and the locks always secure. Or maybe it was because of the occasional gunshots which explode in the night. The news media tells us that Mexico is the most stable country in Latin America, and with the recent oil finds the bankers and the oil men want to keep it that way. I sense, and many know, that in the dark the revolution does not sleep. It is a spirit kept at bay by the high fences and the locked gates, yet it prowls the heart of every man. "Oil will create a new revolution," Justino had told me, "but it's going to be for our people. Mexicans are tired of building gas stations for the gringos from Gringolandia." I understood what he meant: there is much hunger in the country.

I lit a cigarette and walked towards my friend's car which was parked in the driveway near the swimming pool. I approached quietly and peered in. On the back seat with his legs propped on the front seat-back and smoking a cigar sat Justino. Two big, luscious women sat on either side of him, running their fingers through his hair and whispering in his ears. The doors were open to allow a breeze. He looked content. Sitting there he was that famous artist on his way to an afternoon reception in Mexico City, or he was a movie star on his way to the pre-

miere of his most recent movie. Or perhaps it was Sunday and
he was taking a Sunday drive in the country, towards Tepoztlán.
And why shouldn't his two friends accompany him? I had to
smile. Unnoticed I backed away and returned to my room. So
there was quite a bit more than met the eye to this short, dark
Indian from Ocosingo.

In the morning I asked my friend, "What do you know about
Justino?"

"Justino? You mean Vitorino."

"Is that his real name?"

"Sometimes he calls himself Trinidad."

"Maybe his name is Justino Vitorino Trinidad," I suggested.

"I don't know and I don't care," my friend answered. "He told
me he used to be a guide in the jungle. Who knows? The Mexican Indian has an incredible imagination. Really gifted people.
He's a good jardinero, and that's what matters to me. It's difficult to get good jardineros, so I don't ask questions."

"Is he reliable?" I wondered aloud.

"As reliable as a ripe mango," my friend nodded.

I wondered how much he knew, so I pushed a little further.
"And the radio at night?"

"Oh, that. I hope it doesn't bother you. Robberies and break-
ins are increasing here in the colonia. Something we never used
to have. Vitorino said that if he keeps the radio on low the
sound keeps thieves away. A very good idea, don't you think?"

I nodded. A very good idea.

"And I sleep very soundly," my friend concluded, "so I never
hear it."

The following night when I awakened and heard the soft
sound of the music from the radio and heard the splashing of
water, I had only to look from my window to see Justino and his
friends in the pool, swimming nude in the moonlight. They were
joking and laughing softly as they splashed each other, being

quiet so as not to awaken my friend, the patrón who slept so soundly. The women were beautiful. Brown skinned and glistening with water in the moonlight they reminded me of ancient Aztec maidens, swimming around Chac, their god of rain. They teased Justino, and he smiled as he floated on a rubber mattress in the middle of the pool, smoking his cigar, happy because they were happy. When he smiled the gold fleck of a filling glinted in the moonlight.

"¡Qué cabrón!" I laughed and closed my window.

Justino said a Mexican never lies. I believed him. If a Mexican says he will meet you at a certain time and place, he means he will meet you sometime at some place. Americans who retire in Mexico often complain of maids who swear they will come to work on a designated day, then don't show up. They did not lie, they knew they couldn't be at work, but they knew to tell the señora otherwise would make her sad or displease her, so they agree on a date so everyone would remain happy. What a beautiful aspect of character. It's a real virtue which Norteamericanos interpret as a fault in their character, because we are used to asserting ourselves on time and people. We feel secure and comfortable only when everything is neatly packaged in its proper time and place. We don't like the disorder of a free-flowing life.

Someday, I thought to myself, Justino will give a grand party in the sala of his patrón's home. His three wives, or his wife and two mistresses, and his dozens of children will be there. So will the women from the bordellos. He will preside over the feast, smoke his cigars, request his favorite beer-drinking songs from the mariachis, smile, tell stories and make sure everyone has a grand time. He will be dressed in a tuxedo, borrowed from the patrón's closet, of course, and he will act gallant and show everyone that a man who has just come into sudden wealth should share it with his friends. And in the morning he will report to the patrón that something has to be done about the poor mice that are coming in out of the streets and eating everything in the house.

"I'll buy some poison," the patrón will suggest.

"No, no," Justino will shake his head, "a little music from the radio and a candle burning in the sala will do."

And he will be right.

I liked Justino. He was a rogue with class. We talked about the weather, the lateness of the rainy season, women, the role of oil in Mexican politics. Like other workers, he believed nothing was going to filter down to the campesinos. "We could all be real Mexican greasers with all that oil," he said, "but the politicians will keep it all."

"What about the United States?" I asked.

"Oh, I have traveled in the estados unidos to the north. It's a country that's going to the dogs in a worse way than Mexico. The thing I liked the most was your cornflakes."

"Cornflakes?"

"Sí. You can make really good cornflakes."

"And women?"

"Ah, you better keep your eyes open, my friend. Those gringas are going to change the world just like the Suecas changed Spain."

"For better or for worse?"

"Spain used to be a nice country," he winked.

We talked, we argued, we drifted from subject to subject. I learned from him. I had been there a week when he told me the story which eventually led me to B. Traven. One day I was sitting under the orange tree reading the B. Traven novel I had found in the Juárez train station, keeping one eye on the ripe oranges which fell from time to time, my mind wandering as it worked to focus on a story so I could begin to write. After all, that's why I had come to Cuernavaca, to get some writing done, but nothing was coming, nothing. Justino wandered by and asked what I was reading and I replied it was an adventure story, a story of a man's search for the illusive pot of gold at the end of a make-believe rainbow. He nodded, thought awhile and gazed towards Popo, Popocatépetl, the towering volcano which lay to the south, shrouded in mist, waiting for the rains as we waited for the rains, sleeping, gazing at his female counterpart, Itza, who lay sleeping and guarding the valley of Cholula, there, where over four hundred years ago Cortés showed his wrath and executed thousands of Cholulans.

"I am going on an adventure," he finally said, and paused. "I think you might like to go with me."

I said nothing, but I put my book down and listened.

"I have been thinking about it for a long time, and now is the time to go. You see, it's like this. I grew up on the hacienda of don Francisco Jiménez, it's to the south, just a day's drive on the carretera. In my village nobody likes don Francisco, they fear and hate him. He has killed many men and he has taken their fortunes and buried them. He is a very rich man, muy rico. Many men have tried to kill him, but don Francisco is like the devil, he kills them first."

I listened as I always listen, because one never knows when a word or a phrase or an idea will be the seed from which a story sprouts, but at first there was nothing interesting. It sounded like the typical patrón-peón story I had heard so many times before. A man, the patrón, keeps the workers enslaved, in serfdom, and because he wields so much power, soon stories are told about him and he begins to acquire super-human powers. He acquires a mystique, just like the divine right of old. The patrón wields a mean machete, like old King Arthur swung Excalibur. He chops off heads of dissenters and sits on top of the bones-and-skulls pyramid, the king of the mountain, the top macho.

"One day I was sent to look for lost cattle," Justino continued. "I rode back into the hills where I had never been. At the foot of a hill, near a ravine, I saw something move in the bush. I dismounted and moved forward quietly. I was afraid it might be bandidos who steal cattle, and if they saw me they would kill me. When I came near the place I heard a strange sound. Some-body was crying. My back shivered, just like a dog when he sniffs the devil at night. I thought I was going to see witches, brujas who like to go to those deserted places to dance for the devil, or La Llorona."

"La Llorona," I said aloud. My interest grew. I had been hearing Llorona stories since I was a kid, and I was always ready for one more. La Llorona was that archetypal woman of ancient legends who murdered her children, then repentant and demented she has spent the rest of eternity searching for them.

"Sí, La Llorona. You know that poor woman used to drink a lot. She played around with men, and when she had babies she got rid of them by throwing them into la barranca. One day she realized what she had done and went crazy. She started crying and pulling her hair and running up and down the sides of cliffs of the river looking for her children. It's a very sad story."

A new version, I thought, and yes, a sad story. And what of the men who made love to the woman who became La Llorona? Did they ever cry for their children? It doesn't seem fair to have only her suffer, only her crying and doing penance. Perhaps a man should run with her, and in our legends we would call him "El Mero Chingón," he who screwed up everything. Then maybe the tale of love and passion and the insanity it can bring will be complete. Yes, I think someday I will write that story.

"What did you see?" I asked Justino.

"Something worse than La Llorona," he whispered.

To the south a wind mourned and moved the clouds off Popo's crown. The bald, snow-covered mountain thrust its power into the blue Mexican sky. The light glowed like liquid gold around the god's head. Popo was a god, an ancient god. Somewhere at his feet Justino's story had taken place.

"I moved closer, and when I parted the bushes I saw don Francisco. He was sitting on a rock, and he was crying. "From time to time he looked at the ravine in front of him, the hole seemed to slant into the earth. That pozo is called el Pozo de Mendoza. I had heard stories about it before, but I had never seen it. I looked into the pozo, and you wouldn't believe what I saw."

He waited, so I asked, "What?"

"Money! Huge piles of gold and silver coins! Necklaces and bracelets and crowns of gold, all loaded with all kinds of precious stones! Jewels! Diamonds! All sparkling in the sunlight that entered the hole. More money than I have ever seen! A fortune, my friend, a fortune which is still there, just waiting for two adventurers like us to take it!"

"Us? But what about don Francisco? It's his land, his fortune."

"Ah," Justino smiled, "that's the strange thing about this fortune. Don Francisco can't touch it, that's why he was crying. You see, I stayed there, and I watched him closely. Every time he stood up and started to walk into the pozo the money disappeared. He stretched out his hand to grab the gold, and poof, it was gone! That's why he was crying! He murdered all those people and hid their wealth in the pozo, but now he can't touch it. He is cursed."

"El Pozo de Mendoza," I said aloud. Something began to click in my mind. I smelled a story.

"Who was Mendoza?" I asked.

"He was a very rich man. Don Francisco killed him in a quarrel they had over some cattle. But Mendoza must have put a curse on don Francisco before he died, because now don Francisco can't get to the money."

"So Mendoza's ghost haunts old don Francisco."

"Many ghosts haunt him," Justino answered. "He has killed many men."

"And the fortune, the money . . ."

He looked at me and his eyes were dark and piercing. "It's still there. Waiting for us!"

"But it disappears as one approaches it, you said so yourself. Perhaps it's only a hallucination."

"Justino shook his head. "No, it's real gold and silver, not hallucination money. It disappears for don Francisco because the curse is on him, but the curse is not on us." He smiled. He knew he had drawn me into his plot. "We didn't steal the money, so it won't disappear for us. And you are not connected with the place. You are innocent. I've thought very carefully about it, and now is the time to go. I can lower you into the pozo with a rope, in a few hours we can bring out the entire fortune. All we need is a car. You can borrow the patron's car, he is your friend. But he must not know where we're going. We can be there and back in one day, one night." He nodded as if to assure me, then he turned and looked at the sky. "It will not rain today. It will not rain for a week. Now is the time to go."

He winked and returned to watering the grass and flowers of the jardín, a wild Pan among the bougainvillea and the roses, a man possessed by a dream. The gold was not for him, he told me the next day, it was for his women, he would buy them all gifts, bright dresses, and he would take them on a vacation to the United States, he would educate his children, send them to the best colleges. I listened and the germ of a story cluttered my thoughts as I sat beneath the orange tree in the mornings. I couldn't write, nothing was coming, but I knew that there were elements for a good story in Justino's tale. In dreams I saw the lonely hacienda to the south. I saw the pathetic, tormented figure of don Francisco as he cried over the fortune he couldn't touch. I saw the ghosts of the men he had killed, the lonely women who mourned over them and cursed the evil don Francisco. In one dream I saw a man I took to be B. Traven, a grayhaired, distinguished-looking gentleman who looked at me and nodded approvingly.

"Yes, there's a story there, follow it, follow it . . ."

In the meantime, other small and seemingly insignificant details came my way. During a luncheon at the home of my friend, a woman I did not know leaned towards me and asked if I would like to meet the widow of B. Traven. The woman's hair was tinged orange, her complexion was ashen gray. I didn't know who she was or why she would mention B. Traven to me. How did she know Traven had come to haunt my thoughts? Was she a clue which would help unravel the mystery?

I didn't know, but I nodded. Yes, I would like to meet her. I had heard that Traven's widow, Rosa Elena, lived in Mexico City. But what would I ask her? What did I want to know? Would she know Traven's secret? Somehow he had learned that to keep his magic intact he had to keep away from the public.

Like the fortune in the pozo, the magic feel for the story might disappear if unclean hands reached for it. I turned to look at the woman, but she was gone. I wandered to the terrace to finish my beer. Justino sat beneath the orange tree. He yawned. I knew the literary talk bored him. He was eager to be on the way to el Pozo de Mendoza.

I was nervous, too, but I didn't know why. The tension for the story was there, but something was missing. Or perhaps it was just Justino's insistence that I decide whether I was going or not that drove me out of the house in the mornings. Time usually devoted to writing found me in a small cafe in the center of town. From there I could watch the shops open, watch the people cross the zócalo, the main square. I drank lots of coffee, I smoked a lot, I daydreamed, I wondered about the significance of the pozo, the fortune, Justino, the story I wanted to write and B. Traven. In one of these moods I saw a friend from whom I hadn't heard in years. Suddenly he was there, trekking across the square, dressed like an old rabbi, moss and green algae for a beard, and followed by a troop of very dignified Lacandones, Mayan Indians from Chiapas.

"Victor," I gasped, unsure if he was real or a part of the shadows which the sun created as it flooded the square with its light.

"I have no time to talk," he said as he stopped to munch on my pan dulce and sip my coffee. "I only want you to know, for purposes of your story, that I was in a Lacandonian village last month, and a Hollywood film crew descended from the sky. They came in helicopters. They set up tents near the village, and big-bosomed, bikinied actresses emerged from them, tossed themselves on the cut trees which are the atrocity of the giant American lumber companies, and they cried while the director shot his film. Then they produced a gray-haired old man from one of the tents and took shots of him posing with the Indians. Herr Traven, the director called him."

He finished my coffee, nodded to his friends and they began to walk away.

"B. Traven?" I asked.

He turned. "No, an imposter, an actor. Be careful for imposters. Remember, even Traven used many disguises, many names!"

"Then he's alive and well?" I shouted. People around me turned to stare.

"His spirit is with us," were the last words I heard as they moved across the zócalo, a strange troop of near-naked Lacandon Mayans and my friend the Guatemalan Jew, returning to the rain forest, returning to the primal innocent land.

I slumped in my chair and looked at my empty cup. What did it mean? As their trees fall the Lacandones die. Betrayed as B. Traven was betrayed. Does each one of us also die as the trees fall in the dark depths of the Chiapas jungle? Far to the north, in Aztlán, it is the same where the earth is ripped open to expose and mine the yellow uranium. A few poets sing songs and stand in the way as the giant machines of the corporations rumble over the land and grind everything into dust. New holes are made in the earth, pozos full of curses, pozos with fortunes we cannot touch, should not touch. Oil, coal, uranium, from holes in the earth through which we suck the blood of the earth.

There were other incidents. A telephone call late one night, a voice with a German accent called my name, and when I answered the line went dead. A letter addressed to B. Traven came in the mail. It was dated March 26, 1969.

My friend returned it to the post office. Justino grew more and more morose. He sat under the orange tree and stared into space, my friend complained about the garden drying up. Justino looked at me and scowled. He did a little work, then went back to daydreaming. Without the rains the garden withered. His heart was set on the adventure which lay at el pozo.

Finally I said, "Yes, dammit, why not, let's go, neither one of us is getting anything done here," and Justino, cheering like a child, ran to prepare for the trip. But when I asked my friend for the weekend loan of the car he reminded me that we were invited to a tertulia, an afternoon reception, at the home of Señora Ana R. Many writers and artists would be there. It was in my honor, so I could meet the literati of Cuernavaca. I had to tell Justino I couldn't go.

Now it was I who grew morose. The story growing within would not let me sleep. I awakened in the night and looked out the window, hoping to see Justino and women bathing in the pool, enjoying themselves. But all was quiet. No radio played. The still night was warm and heavy. From time to time gunshots sounded in the dark, dogs barked, and the presence of a Mexico which never sleeps closed in on me.

Saturday morning dawned with a strange overcast. Perhaps

the rains will come, I thought. In the afternoon I reluctantly accompanied my friend to the reception. I had not seen Justino all day, but I saw him at the gate as we drove out. He looked tired, as if he, too, had not slept. He wore the white shirt and baggy pants of a campesino. His straw hat cast a shadow over his eyes. I wondered if he had decided to go to the pozo alone. He didn't speak as we drove through the gate, he only nodded. When I looked back I saw him standing by the gate, looking after the car, and I had a vague, uneasy feeling that I had lost an opportunity.

The afternoon gathering was a pleasant affair, attended by a number of affectionate artists, critics and writers who enjoyed the refreshing drinks which quenched the thirst.

But my mood drove me away from the crowd. I wandered around the terrace and found a foyer surrounded by green plants, huge fronds and ferns and flowering bougainvillea. I pushed the green aside and entered a quiet, very private alcove. The light was dim, the air was cool, a perfect place for contemplation.

At first I thought I was alone, then I saw the man sitting in one of the wicker chairs next to a small wrought-iron table. He was an elderly white-haired gentleman. His face showed he had lived a full life, yet he was still very distinguished in his manner and posture. His eyes shone brightly.

"Perdón," I apologized, and turned to leave. I did not want to intrude.

"No, no, please," he motioned to the empty chair, "I've been waiting for you." He spoke English with a slight German accent. Or perhaps it was Norwegian, I couldn't tell the difference. "I can't take the literary gossip. I prefer the quiet."

I nodded and sat. He smiled and I felt at ease. I took the cigar he offered and we lit up. He began to talk and I listened. He was a writer also, but I had the good manners not to ask his titles.

He talked about the changing Mexico, the change the new oil would bring, the lateness of the rains and how they affected the people and the land, and he talked about how important a woman was in a writer's life. He wanted to know about me, about the Chicanos of Aztlán, about our work. It was the workers, he said, who would change society. The artist learned from the worker. I talked, and sometime during the conversation I told him the name of the friend with whom I was staying. He laughed and wanted to know if Vitorino was still working for him.

"Do you know Justino?" I asked.

"Oh, yes, I know that old guide. I met him many years ago, when I first came to Mexico," he answered. "Justino knows the campesino very well. He and I traveled many places together, he in search of adventure, I in search of stories."

I thought the coincidence strange, so I gathered the courage and asked, "Did he ever tell you the story of the fortune at el Pozo de Mendoza?"

"Tell me?" the old man smiled. "I went there."

"With Justino?"

"Yes, I went with him. What a rogue he was in those days, but a good man. If I remember correctly I even wrote a story based on that adventure. Not a very good story. Never came to anything. But we had a grand time. People like Justino are the writer's source. We met interesting people and saw fabulous places, enough to last me a lifetime. We were supposed to be gone for one day, but we were gone nearly three years. You see, I wasn't interested in the pots of gold he kept saying were just over the next hill: I went because there was a story to write."

"Yes, that's what interested me," I agreed.

"A writer has to follow a story if it leads him to hell itself. That's our curse. Ay, and each one of us knows our own private hell."

I nodded. I felt relieved. I sat back to smoke the cigar and sip from my drink. Somewhere to the west the sun bronzed the evening sky. On a clear afternoon, Popo's crown would glow like fire.

"Yes," the old man continued, "a writer's job is to find and follow people like Justino. They're the source of life. The ones you have to keep away from are the dilettantes like the ones in there." He motioned in the general direction of the noise of the party. "I stay with people like Justino. They may be illiterate, but they understand our descent into the pozo of hell, and they understand us because they're willing to share the adventure with us. You seek fame and notoriety and you're dead as a writer."

I sat upright. I understood now what the pozo meant, why Justino had come into my life to tell me the story. It was clear. I rose quickly and shook the old man's hand. I turned and parted the palm leaves of the alcove. There, across the way, in one of the streets that led out of the maze of the town towards the south, I saw Justino. He was walking in the direction of Popo, and he was followed by women and children, a rag-tail army of adventurers, all happy, all singing. He looked up to where I stood on the terrace, and he smiled as he waved. He paused to light the stub of a cigar. The women turned, and the children turned, and all waved to me. Then they continued their walk, south, towards the foot of the volcano. They were going to the Pozo de Mendoza, to the place where the story originated.

I wanted to run after them, to join them in the glorious light which bathed the Cuernavaca valley and the majestic snow-covered head of Popo. The light was everywhere, a magnetic element which flowed from the clouds. I waved as Justino and his followers disappeared in the light. Then I turned to say something to the old man, but he was gone. I was alone in the alcove. Somewhere in the background I heard the tinkling of glasses and the laughter which came from the party, but that was not for me.

I left the terrace and crossed the lawn, found the gate and walked down the street. The sounds of Mexico filled the air. I felt light and happy. I wandered aimlessly through the curving, narrow streets, then I quickened my pace because suddenly the story was overflowing and I needed to write. I needed to get to my quiet room and write the story about B. Traven being alive and well in Cuernavaca.

Contemporary Mexican Voices

Excerpt from *The Death of Artemio Cruz*

I wake up . . . The touch of that cold object against my penis wakes me up. I didn't know I could urinate without being aware of it. I keep my eyes shut. I can't even make out the nearest voices. If I opened my eyes, would I be able to hear them? . . . But my eyelids are so heavy: two pieces of lead, coins on my tongue, hammers in my ears, a . . . a something like tarnished silver in my breath. It all tastes metallic. Or mineral. I urinate without knowing I'm doing it. I remember with a shock that I've been unconscious—maybe I ate and drank without knowing it. Because it was just getting light when I reached out my hand and accidentally knocked the telephone on the floor. Then I just lay there, face down on the bed, with my arms hanging, the veins in my wrist tingling. Now I'm waking up, but I don't want to open my eyes. Even so, I see something shining near my face. Something that turns into a flood of black lights and blue circles behind my closed lids. I tighten my face muscles, I open my right eye, and I see it reflected in the squares of glass sewn onto a woman's handbag. That's what I am. That's what I am. That old man whose features are fragmented by the uneven squares of glass. I am that eye. I am that eye. I am that eye furrowed by accumulated rage, an old, forgotten, but always renewed rage. I am that puffy green eye set between those eyelids. Eyelids. Eyelids. Oily eyelids. I am that nose. That nose. That nose. Broken. With wide nostrils. I am those cheekbones. Cheekbones. Where my white beard starts. Starts. Grimace. Grimace. Grimace. I am that grimace that has nothing to do with old age or pain. Grimace. My teeth discolored by tobacco. Tobacco. Tobacco. My bre-bre-breathing fogs the squares of glass, and someone removes the handbag from the night table.

"Look, Doctor, he's just faking . . ."

"Mr. Cruz . . ."

"Even now in the hour of his death he has to trick us!"

I don't want to talk. My mouth is stuffed with old pennies, with that taste. But I open my eyes a little more, and between my eyelashes I can make out the two women, the doctor who smells of aseptic things: his sweaty hands, stinking of alcohol, are now tapping my chest under my shirt. I try to push that hand away.

"Easy now, Mr. Cruz, easy . . ."

No. I am not going to open my mouth, or that wrinkled line with no lips reflected in the glass. I'll keep my arms stretched out on top of the sheets. The covers reach my stomach. My stomach . . . ah . . . And my legs stay spread, with that cold gadget between my thighs. And my chest stays asleep, with the same dull tingling that I feel . . . that . . . I felt when I would sit in one position for a long time in the movies. Bad circulation, that's all it is. Nothing more. Nothing more. Nothing serious. Nothing more serious than that. I have to think about my body. Thinking about your body wears you out. Your own body. Your body, whole. It wears you out. Better not to think. There it is. I do think about this flight of nerves and scales, of cells and scattered globules. My body, on which the doctor taps his fingers. Fear. I'm afraid of thinking about my own body. And my face? Teresa removed the handbag that reflected it. I'm trying to remember it in the reflection. It was a face broken by asymmetrical pieces of glass, with one eye very close to an ear and far away from the other eye, with the grimace spread out on three encircling mirrors. Sweat is pouring down my forehead. I close my eyes again, and I ask, ask that my face and body be given back to me. I ask, but I feel that hand caressing me, and I would like to get away from its touch, but I don't have the strength.

"Feeling better?"

I don't see her. I don't see Catalina. I see farther off. Teresa is sitting in the armchair. She has an open newspaper in her hands. My newspaper. It's Teresa, but she has her face hidden behind the open pages.

"Open the window."

"No, no. You might catch cold and make everything worse."

"Forget it, Mama. Can't you see he's fooling around?"

Ah. I smell that incense. Ah. The murmuring at the door. Here he comes with that smell of incense, with his black cassock, and with the hyssop out in front, a farewell so harsh it's really a threat. Ha, they fell into the trap.

"Isn't Padilla here?"

"Yes, he is. He's outside."

"Have him sent in."

"But . . .

"First Padilla."

Ah, Padilla, come closer. Did you bring the tape recorder? If you knew what was good for you, you'd have brought it here the way you brought it to my house in Coyoacán every night. Today, more than ever, you should be trying to trick me into thinking that everything's the same as it's always been. Don't disturb the rituals, Padilla. That's right, come closer. They don't want you to.

"Go over to him, so he can see who you are. Tell him your name."

"I am . . . I'm Gloria . . ."

If I could only see her face better. If I could only see her grimace better. She must notice this smell of dead scales; she must be looking at this sunken chest, this gray, messy beard, this fluid running out of my nose, these . . .

They take her away from me.

The doctor checks my pulse.

"I'll have to talk this over with the other doctors on the case."

Catalina brushes my hand with hers. What a useless caress. I can't see her very well, but I try to fix my eyes on hers. I catch her. I hold her frozen hand.

"That morning I waited for him with pleasure. We crossed the river on horseback."

"What's that? Don't try to talk. Don't wear yourself out. I don't understand what you're saying."

"I'd like to go back there, Catalina. How useless."

Yes: the priest kneels next to me. He whispers his words. Padilla plugs in the recorder. I hear my voice, my words. Ay, a shout. Ay, I shout. Ay, I survived. There are two doctors standing in the doorway. I survived. Regina, it hurts, it hurts, Regina, I realize that it hurts. Regina. Soldier. Hug me; it hurts. Someone has stuck a long, cold dagger into my stomach; there is someone, there is someone else who has stuck a blade into my guts: I smell that incense and I'm tired. I let them do as they please. I let them lift me up heavily as I groan. I don't owe my life to you. I can't, I can't, I didn't choose, the pain bends my waist, I touch my frozen feet, I don't want those blue toenails, my new blue toenails, aaaah ayyyy, I survived. What did I do yesterday? If I think about what I did yesterday, I'll stop thinking about what's happening to me now. That's a good idea. Very good. Think yesterday. You aren't so crazy; you aren't in so much pain; you were able to think that. Yesterday yesterday yesterday. Yesterday Artemio Cruz flew from Hermosillo to Mexico City. Yes. Yesterday Artemio Cruz . . . Before he got sick, yesterday Artemio Cruz . . . No, he didn't get sick. Yesterday Artemio Cruz was in his office and he felt very sick. Not yesterday. This morning. Artemio Cruz. Not sick, no. Not Artemio Cruz, no. Another man. In a mirror hanging across from the sick man's bed. The other man. Artemio Cruz. His twin. Artemio Cruz is sick. The other one. Artemio Cruz is sick. He isn't living. He certainly is living. Artemio Cruz lived. He lived for some years . . . Years he didn't miss, years he didn't. He lived for a few days. His twin. Artemio Cruz. His double. Yesterday Artemio Cruz, the one who only lived a few days before dying, yesterday Artemio Cruz . . . That's me . . . and it's another man . . . Yesterday . . .

Yesterday you did what you do every day. You don't know if it's worthwhile remembering it. You only want to remember, lying back there in the twilight of your bedroom, what's going to happen: you don't want to foresee what has already happened. In your twilight, your eyes see ahead; they don't know how to guess the past. Yes; yesterday you will fly from Hermosillo, yesterday, April 9, 1959, on the Compañía Mexicana de Aviación shuttle, which will depart from the capital of Sonora, where it will be hot as hell, at 9:55 a.m., and will reach Mexico City exactly on time at 4:30 p.m. From your seat on the four-motor plane, you will see a flat, gray city, a belt of adobe and tin roofs. The hostess will offer you a Chiclet wrapped in cellophane—you will remember that in particular because she will be (she has to be, don't think everything in the future tense from now on) a very pretty girl and you will always have a good eye for such things even if your age condemns you to imagine rather than do (you're using words incorrectly: of course, you will never feel condemned to that, even if you can only imagine it). The bright sign NO SMOKING, FASTEN SEAT BELTS will go on just when the plane, entering the Valley of Mexico, abruptly descends, as if it has lost the power to stay aloft in the thin air; then it suddenly leans to the right, and packages, jackets, suitcases will fall and a collective shout will ring out, cut off by a low sob, and the flames will sputter, until the fourth motor on the right wing stops, and everyone goes on shouting and only you stay calm, unmoved, chewing your gum and watching the legs of the hostess, who will run up and down the aisle calming the passengers. The internal fire extinguisher will work and the plane will land with no difficulty, but no one will have realized that only you, an old man of seventy-one, maintained his composure. You will feel proud of yourself, without showing it. You will think that you have done so many cowardly things that it's easy for you to be brave. You will smile and say to yourself no, no, it isn't a paradox: it's the truth and perhaps even a general truth. You will have made the trip to Sonora by car—a 1959 Volvo, license plate DF 712—because some government officials were misbehaving badly and you would have to go all that way just to make sure those people remain loyal, the people you bought—bought, that's right, you will not fool yourself with words from your own annual speeches: I'll convince them, I'll persuade them. No, you'll buy them—and then they'll impose tariffs (another ugly word) on the truckers who carry fish on the Sonora–Sinaloa–Mexico City route. You will give the inspectors ten percent, and because of those middlemen, the fish will be expensive when they reach the city, and your personal profit will be twenty times larger than the original value of the fish. You will try to remember all this, and you will carry out your desire even if all this seems a fit subject for an editorial in your newspaper and you think that, after all, you're wasting your time

of the vast network of businesses you control: the newspaper,
the real-estate investments—Mexico City, Puebla, Guadalajara,
Monterrey, Culiacán, Hermosillo, Guaymas, Acapulco—the
sulphur domes in Jáltipan, the mines in Hidalgo, the logging
concessions in Tarahumara, your stock in the chain of hotels,
the pipe factory, the fish business, financing of financing, the
net of stock operations, the legal representation of U.S. companies, the administration of the railroad loans, the advisory posts
in fiduciary institutions, the shares in foreign corporations—
dyes, steel, detergents—and one fact that does not appear on the
diagram: $15 million deposited in London, New York, and
Zurich. You will light a cigarette, despite the doctor's warnings,
and you will recite to Padilla the steps that led to this wealth.
Short-term loans at high interest to the peasants in the state of
Puebla at the end of the Revolution; acquisition of property
near the city of Puebla, foreseeing its growth, thanks to the
friendly intervention of whichever President happened to be in
power at the time; property for subdivisions in Mexico City;
acquisition of the metropolitan daily; purchase of mining stocks
and the creation of joint Mexican–U.S. corporations in which
you were the front man, to comply with the letter of the law; the
man on whom U.S. investors depended; intermediary between
Chicago, New York, and the Mexican government; manipula-
tion of the bond market to raise or lower prices, sell or buy
according to your wish or need; a cozy, tight relationship with
President Alemán; acquisition of communal properties stripped
from the peasants to create new subdivisions in the cities of
the interior; logging concessions. Yes—you will sigh as you ask
Padilla for a match—twenty years of confidence, social peace,
class collaboration; twenty years of progress after Lázaro Cárde-
nas's demagoguery; twenty years of protection for the company's
interests; twenty years of submissive union leaders and broken
strikes. And then you will raise your hands to your stomach, and

your head, with its unruly gray hair, will land with a hollow thud on the glass tabletop, and once again, now from up close, you will see that reflection of your sick twin, while all noise pours out of your head, in laughter, and the sweat of all those people envelops you, the flesh of all those people suffocates you, makes you lose consciousness. The reflected twin will join the other, which is you, the old man seventy-one years of age who will lie unconscious between the desk chair and the big metal desk, and you will be here but not know which facts will get into your biography and which will be hushed up, hidden. You will not know. They are vulgar facts and you will not be the first or only person to possess such a service record. You will have had a good time. You will have remembered that. But you will recall other things, other days, you will have to remember them, too. They are days that, far back, recent, pushed toward oblivion, etched in memory—meeting and rejection, fleeting love, freedom, anger, failure, will—were and will be something more than the names you might give them: days in which your destiny will pursue you like a bloodhound, will find you, will charge you dearly, will incarnate you with words and acts, complex, opaque, adipose matter, woven forever with the other, the impalpable, the substance of your spirit absorbed by matter: a love of cool quinces, the ambition of growing fingernails, the tedium of progressive baldness, the melancholy of sun and desert, the abulia of dirty dishes, the distraction of tropical rivers, the fear of sabers and gunpowder, the loss of clean sheets, the youth of black horses, the old age of an abandoned beach, the discovery of the envelope and the foreign stamp, the repugnance toward incense, the reaction to nicotine, the pain of red earth, the tenderness of the afternoon patio, the spirit of all objects, the matter of all souls: the sundering of your memory, which separates the two halves; the solder of life that reunites them once again, that dissolves them, that pursues them, that finds them. The fruit has

Introduction from
Here's to You, Jesusa!

Over there where Mexico City starts getting smaller, where the streets get lost and are deserted, that's where Jesusa lives. It's so warm there's no ice left in the freezers, just water, and the Victoria and Superior beers just float around. The women's hair sticks against the nape of their necks, beaten down by sweat. Sweat dampens the air, clothes, armpits, foreheads. The heat buzzes, like the flies. The air in those parts is greasy, dirty; the people live in the very frying pans where they cook *garnachas*, those thick, filled tortillas covered in chile sauce, and potato or pumpkin-flower quesadillas, the daily bread that the women heap on tables with uneven legs along the street. The dust is the only dry thing, that and a few gourds.

Jesusa is dried up, too. She's as old as the century. She's eighty-seven and the years have made her smaller, as it has the houses, bending their backbones. They say that old people get smaller so they'll take up the least possible space inside the earth when they're done living on top of it. Jesusa's eyes, with little red veins, are tired; they've gotten gritty, gray around the pupil, the brown fading a little bit at a time. Tears no longer reach her eyes and the bright red lacrimal ducts are the most intense parts of her face. There's no water under her skin either. Jesusa constantly says: "I'm turning into parchment." But the skin remains stretched over her prominent cheekbones. "Every time I move I lose scales." She lost a front tooth and she decided: "When I go out somewhere, if I ever do go out, I'll put a Chiclet there, I'll chew it up real good and I'll stick it on."

I met her in 1964. She lived near Morazán and Ferrocarril-Cintura, a poor neighborhood in Mexico City, whose main attraction was the Penitentiary, called El Palacio Negro de Lecumberri, the Black Palace of Lecumberri. The prison was the most important place in the area; around it swarmed the women who sold quesadillas, steaming pots of chile, sweet and butter tamales, the ones who sold *sopes*, the tortillas drenched in chile sauce, and hot *garnachas*, the big-bellied attorneys with their suits, ties, beards, and briefcases, the paperboys, the buses, the relatives of the prisoners, and those bureaucrats who always flutter around misfortune, the morbid, the curious. Jesusa lived in a tenement close to the Peni. You could hear the constant humming of a typewriter. Or maybe it was several. It smelled like dampness, fermentation.

—What do you want? What business do you have with me?
   —I want to talk to you.
   —To me? Listen, I work. If I don't work, I don't eat. I don't have time to hang around chatting.
   Irascibly, Jesusa agreed to let me visit with her on the only free day she had during the week: Wednesday from four to six. I started living from Wednesday to Wednesday. Jesusa, on the

other hand, never gave up her hostile attitude. When the neigh-bors would yell to her from the doorway to hold the dog so I could come in, she'd say in a bad-tempered tone: "Oh, it's you." As I skirted around the dog carrying a big square tape recorder, I could feel its breath hot on my ankles. Its barks were as gruff as Jesusa's disposition.

The tenement had a main hallway and rooms on either side. The two waterless "toilets" set up in the back were filled to the top, and the dirty papers were piled up on the floor. Jesusa's place got very little sun, and the gas from the grill made your eyes water. The walls were rotting, and although the hallway was quite narrow, half a dozen bare-bottomed little ones played there and peeked into the neighbors' rooms. Jesusa would say: "Do you want a taco? . . . No? Then don't stand around begging in doorways." The rats peered in too.

Back in those days Jesusa wasn't home much because she left early for work at the printshop. She closed up her room tightly since there was no lock, her animals asphyxiating inside, her plants too. She cleaned at the printshop, swept, picked up, dusted, rinsed and drained the metal pieces. She took the work-ers' overalls home and often even their everyday clothes, and she labored a second shift at her washboard. In the evening she fed her cats, chickens, and rabbit, watered her plants, and tidied up the place.

The first time I asked her to tell me her life story (because I'd heard her talking on a rooftop and the language she used was extraordinary, but above all because I was drawn to her capacity for indignation) she answered: "I don't have time." She showed me the piled-up overalls, the five chickens that had to be taken out to get some sun, the dog and the cats that had to be fed, the two birds that looked like sparrows, imprisoned inside a cage that got smaller every day.

—You see what I mean? Are you going to help me?

—Yes, I answered.

—All right, then put those overalls in gasoline.

That's when I learned what overalls really were. They were hard and stiff and full of grime with big grease stains. I put them in a washbasin to soak. The liquid wouldn't cover them because they were so rigid; the overalls were an island in the middle of water, a rock. Jesusa ordered: "While they're soaking, take the chickens out to the sidewalk." So I did, but the hens started to peck the cement, looking for the improbable. Then they jumped off the sidewalk and scattered into the street. I got scared and ran back to Jesusa.

—They're going to get run over by a car!

—*Pues*, don't you know how to put chickens out? Didn't you see the little string? You had to tie them by the leg.

She quickly got her hens back inside and scolded me again:

—Who would think of letting chickens out like that?

Upset, I answered:

—What else can I help you with?

—Let the chickens out on the roof, even if it's just for a little while!

I did so but with some apprehension. The house was so low that even I—and I'm about as tall as a sitting dog—could see them ruffling their feathers. They seemed to be happy pecking at the roof. I liked it. I thought: "Well, at least I did something right." The black dog in the doorway was annoyed, and Jesusa yelled at me again:

—What happened to the overalls?

I took them out of the gasoline. When I asked her where the sink was, Jesusa pointed to a corrugated washboard that was barely twenty or twenty-five centimeters wide by fifty long:

—A sink? Like you'd find one of those around here! Scrub on that!

She took a washbasin out from under her bed and looked at

me sarcastically: she knew it was impossible for me to scrub anything. The overalls were so stiff you couldn't even grab hold of
them. Jesusa exclaimed:

—It's obvious that you're high-class and useless.

She pushed me aside, and then she realized that the overalls
needed to soak in the gasoline overnight and she ordered:

—Let's go get meat for my animals now.

—We'll take my car.

—No, it's right here on the corner.

She walked fast, her change purse in her hand, not looking at
me. In contrast to her taciturn behavior with me, she joked with
the butcher, going out of her way to be pleasant, and bought a
pile of wretched carcasses wrapped in paper that immediately
got bloody. At her place she threw the animal parts on the floor
and the cats were right on top of them, electrified, with their
tails up straight. The dogs were slower. The birds chirped. Like
a fool, I asked her if they ate meat too.

—What country are you from?

I plugged in my tape recorder. It looked like a navy-blue coffin with a huge dance-hall speaker. Jesusa protested: "Are you
going to pay for the electricity?" Then she gave in: "Where are
you going to put that animal? I'll have to move all this crap." I
told her the tape recorder was on loan to me: "Why are you
using something that isn't yours? Aren't you afraid?" The following Wednesday I asked her the same questions again.

—Didn't I tell you about that last week?

—Yes, but it didn't record.

—That big animal doesn't work?

—Sometimes I don't notice if it's taping or not.

—Then don't bring it anymore.

—I don't write fast and we'd waste a lot of time.

—That's it then. It'd be better if we stopped here. After all,
neither you nor I have anything to gain from this.

So I started to write in a notebook and Jesusa made fun of my handwriting: "So many years of school to end up with that scribble-scrabble!" This method worked for me, for when I got home at night, I'd re-create what she'd told me. I was always afraid that on the day when I least expected it she'd cut me off like a spurned lover. She didn't like the neighbors to see me, or for me to greet them. One day when I asked about the smiling girls who had been at the door, she insisted: "Don't call them girls, call them whores, yes, little whores, that's what they are."

One Wednesday I found Jesusa wrapped in a bright red, yellow, and parrot-green serape with wide flashy stripes. She had been lying on her bed and had only gotten up to open the door for me. Then she went back to bed to lie down, with the serape covering her whole head. She usually sat in front of the radio in the dark, like a little bundle of old age and loneliness listening, attentive, alert, critical.

I looked at the big serape, which I hadn't seen before, as I sat in a little chair at the foot of the bed. Jesusa didn't say a word. Even the radio, which was always on during our conversations, was turned off. I waited something like half an hour in the dark. Every now and then I'd ask her:

—Jesusa, do you feel sick?

There was no answer.

—Jesusa, don't you want to talk?

She didn't move.

—Are you angry?

Total silence. I decided to be patient. Many times, when we started our interviews Jesusa would be in a bad mood. After a while she settled in, but she never lost her grouchiness and her ever-present scorn.

—Have you been sick? Have you been going to work?

—No.

—Why not?

—I haven't gone in two weeks.

We went back to the most absolute silence. The birds, which always made their presence known with a humble and trivial "here I am" under the rags she covered the cage with, weren't even chirping. Discouraged, I waited a long time, dusk fell, I kept waiting, the sky turned lilac. Cautiously, I returned to the task at hand:

—Aren't you going to talk to me?

She didn't answer.

—Do you want me to leave?

Then she pulled the serape down below her eyes, then under her chin, and said with annoyance:

—Listen, you've been coming here and screwing around and annoying me for two years and you still don't understand anything. So it's better if we just stop now.

I left with my notebook pressed against my chest, like a shield. In the car I thought "My God! What a marvelous old woman she is! She doesn't have anyone in her life, I'm the only person who visits her, and she still can tell me to go to hell."

The next Wednesday I was late (perhaps I was unconsciously getting even) and she was waiting outside on the sidewalk.

She muttered:

—Well, what's wrong with you? You don't seem to understand. When you leave, I go to the stable for my milk, I go get my bread. You screw me up if you're late.

So I went to the stable with her. In the poor neighborhoods the countryside spills over the city's boundaries, or maybe it's the other way around, even though nothing smells like fields and everything tastes like dust, like garbage, rotten. "When we poor people drink milk we get it right from the cow, not that crap in bottles and boxes that you all drink." At the bakery, Jesusa bought four rolls: "Not sweet rolls, those don't fill you up and cost more."

I came to understand poverty through Jesusa, real poverty, where water is collected in buckets and carried very carefully so it doesn't spill, where the washing is done on a metal washboard because there is no sink, where a neighbor will tap into another's electric line, where the hens lay eggs without shells, "just membrane," because a lack of sun keeps them from hardening. Jesusa was one of the millions of men and women who don't live so much as they survive. Just getting through the day is so much work, the hours and the energy lost makes life so difficult for poor people. Survival means staying afloat, breathing calmly, even if it's only for a moment in the evening when the chickens no longer cackle in their cages and the cat stretches out on the trampled earth.

On Wednesday afternoons, as the sun set and the blue sky changed to orange, in that semidark little room, in the midst of the shrieking of the children, the slamming doors, the shouting, and the radio going full blast, another life emerged—that of Jesusa Palancares, the one that she relived as she retold it. Through a tiny crack, we watched the sky, its colors, blue, then orange, and finally black. A sliver of sky. I squinted so my gaze would fit through that crack, and we would enter the other life.

Listening to Jesusa, I imagined her as young, fast, independent, severe, and I lived her rages and her pains, her legs that became numb from the cold snow up north, her hands reddened from washing. Watching her act out her story, able to make her own decisions, made my own lack of character more obvious to me. More than anything, I liked to imagine her in the ocean, her hair loose, her bare feet on the sand, sucked in by the water, her hands made into shells to taste it, to discover its saltiness, its sting. "You know, the sea is an immensity!" I also saw her running as a child, her petticoats between her legs, stuck to her strong body, her radiant face, her beautiful head, sometimes covered with a straw hat made of *soyate*, sometimes with a rebozo. Watching her fight in the marketplace was a pleasure, a right cross, hit her lower, kick her in the back, you knocked the wind out of her, a hook to the liver, don't forget her jaw, now, get it over with, hard, throw another one, good judgment, Jesusa. But the most endearing image was that of her small figure, very straight, next to the other *adelitas*, the camp followers who rode on top of the train, her cartridge belts across her chest, Captain Pedro Aguilar's wide sombrero protecting her from the sun.

As she talked, such images gave me great joy. I felt strength from all the things I hadn't lived through. When I got home I'd say: "Something is being born inside me, something new that wasn't there before," but no one ever answered me. I wanted to tell them: "I get stronger each time, I'm growing, I'm finally going to be a woman." What was growing, although it may have been there for years, was my Mexican being, my becoming Mexican; feeling Mexico inside me, the same one that was inside Jesusa. I wasn't the eight-year-old girl who had arrived on a refugee ship, the *Marqués de Comilla*, the daughter of eternally absent parents, of transatlantic travelers, the daughter of trains. Now Mexico was inside me, it was a huge animal (as Jesusa called the tape recorder), a strong animal, energetic, one that got bigger and bigger until it filled the entire space. Discovering it was like suddenly having a truth in your hands, like a lamp that shines brightly and casts its circle of light on the floor. Before, I'd only seen floating lights that got lost in the darkness, the light from the switchman's kerosene lamp that eventually disappeared. But this stable, immobile lamp gave me security, like an anchor. My grandparents and my great-grandparents always repeated a phrase in English that they thought was poetic: "I don't belong." Maybe it was their way of distinguishing themselves from the rabble, not being like the rest. One night, before to write back. She'd go to the scribes at the Plaza de Santo Domingo and dictate her letter and she'd send it first-class. She wrote about the things she thought I'd be most interested in, like the president of Czechoslovakia's trip to Mexico, the foreign debt, highway accidents; we never talked about the news in the papers when I was with her. Jesusa was always unpredictable. One afternoon I found her glued to the radio, a notebook on her lap, a pencil in her hand. She was writing an upside-down U and a three-legged N; and it was extremely awkward for her. She was taking writing lessons from the radio. Stupidly I asked:

—Why do you want to learn how to do that now?

—Because I want to die knowing how to read and write.

I tried to take her out on several occasions:

—Let's go to the movies, Jesusa.

—No, I don't see well . . . I used to like the serials, the Lon Chaney ones.

—Then let's take a ride.

—And the chores? Obviously you don't have anything to do.

I suggested a trip to Tehuantepec to see her homeland again, something that I thought would please her, until I realized that the hope of something better unsettled her, it made her hostile. Jesusa was so used to her condition, so ruined by loneliness and poverty that the possibility of change seemed an insult: "Get out of here. What do you understand? I said get out. Leave me alone." I understood then that there is a point when you've suffered so much that you can't stop suffering. The only break Jesusa allowed herself was the cigarette she smoked leisurely at around six in the evening, her radio always on. She unwrapped gifts and then rewrapped them carefully. "So they don't get damaged." That's how I learned about her carton of dolls, all new, untouched. "There are four. I bought them for myself. Since I never had any as a child . . ."

In her book *Soldaderas in the Mexican Military*, Elizabeth Salas states that in 1914, between January and September, at Fort Bliss and then at Fort Wingate, 3,359 officers and soldiers were incarcerated, as well as 1,256 *soldaderas* and 554 children. The *soldaderas* were called that because they welcomed the soldiers, took care of them, never hesitating to take up a rifle and shoot when their man was eating or taking care of his business. They, on the other hand, had to watch their own backs. They gave birth on the road and kept on walking. They fought in the trenches. One of Jesusa's friends had her child in a trench, another in a desert up north, but it died from lack of water. Jesusa, Captain Pedro Aguilar's wife, not only knew the rails, the steady gunfire, the arguments between the troublemaker *soldaderas;* she also experienced the glories of battle, taking out the enemy with a single shot. The bullets in the blue air exploded like little white balls, clouds of deafening smoke covered the sky and enlivened Jesusa.

Without the *soldaderas* the Revolution would not have survived. Who would have looked after the soldiers? Without them everyone would have deserted. They made hearth and home and they buried their soldier, their Juan, when the worst happened, just as God commands. They carried their children on their backs, tied up in their rebozos, and at dawn somehow they worked it so that even under the worst circumstances the camp would awaken to the fragrant smell of coffee. Many of them died from tuberculosis, peritonitis, and diarrhea, but that didn't take away their sense of adventure. Blessed *soldaderas* so maligned! They recklessly challenged death.

What an atmosphere the *soldaderas* created! Besides casseroles, chickens, piglets, pots, serapes, pans, ammunition, baby bottles, rifles, metates, and pups that they raised, they carried guitars and sang around the campfires at night. They walked for hours without tiring, stronger than the Tameme Indians, the natives that carried huge loads on their backs. If they happened to kill a steer with a stray bullet, then they had food for several days.

They were maternal, they sheltered their man, they made him laugh, they entertained him. They built fires with carefully chosen stones, they ground corn, patted out thin tortillas, and still found a way to bathe and braid their tresses with colored ribbons to brighten their Juan's day. Their men could very easily have forgotten they were women, always seeing them dressed as men.

I had a dilemma when I wrote *Hasta no verte Jesús mío* in Spanish: the curse words. In a first version, Jesusa never said a bad word and I liked to think of her as modest, reserved; I was writing the story without "haughty words," but as our trust of each other grew, which happened after I returned from my year in France, Jesusa let loose. She brought me into her world, she no longer watched what she said and she'd admonish me: "Don't be such an asshole, you're the only one who believes in people, you're the only one who thinks people are good." I had to look up some of the words she used in a dictionary of Mexicanisms; others dated back to an archaic Spanish. She threw my absence in my face: "You look out for your own interests! You'll come see me as long as you can get what you want out of me, then there'll be neither hide nor hair of you. That's how it always is, everyone uses whoever they can." Like all old people, she had a long string of ailments and complaints; her rotting backside, her aching muscles, how badly the buses ran, the horrible quality of the food, the rent that was no longer affordable, the lazy and drunk neighbors. She'd repeat the same thing over and over, sitting on her bed, her legs hanging because it was set up on bricks; the water flooded the rooms during the rainy season and Doña Casimira, the owner, never bothered to have the patio drains unclogged.

Jesusa tolerated Casimira, the "rich one," like an enemy, someone who was there just to annoy her. The owner represented authority, and Jesusa believed that authority never helped the poor, they'd rather see them three feet under. She'd experienced enough with Don Venustiano Carranza, who stole her widow's pay.

Each meeting was really a long interview. When it was over I was left with a feeling of loss because I couldn't make her spirit visible, I couldn't reveal the intensity of Jesusa's character. Looking back now, I think I got caught up in the adventures, going from one anecdote to another. I liked her picaresque life. I never made her answer anything she didn't want to. I couldn't pry into her privacy. There was no way to present those moments when we were both silent, not even thinking, waiting for a miracle. We were always a little feverish, wishing for hallucinations. I heard my nanny's voice in Jesusa's, the woman who taught me Spanish, the voices of all the maids who passed through our house like air currents, their expressions, their view of life, if you could even call it that, because they lived for the day, they had no reason to hope for anything.

The voices of these other marginalized women sang a chorus to Jesusa Palancares's melody, and that's why there are words, idiomatic expressions and proverbs in the text, that come not only from Oaxaca, Jesusa's home state, but from the whole Republic, Jalisco, Veracruz, Guerrero, the sierra of Puebla. There were Wednesdays when Jesusa talked of nothing but her obsession of that day, but in the inactivity of the routine, the difficulty of everyday living, there were moments of pleasant, unexpected respite, such as when we took the chickens out of their cages and set them on the bed like little children.

I went to see Jesusa on Wednesday afternoons and when I got home I'd accompany my mother to cocktail parties at one embassy or another. I always tried to maintain a balance between the extreme poverty that I shared at Jesusa's tenement and the splendor of the receptions. My socialism was in name only. As I got into the tub of hot water, I'd remember the washbasin under the bed where Jesusa rinsed the overalls and bathed herself on Saturdays. I was ashamed: "I hope she never sees my house or how I live." When she did, she said: "I'm never coming back, I don't want you thinking I'm a beggar." But the friendship survived, the bond had been established. Jesusa and I loved each other. Never, however, did she stop judging me. "I knew from the beginning that you were high society." When I was in the hospital, she wanted to spend the night: "I'll lie down right at the foot of your bed." I've never received so much from anyone, I've never felt more guilty. I moved over a little in the bed:

"Come on, Jesusita, there's room for both of us," but she wouldn't. She left at five in the morning while I was still saying: "Ay, but there's room for both of us." She said: "No, the only bed we both fit in is mine because it's a poor person's bed."

When I'd typed up the first clean version of her life, I took it to her bound in sky-blue covers. She said: "What do I want this for? Get that piece of shit out of here. Can't you see it's in my way?" I thought she'd like it because it was so big. When it was to be published, I chose the Niño de Atocha, the little Jesus that presided over the semidarkness of her room, for the cover of the book, and when she saw it she asked me for twenty copies, which she gave to the men at the shop so they'd know about her life, the many precipices she had crossed, and so they'd have an idea of what the Revolution was really like.

Her difficult childhood, the abuse she suffered from her stepmother, Señora Evarista, and loneliness made her suspicious, proud; she was a skittish mare who avoided any expression of affection, of possible closeness. She never spoke of her love life.

I tried to emphasize Jesusa's personal qualities in the novel, things that differentiated her from the traditional image of the

The Day of the Dead

The solitary Mexican loves fiestas and public gatherings. Any occasion for getting together will serve, any pretext to stop the flow of time and commemorate men and events with festivals and ceremonies. We are a ritual people, and this characteristic enriches both our imaginations and our sensibilities, which are equally sharp and alert. The art of the fiesta has been debased almost everywhere else, but not in Mexico. There are few places in the world where it is possible to take part in a spectacle like our great religious fiestas with their violent primary colors, their bizarre costumes and dances, their fireworks and ceremonies, and their inexhaustible welter of surprises: the fruit, candy, toys, and other objects sold on these days in the plazas and open-air markets.

Our calendar is crowded with fiestas. There are certain days when the whole country, from the most remote villages to the largest cities, prays, shouts, feasts, gets drunk, and kills, in honor of the Virgin of Guadalupe or Benito Juárez. Each year on the fifteenth of September, at eleven o'clock at night, we celebrate the fiesta of the *Grito*[1] in all the plazas of the Republic, and the excited crowds actually shout for a whole hour . . . the better, perhaps, to remain silent for the rest of the year. During the days before and after the twelfth of December,[2] time comes to a full stop, and instead of pushing us toward a deceptive tomorrow that is always beyond our reach, offers us a complete and perfect today of dancing and revelry, of communion with the most ancient and secret Mexico. Time is no longer succession, and becomes what it originally was and is: the present, in which past and future are reconciled.

But the fiestas which the Church and State provide for the country as a whole are not enough. The life of every city and village is ruled by a patron saint whose blessing is celebrated with devout regularity. Neighborhoods and trades also have their annual fiestas, their ceremonies and fairs. And each one of us—atheist, Catholic, or merely indifferent—has his own saint's day, which he observes every year. It is impossible to calculate how many fiestas we have and how much time and money we spend on them. I remember asking the mayor of a village near Mitla, several years ago, "What is the income of the village government?" "About 3,000 pesos a year. We are very poor. But the Governor and the Federal Government always help us to meet our expenses." "And how are the 3,000 pesos spent?" "Mostly on fiestas, señor. We are a small village, but we have two patron saints."

This reply is not surprising. Our poverty can be measured by the frequency and luxuriousness of our holidays. Wealthy countries have very few: there is neither the time nor the desire for them, and they are not necessary. The people have other things to do, and when they amuse themselves they do so in small

[1]Padre Hidalgo's call-to-arms against Spain, 1810.—*Tr.*
[2]Fiesta of the Virgin of Guadalupe.—*Tr.*

groups. The modern masses are agglomerations of solitary individuals. On great occasions in Paris or New York, when the populace gathers in the squares or stadiums, the absence of people, in the sense of *a* people, is remarkable: there are couples and small groups, but they never form a living community in which the individual is at once dissolved and redeemed. But how could a poor Mexican live without the two or three annual fiestas that make up for his poverty and misery? Fiestas are our only luxury. They replace, and are perhaps better than, the theater and vacations, Anglo-Saxon weekends and cocktail parties, the bourgeois reception, the Mediterranean café.

In all of these ceremonies—national or local, trade or family—the Mexican opens out. They all give him a chance to reveal himself and to converse with God, country, friends, or relations. During these days the silent Mexican whistles, shouts, sings, shoots off fireworks, discharges his pistol into the air. He discharges his soul. And his shout, like the rockets we love so much, ascends to the heavens, explodes into green, red, blue, and white lights, and falls dizzily to earth with a trail of golden sparks. This is the night when friends who have not exchanged more than the prescribed courtesies for months get drunk together, trade confidences, weep over the same troubles, discover that they are brothers, and sometimes, to prove it, kill each other. The night is full of songs and loud cries. The lover wakes up his sweetheart with an orchestra. There are jokes and conversations from balcony to balcony, sidewalk to sidewalk. Nobody talks quietly. Hats fly in the air. Laughter and curses ring like silver pesos. Guitars are brought out. Now and then, it is true, the happiness ends badly, in quarrels, insults, pistol shots, stabbings. But these too are part of the fiesta, for the Mexican does not seek amusement: he seeks to escape from himself, to leap over the wall of solitude that confines him during the rest of the year. All are possessed by violence and frenzy. Their souls explode like the colors and voices and emotions. Do they forget themselves and show their true faces? Nobody knows. The important thing is to go out, open a way, get drunk on noise, people, colors. Mexico is celebrating a fiesta. And this fiesta, shot through with lightning and delirium, is the brilliant reverse to our silence and apathy, our reticence and gloom.

According to the interpretation of French sociologists, the fiesta is an excess, an expense. By means of this squandering the community protects itself against the envy of the gods or of men. Sacrifices and offerings placate or buy off the gods and the patron saints. Wasting money and expending energy affirms the community's wealth in both. This luxury is a proof of health, a show of abundance and power. Or a magic trap. For squandering is an effort to attract abundance by contagion. Money calls to money. When life is thrown away it increases; the orgy, which is sexual expenditure, is also a ceremony of regeneration; waste gives strength. New Year celebrations, in every culture, signify something beyond the mere observance of a date on the calendar. The day is a pause: time is stopped, is actually annihilated. The rites that celebrate its death are intended to provoke its rebirth, because they mark not only the end of an old year but also the beginning of a new. Everything attracts its opposite. The fiesta's function, then, is more utilitarian than we think: waste attracts or promotes wealth, and is an investment like any other, except that the returns on it cannot be measured or counted. What is sought is potency, life, health. In this sense the fiesta, like the gift and the offering, is one of the most ancient of economic forms.

This interpretation has always seemed to me to be incomplete. The fiesta is by nature sacred, literally or figuratively, and above all it is the advent of the unusual. It is governed by its own special rules, that set it apart from other days, and it has a logic, an ethic, and even an economy that are often in conflict with everyday norms. It all occurs in an enchanted world: time is transformed to a mythical past or a total present; space, the scene of the fiesta, is turned into a gaily decorated world of its own; and the persons taking part cast off all human or social rank and become, for the moment, living images. And everything takes place as if it were not so, as if it were a dream. But whatever happens, our actions have a greater lightness, a different gravity. They take on other meanings and with them we contract new obligations. We throw down our burdens of time and reason.

In certain fiestas the very notion of order disappears. Chaos comes back and license rules. Anything is permitted: the customary hierarchies vanish, along with all social, sex, caste, and trade distinctions. Men disguise themselves as women, gentlemen as slaves, the poor as the rich. The army, the clergy, and the law are ridiculed. Obligatory sacrilege, ritual profanation is committed. Love becomes promiscuity. Sometimes the fiesta becomes a Black Mass. Regulations, habits, and customs are violated. Respectable people put away the dignified expressions and conservative clothes that isolate them, dress up in gaudy colors, hide behind a mask, and escape from themselves.

Therefore the fiesta is not only an excess, a ritual squandering of the goods painfully accumulated during the rest of the year; it is also a revolt, a sudden immersion in the formless, in pure being. By means of the fiesta society frees itself from the norms it has established. It ridicules its gods, its principles, and its laws: it denies its own self.

The fiesta is a revolution in the most literal sense of the word. In the confusion that it generates, society is dissolved, is drowned, insofar as it is an organism ruled according to certain laws and principles. But it drowns in itself, in its own original chaos or liberty. Everything is united: good and evil, day and night, the sacred and the profane. Everything merges, loses shape and individuality and returns to the primordial mass. The fiesta is a cosmic experiment, an experiment in disorder, reuniting contradictory elements and principles in order to bring about a renascence of life. Ritual death promotes a rebirth; vomiting increases the appetite; the orgy, sterile in itself, renews the fertility of the mother or of the earth. The fiesta is a return to a remote and undifferentiated state, prenatal or presocial. It is a return that is also a beginning, in accordance with the dialectic that is inherent in social processes.

The group emerges purified and strengthened from this plunge into chaos. It has immersed itself in its own origins, in the womb from which it came. To express it in another way, the fiesta denies society as an organic system of differentiated forms and principles, but affirms it as a source of creative energy. It is a true "re-creation," the opposite of the "recreation" characterizing modern vacations, which do not entail any rites or ceremonies whatever and are as individualistic and sterile as the world that invented them.

Society communes with itself during the fiesta. Its members return to original chaos and freedom. Social structures break down and new relationships, unexpected rules, capricious hierarchies are created. In the general disorder everybody forgets himself and enters into otherwise forbidden situations and places. The bounds between audience and actors, officials and servants, are erased. Everybody takes part in the fiesta, everybody is caught up in its whirlwind. Whatever its mood, its character, its meaning, the fiesta is participation, and this trait distinguishes it from all other ceremonies and social phenomena. Lay or religious, orgy or saturnalia, the fiesta is a social act based on the full participation of all its celebrants.

Thanks to the fiesta the Mexican opens out, participates, communes with his fellows and with the values that give meaning to his religious or political existence. And it is significant that a country as sorrowful as ours should have so many and such joyous fiestas. Their frequency, their brilliance and excitement, the enthusiasm with which we take part, all suggest that without them we would explode. They free us, if only momentarily, from the thwarted impulses, the inflammable desires that we carry within us. But the Mexican fiesta is not merely a return to an original state of formless and normless liberty: the Mexican is not seeking to return, but to escape from himself, to exceed himself. Our fiestas are explosions. Life and death, joy and sorrow, music and mere noise are united, not to re-create or recognize themselves, but to swallow each other up. There is nothing so joyous as a Mexican fiesta, but there is also nothing so sorrowful. Fiesta night is also a night of mourning.

If we hide within ourselves in our daily lives, we discharge ourselves in the whirlwind of the fiesta. It is more than an opening out: we rend ourselves open. Everything—music, love, friendship—ends in tumult and violence. The frenzy of our festivals shows the extent to which our solitude closes us off from communication with the world. We are familiar with delirium, with songs and shouts, with the monologue . . . but not with the dialogue. Our fiestas, like our confidences, our loves, our attempts to reorder our society, are violent breaks with the old or the established. Each time we try to express ourselves we have to break with ourselves. And the fiesta is only one example, perhaps the most typical, of this violent break. It is not difficult to name others, equally revealing: our games, which are always a going to extremes, often mortal; our profligate spending, the reverse of our timid investments and business enterprises; our confessions. The somber Mexican, closed up in himself, suddenly explodes, tears open his breast and reveals himself, though not without a certain complacency, and not without a stopping place in the shameful or terrible mazes of his intimacy. We are not frank, but our sincerity can reach extremes that horrify a European. The explosive, dramatic, sometimes even suicidal manner in which we strip ourselves, surrender ourselves, is evidence that something inhibits and suffocates us. Something impedes us from being. And since we cannot or dare not confront our own selves, we resort to ' ⁻ f ˍsta. It fires us into the void; it is a drunken rapture that burns itself out, a pistol shot in the air, a skyrocket.

Death is a mirror which reflects the vain gesticulations of the living. The whole motley confusion of acts, omissions, regrets, and hopes which is the life of each one of us finds in death, not meaning or explanation, but an end. Death defines life; a death depicts a life in immutable forms; we do not change except to disappear. Our deaths illuminate our lives. If our deaths lack meaning, our lives also lacked it. Therefore we are apt to say, when somebody has died a violent death, "He got what he was looking for." Each of us dies the death he is looking for, the death he has made for himself. A Christian death or a dog's death are ways of dying that reflect ways of living. If death betrays us and we die badly, everyone laments the fact, because we should die as we have lived. Death, like life, is not transferable. If we do not die as we lived, it is because the life we lived was not really ours: it did not belong to us, just as the bad death that kills us does not belong to us. Tell me how you die and I will tell you who you are.

The opposition between life and death was not so absolute to the ancient Mexicans as it is to us. Life extended into death, and vice versa. Death was not the natural end of life but one phase of an infinite cycle. Life, death, and resurrection were stages of a cosmic process which repeated itself continuously. Life had no higher function than to flow into death, its opposite and complement; and death, in turn, was not an end in itself: man fed the insatiable hunger of life with his death. Sacrifices had a double purpose: on the one hand man participated in the creative process at the same time paying back to the gods the debt contracted by his species; on the other hand he nourished cosmic life and also social life, which was nurtured by the former.

Perhaps the most characteristic aspect of this conception is the impersonal nature of the sacrifice. Since their lives did not belong to them, their deaths lacked any personal meaning. The dead—including warriors killed in battle and women dying in childbirth, companions of Huitzilopochtli the sun god—disappeared at the end of a certain period, to return to the undifferentiated country of the shadows, to be melted into the air, the earth, the fire, the animating substance of the universe. Our indigenous ancestors did not believe that their deaths belonged to them, just as they never thought that their lives were really theirs in the Christian sense. Everything was examined to determine, from birth, the life and death of each man: his social class, the year, the place, the day, the hour. The Aztec was as little responsible for his actions as for his death.

Space and time were bound together and formed an inseparable whole. There was a particular "time" for each place, each of the cardinal points and the center in which they were immobilized. And this complex of space-time possessed its own virtues and powers, which profoundly influenced and determined human life. To be born on a certain day was to pertain to a place, a time, a color, and a destiny. All was traced out in advance. Where we dissociate space and time, mere stage sets for the actions of our lives, there were as many "space-times" for the Aztecs as there were combinations in the priestly calendar, each one endowed with a particular qualitative significance, superior to human will.

Religion and destiny ruled their lives, as morality and

freedom rule ours. We live under the sign of liberty, and everything—even Greek fatality and the grace of the theologians—is election and struggle, but for the Aztecs the problem reduced itself to investigating the never-clear will of the gods. Only the gods were free, and only they had the power to choose—and therefore, in a profound sense, to sin. The Aztec religion is full of great sinful gods—Quetzalcóatl is the major example—who grow weak and abandon their believers, in the same way that Christians sometimes deny God. The conquest of Mexico would be inexplicable without the treachery of the gods, who denied their own people.

The advent of Catholicism radically modified this situation. Sacrifice and the idea of salvation, formerly collective, became personal. Freedom was humanized, embodied in man. To the ancient Aztecs the essential thing was to assure the continuity of creation; sacrifice did not bring about salvation in another world, but cosmic health; the universe, and not the individual, was given life by the blood and death of human beings. For Christians it is the individual who counts. The world—history, society—is condemned beforehand. The death of Christ saved each man in particular. Each one of us is Man, and represents the hopes and possibilities of the species. Redemption is a personal task.

Both attitudes, opposed as they may seem, have a common note: life, collective or individual, looks forward to a death that in its way is a new life. Life only justifies and transcends itself when it is realized in death, and death is also a transcendence, in that it is a new life. To Christians death is a transition, a somersault between two lives, the temporal and the otherworldly; to the Aztecs it was the profoundest way of participating in the continuous regeneration of the creative forces, which were always in danger of being extinguished if they were not provided with blood, the sacred food. In both systems life and death lack autonomy, are the two sides of a single reality. They are references to the invisible realities.

Modern death does not have any significance that transcends it or that refers to other values. It is rarely anything more than the inevitable conclusion of a natural process. In a world of facts, death is merely one more fact. But since it is such a disagreeable fact, contrary to all our concepts and to the very meaning of our lives, the philosophy of progress ("Progress toward what, and from what?" Scheler asked) pretends to make it disappear, like a magician palming a coin. Everything in the modern world functions as if death did not exist. Nobody takes it into account, it is suppressed everywhere: in political pronouncements, commercial advertising, public morality, and popular customs; in the promise of cut-rate health and happiness offered to all of us by hospitals, drugstores, and playing fields. But death enters into everything we undertake, and it is no longer a transition but a great gaping mouth that nothing can satisfy. The century of health, hygiene, and contraceptives, miracle drugs and synthetic foods, is also the century of the concentration camp and the police state, Hiroshima and the murder story. Nobody thinks about death, about his own death, as Rilke asked us to do, because nobody lives a personal life. Collective slaughter is the fruit of a collectivized way of life.

Death also lacks meaning for the modern Mexican. It is no longer a transition, an access to another life more alive than our own. But although we do not view death as a transcendence, we have not eliminated it from our daily lives. The word death is not pronounced in New York, in Paris, in London, because it burns the lips. The Mexican, in contrast, is familiar with death, jokes about it, caresses it, sleeps with it, celebrates it; it is one of his favorite toys and his most steadfast love. True, there is perhaps as much fear in his attitude as in that of others, but at least death is not hidden away: he looks at it face to face, with impatience, disdain, or irony. "If they are going to kill me tomorrow, let them kill me right away.[3]

The Mexican's indifference toward death is fostered by his indifference toward life. He views not only death but also life as nontranscendent. Our songs, proverbs, fiestas, and popular beliefs show very clearly that the reason death cannot frighten us is that "life has cured us of fear." It is natural, even desirable, to die, and the sooner the better. We kill because life—our own or another's—is of no value. Life and death are inseparable, and when the former lacks meaning, the latter becomes equally meaningless. Mexican death is the mirror of Mexican life. And the Mexican shuts himself away and ignores both of them.

Our contempt for death is not at odds with the cult we have made of it. Death is present in our fiestas, our games, our loves and our thoughts. To die and to kill are ideas that rarely leave us. We are seduced by death. The fascination it exerts over us is the result, perhaps, of our hermit-like solitude and of the fury with which we break out of it. The pressure of our vitality, which can only express itself in forms that betray it, explains the deadly nature, aggressive or suicidal, of our explosions. When we explode we touch against the highest point of that tension, we graze the very zenith of life. And there, at the height of our frenzy, suddenly we feel dizzy: it is then that death attracts us.

Another factor is that death revenges us against life, strips it of all its vanities and pretensions and converts it into what it really is: a few neat bones and a dreadful grimace. In a closed world where everything is death, only death has value. But our affirmation is negative. Sugar-candy skulls, and tissue-paper skulls and skeletons strung with fireworks . . . our popular images always poke fun at life, affirming the nothingness and insignificance of human existence. We decorate our houses with

[3]From the popular folk song *La Valentina.*—Tr.

death's heads, we eat bread in the shape of bones on the Day of the Dead, we love the songs and stories in which death laughs and cracks jokes, but all this boastful familiarity does not rid us of the question we all ask: What is death? We have not thought up a new answer. And each time we ask, we shrug our shoulders: Why should I care about death if I have never cared about life?

Does the Mexican open out in the presence of death? He praises it, celebrates it, cultivates it, embraces it, but he never surrenders himself to it. Everything is remote and strange to him, and nothing more so than death. He does not surrender himself to it because surrender entails a sacrifice. And a sacrifice, in turn, demands that someone must give and someone receive. That is, someone must open out and face a reality that transcends him. In a closed, nontranscendent world, death neither gives nor receives: it consumes itself and is self-gratifying. Therefore our relations with death are intimate—more intimate, perhaps, than those of any other people—but empty of meaning and devoid of erotic emotion. Death in Mexico is sterile, not fecund like that of the Aztecs and the Christians.

Nothing is more opposed to this attitude than that of the Europeans and North Americans. Their laws, customs, and public and private ethics all tend to preserve human life. This protection does not prevent the number of ingenious and refined murders, of perfect crimes and crime-waves, from increasing. The professional criminals who plot their murders with a precision impossible to a Mexican, the delight they take in describing their experiences and methods, the fascination with which the press and public follow their confessions, and the recognized inefficiency of the systems of prevention, show that the respect for life of which Western civilization is so proud is either incomplete or hypocritical.

The cult of life, if it is truly profound and total, is also the cult of death, because the two are inseparable. A civilization that denies death ends by denying life. The perfection of modern crime is not merely a consequence of modern technical progress and the vogue of the murder story: it derives from the contempt for life which is inevitably implicit in any attempt to hide death away and pretend it does not exist. It might be added that modern technical skills and the popularity of crime stories are, like concentration camps and collective extermination, the results of an optimistic and unilateral conception of existence. It is useless to exclude death from our images, our words, our ideas, because death will obliterate all of us, beginning with those who ignore it or pretend to ignore it.

When the Mexican kills—for revenge, pleasure or caprice—he kills a person, a human being. Modern criminals and statesmen do not kill: they abolish. They experiment with beings who have lost their human qualities. Prisoners in the concentration camps are first degraded, changed into mere objects; then they are exterminated en masse. The typical criminal in the large cities—beyond the specific motives for his crimes—realizes on a small scale what the modern leader realizes on a grand scale. He too experiments, in his own way: he poisons, destroys corpses with acids, dismembers them, converts them into objects. The ancient relationship between victim and murderer, which is the only thing that humanizes murder, that makes it even thinkable, has disappeared. As in the novels of Sade, there is no longer anything except torturers and objects, instruments of pleasure and destruction. And the nonexistence of the victim makes the infinite solitude of the murderer even more intolerable. Murder is still a relationship in Mexico, and in this sense it has the same liberating significance as the fiesta or the confession. Hence its drama, its poetry, and—why not say it?—its grandeur. Through murder we achieve a momentary transcendence.

. . .

At the beginning of his eighth Duino Elegy, Rilke says that the "creature," in his condition of animal innocence, "beholds the open" . . . unlike ourselves, who never look forward, toward the absolute. Fear makes us turn our backs on death, and by refusing to contemplate it we shut ourselves off from life, which is a totality that includes it. The "open" is where contraries are reconciled, where light and shadow are fused. This conception restores death's original meaning: death and life are opposites that complement each other. Both are halves of a sphere that we, subjects of time and space, can only glimpse. In the prenatal world, life and death are merged; in ours, opposed; in the world beyond, reunited again, not in the animal innocence that precedes sin and the knowledge of sin, but as in innocence regained. Man can transcend the temporal opposition separating them (and residing not in them but in his own consciousness) and perceive them as a superior whole. This recognition can take place only through detachment: he must renounce his temporal life and his nostalgia for limbo, for the animal world. He must open himself out to death if he wishes to open himself out to life. Then he will be "like the angels."

Thus there are two attitudes toward death: one, pointing forward, that conceives of it as creation; the other, pointing backward, that expresses itself as a fascination with nothingness or as a nostalgia for limbo. No Mexican or Spanish-American poet, with the possible exception of César Vallejo, approaches the first of these two concepts. The absence of a mystic—and only a mystic is capable of offering insights like those of Rilke—indicates the extent to which modern Mexican culture is insensible to religion. But two Mexican poets, José Gorostiza and Xavier Villaurrutia, represent the second of these two attitudes. For Gorostiza life is a "death without end," a perpetual falling into nothingness; for Villaurrutia it is no more than a "nostalgia for death."

The phrase that Villaurrutia chose for his book, *Nostalgia de la Muerte,* is not merely a lucky hit. The author has used it in order to tell us the ultimate meaning of his poetry. Death as nostalgia, rather than as the fruition or end of life, is death as origin. The ancient, original source is a bone, not a womb. This statement runs the risk of seeming either an empty paradox or an old commonplace: "For thou art dust, and unto dust shalt thou return." I believe that the poet hopes to find in death (which is, in effect, our origin) a revelation that his temporal life has denied him: the true meaning of life. When we die,

> *The second hand*
> *will race around its dial,*
> *all will be contained in an instant . . .*
> *and perhaps it will be possible*
> *to live, even after death.*

A return to original death would be a return to the life before life, the life before death: to limbo, to the maternal source.

Muerte sin Fin, the poem by José Gorostiza, is perhaps the best evidence we have in Latin America of a truly modern consciousness, one that is turned in upon itself, imprisoned in its own blinding clarity. The poet, in a sort of lucid fury, wants to rip the mask off existence in order to see it as it is. The dialogue between man and the world, which is as old as poetry and love, is transformed into a dialogue between the water and the glass that contains it, between the thought and the form into which it is poured and which it eventually corrodes. The poet warns us from his prison of appearances—trees and thoughts, stones and emotions, days and nights and twilights are all simply metaphors, mere colored ribbons—that the breath which informs matter, shaping it and giving it form, is the same breath that corrodes and withers and defeats it. It is a drama without personae, since all are merely reflections, the various disguises of a suicide who talks to himself in a language of mirrors and echoes, and the mind also is nothing more than a reflection of death, of death in love with itself. Everything is immersed in its own clarity and brilliance, everything is directed toward this transparent death: life is only a metaphor, an invention with which death—death too!—wants to deceive itself. The poem is a variation on the old theme of Narcissus, although there is no allusion to it in the text. And it is not only the consciousness that contemplates itself in its empty, transparent water (both mirror and eye at the same time, as in the Valéry poem): nothingness, which imitates form and life, which feigns corruption and death, strips itself naked and turns in upon itself, loves itself, falls into itself: a tireless death without end.

If we open out during fiestas, then, or when we are drunk or exchanging confidences, we do it so violently that we wound ourselves. And we shrug our shoulders at death, as at life, confronting it in silence or with a contemptuous smile. The fiesta, the crime of passion, and the gratuitous crime reveal that the equilibrium of which we are so proud is only a mask, always in danger of being ripped off by a sudden explosion of our intimacy.

All of these attitudes indicate that the Mexican senses the presence of a stigma both on himself and on the flesh of his country. It is diffused but none the less living, original, and ineradicable. Our gestures and expressions all attempt to hide this wound, which is always open, always ready to catch fire and burn under the rays of a stranger's glance.

Now, every separation causes a wound. Without stopping to investigate how and when the separation is brought about, I want to point out that any break (with ourselves or those around us, with the past or the present) creates a feeling of solitude. In extreme cases—separation from one's parents, matrix, or native land, the death of the gods, or a painful self-consciousness—solitude is identified with orphanhood. And both of them generally manifest themselves as a sense of sin. The penalties and guilty feelings inflicted by a state of separation can be considered, thanks to the ideas of expiation and redemption, as necessary sacrifices, as pledges or promises of a future communion that will put an end to the long exile. The guilt can vanish, the wound heal over, the separation resolve itself in communion. Solitude thus assumes a purgative, purifying character. The solitary or isolated individual transcends his solitude, accepting it as a proof or promise of communion.

The Mexican does not transcend his solitude. On the contrary, he locks himself up in it. We live in our solitude like Philoctetes on his island, fearing rather than hoping to return to the world. We cannot bear the presence of our companions. We hide within ourselves—except when we rend ourselves open in our frenzy—and the solitude in which we suffer has no reference either to a redeemer or a creator. We oscillate between intimacy and withdrawal, between a shout and a silence, between a fiesta and a wake, without ever truly surrendering ourselves. Our indifference hides life behind a death mask; our wild shout rips off this mask and shoots into the sky, where it swells, explodes, and falls back in silence and defeat. Either way, the Mexican shuts himself off from the world: from life and from death.

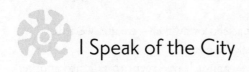

I Speak of the City

for Eliot Weinberger

news today and tomorrow a ruin, buried and resurrected
every day,

lived together in streets, plazas, buses, taxis, movie houses,
theaters, bars, hotels, pigeon coops and catacombs,

the enormous city that fits in a room three yards square,
and endless as a galaxy,

the city that dreams us all, that all of us build and unbuild
and rebuild as we dream,

the city we all dream, that restlessly changes while we
dream it,

the city that wakes every hundred years and looks at itself
in the mirror of a word and doesn't recognize itself and goes
back to sleep,

the city that sprouts from the eyelids of the woman who
sleeps at my side, and is transformed,

with its monuments and statues, its histories and legends,

into a fountain made of countless eyes, and each eye reflects
the same landscape, frozen in time,

before schools and prisons, alphabets and numbers, the altar
and the law:

the river that is four rivers, the orchard, the tree, the Female
and Male, dressed in wind—

to go back, go back, to be clay again, to bathe in that light,
to sleep under those votive lights,

   to float on the waters of time like the flaming maple leaf
the current drags along,

   to go back—are we asleep or awake?—we are, we are
nothing more, day breaks, it's early,

   we are in the city, we cannot leave except to fall into another
city, different yet identical,

   I speak of the immense city, that daily reality composed of
two words: *the others*,

   and in every one of them there is an I clipped from a we, an
I adrift,

   I speak of the city built by the dead, inhabited by their
stern ghosts, ruled by their despotic memory,

   the city I talk to when I talk to nobody, the city that
dictates these insomniac words,

   I speak of towers, bridges, tunnels, hangars, wonders and
disasters,

   the abstract State and its concrete police, the schoolteachers,
jailers, preachers,

   the shops that have everything, where we spend everything,
and it all turns to smoke,

   the markets with their pyramids of fruit, the turn of the
seasons, the sides of beef hanging from the hooks, the hills of
spices and the towers of bottles and preserves,

   all of the flavors and colors, all the smells and all the stuff,
the tide of voices—water, metal, wood, clay—the bustle, the
haggling and conniving as old as time,

   I speak of the buildings of stone and marble, of cement,
glass and steel, of the people in the lobbies and doorways, of
the elevators that rise and fall like the mercury in
thermometers,

   of the banks and their boards of directors, of factories and
their managers, of the workers and their incestuous machines,

   I speak of the timeless parade of prostitution through
streets long as desire and boredom,

of the coming and going of cars, mirrors of our anxieties, business, passions (why? toward what? for what?),

of the hospitals that are always full, and where we always die alone,

I speak of the half-light of certain churches and the flickering candles at the altars,

the timid voices with which the desolate talk to saints and virgins in a passionate, failing language,

I speak of dinner under a squinting light at a limping table with chipped plates,

of the innocent tribes that camp in the empty lots with their women and children, their animals and their ghosts,

of the rats in the sewers and the brave sparrows that nest in the wires, in the cornices and the martyred trees,

of the contemplative cats and their libertine novels in the light of the moon, cruel goddess of the rooftops,

of the stray dogs that are our Franciscans and *bhikkus*, the dogs that scratch up the bones of the sun,

I speak of the anchorite and the libertarian brotherhood, of the secret plots of law enforcers and of bands of thieves,

of the conspiracies of levelers and the Society of Friends of Crime, of the Suicide Club, and of Jack the Ripper,

of the Friend of the People, sharpener of the guillotine, of Caesar, Delight of Humankind,

I speak of the paralytic slum, the cracked wall, the dry fountain, the graffitied statue,

I speak of garbage heaps the size of mountains, and of melancholy sunlight filtered by the smog,

of broken glass and the desert of scrap iron, of last night's crime, and of the banquet of the immortal Trimalchio,

of the moon in the television antennas, and a butterfly on a filthy jar,

I speak of dawns like a flight of herons on the lake, and the sun of transparent wings that lands on the rock foliage of the churches, and the twittering of light on the glass stalks of the palaces,

I speak of certain afternoons in early fall, waterfalls of immaterial gold, the transformation of this world, when everything loses its body, everything is held in suspense,

and the light thinks, and each one of us feels himself thought by that reflective light, and for one long moment time dissolves, we are air once more,

I speak of the summer, of the slow night that grows on the horizon like a mountain of smoke, and bit by bit it crumbles, falling over us like a wave,

the elements are reconciled, night has stretched out, and its body is a powerful river of sudden sleep, we rock in the waves of its breathing, the hour is tangible, we can touch it like a fruit,

they have lit the lights, and the avenues burn with the brilliancy of desire, in the parks electric light breaks through the branches and falls over us like a green and phosphorescent mist that illuminates but does not wet us, the trees murmur, they tell us something,

there are streets in the half-light that are a smiling insinuation, we don't know where they lead, perhaps to the ferry for the lost islands,

I speak of the stars over the high terraces and the indecipherable sentences they write on the stone of the sky,

I speak of the sudden downpour that lashes the windowpanes and bends the trees, that lasted twenty-five minutes and now, up above, there are blue slits and streams of light, steam rises from the asphalt, the cars glisten, there are puddles where ships of reflections sail,

I speak of nomadic clouds, and of a thin music that lights a room on the fifth floor, and a murmur of laughter in the middle of the night like water that flows far-off through roots and grasses,

I speak of the longed-for encounter with that unexpected form with which the unknown is made flesh, and revealed to each of us:

eyes that are the night half-open and the day that wakes, the sea stretching out and the flame that speaks, powerful breasts: lunar tide,

lips that say *sesame,* and time opens, and the little room becomes a garden of change, air and fire entwine, earth and water mingle,

or the arrival of that moment there, on the other side that is really here, where the key locks and time ceases to flow:

the moment of *until now,* the last of the gasps, the moaning, the anguish, the soul loses its body and crashes, through a hole in the floor, falling in itself, and time has run aground, and we walk through an endless corridor, panting in the sand,

is that music coming closer or receding, are those pale lights just lit or going out? space is singing, time has vanished: it is the gasp, it is the glance that slips through the blank wall, it is the wall that stays silent, the wall,

I speak of our public history, and of our secret history, yours and mine,

I speak of the forest of stone, the desert of the prophets, the ant-heap of souls, the congregation of tribes, the house of mirrors, the labyrinth of echoes,

I speak of the great murmur that comes from the depths of time, the incoherent whisper of nations uniting or splitting apart, the wheeling of multitudes and their weapons like boulders hurling down, the dull sound of bones falling into the pit of history,

I speak of the city, shepherd of the centuries, mother that gives birth to us and devours us, that creates us and forgets.

Excerpt from
The Book of Lamentations

San Juan, the Guarantor, he who was there when the worlds first appeared, who spoke the yes that started the century on its way and is one of the pillars that keep stable what is stable, stooped down one day to contemplate the land of men.

His eyes travelled from the sea where the fish glides to the mountaintop where the snow sleeps. They passed over the flatlands where the fluttering wind scuffles, over the beaches' buzzing sands, over the forests, refuge of wary animals. Over the valleys.

The gaze of San Juan Guarantor paused at the valley called Chamula. He was pleased by the gentle slope of the hills that come there from far away to meet, their ravines gently heaving. He was pleased by the sky, hovering near in the early morning mists. There rose up in the soul of San Juan a desire to be worshiped in this place. That was why he turned all the white sheep in the flocks grazing in that valley to stone: so there would be no lack of materials to build his church and so his church would be white.

And there the rocky outcrop remained, silent and unmoving, sign of a divine desire. But the tribes that dwelled in the valley of Chamula, those called Tzotzils, the People of the Bat, did not know how to interpret this marvel. Neither the eldest among the elders nor the men of the Council were able to express a worthy opinion; they produced only confused stammerings, lowered eyelids, arms falling in gestures of fear.

That was why the other men had to come, later. And it was as if they came from another world. They carried the sun in their faces and spoke an arrogant language, a language that wrenches the hearts of those who hear it. A language not like Tzotzil (which is also spoken in dreams), but like an iron instrument of mastery, a weapon of conquest, the striking lash of the law's whip. For how could orders be given or condemnations passed down, if not in Castilla? How could punishments or rewards be meted out, if not in Castilla?

The newcomers did not fully understand the enigma of the petrified sheep either. They understood only the command that work be done. So they with their heads and the Indians with their hands began to construct a church. By day they dug the foundations, but at night the foundations filled in and became level again. By day they built the walls, and at night the walls fell down. San Juan Guarantor had to come in person, pushing the stones himself, rolling them down the slopes one by one until they were all gathered in the place they would remain. Only then did the men's efforts come to fruition.

The building is white, as San Juan Guarantor wanted. In the air consecrated by its vault resound the prayers and chants of the Caxlán, the pleas and laments of the Indian. Wax burns in perfect self-immolation; incense exhales its fervent soul; a carpet of pine needles clears and perfumes the air. From the altar's most conspicuous niche, the refined profile of the brightly painted wooden image of San Juan looks down, larger than the other images: Santa Margarita, the smallfooted maiden who pours out blessings; San Agustín, tranquil and robust; San Jerónimo, with a tiger in his belly, the secret protector of brujos; the Virgen Dolorosa, with a storm cloud darkening her horizon; the enormous Good Friday cross, expectant of its annual victim, leaning precariously, ready to drop like a catastrophe. There are also hostile powers that had to be tied down to keep their forces from erupting; anonymous virgins, mutilated apostles, inept angels fallen from the altar to the portable platforms and from there to the ground where they were knocked over: inanimate matter, forgotten by piety and disdained by oblivion. Hearing dulled, heart indifferent, hand closed.

These, it is said, are the things that have taken place since the beginning. It is no lie. There are witnesses. All of it can be read in the three arches of the church portal, where the sun takes its leave of the valley.

This is the center. Around it are the three sections of Chamula, the principal town of the municipality: a town with both religious and political roles, a ceremonial city.

The leading men of even the most distant regions of the Chiapas highlands where Tzotzil is spoken come to Chamula. Here they take up the burden of their duties.

The greatest responsibility falls on the president, and after him, the secretary. The two of them are assisted by alcaldes, regidores, elders, gobernadores and síndicos. The mayordomos are there to supervise the worship of the saints, the alféreces to organize the celebration of holy days. The pasiones are assigned their tasks for Carnival.

These duties last twelve months and those who carry them out, transitory inhabitants of Chamula, live in the huts scattered along the hillsides and the valley floor, supporting themselves by working the land, raising animals and guarding flocks of sheep.

When their term is over, these representatives return to the places they came from, enveloped in dignity and prestige. Now they are "former authorities." They have deliberated in the presence of their president and their deliberations were entered into the record by the secretary, inscribed on the paper that talks. They have established boundaries, mediated rivalries, dispensed justice, formalized and dissolved marriages. Most importantly, they were custodians of the divine. They saw to it that no one was remiss in care and reverence. This is why the chosen ones, the elite of the race, are not permitted to enter the day in the spirit of labor: they must enter it in the spirit of prayer. Before commencing any task, before pronouncing any word, the man who serves as an example to others must prostrate himself before his father, the sun.

Morning comes late to Chamula. The cock crows to chase away the darkness. As the men grope toward wakefulness, the women find their way to the ashes where they bend and blow to reveal the embers. The wind circles the hut, and below the roof of palm fronds, between the four walls of mud and twigs, cold is the guest of honor.

Pedro González Winiktón spread apart the hands that had been joined in meditation and let them fall along his body. He was an Indian of good height and solid muscles. Despite his youth (marked by the early severity typical of his people), others looked up to him as an elder brother. The wisdom of his decisions, the energy of his commands and the purity of his habits ranked him among men of respect, and only there did his heart expand. So he was content when, obliged to accept investiture as a judge, he took his oath before the cross in the portal of the church of San Juan Chamula. His wife, Catalina Díaz Puiljá, wove a serape of thick, black wool that amply covered him down to his ankles, to make those assembled hold him in greater esteem.

Consequently, after December 31st of that year, Pedro González Winiktón and Catalina Díaz Puiljá came to Chamula.
They were given a hut to live in, a plot of land to farm. The
cornfield was there, already green and promising a good harvest.
What more could Pedro wish for? He had material abundance,
prestige among his equals, the devotion of his wife. A smile
lasted only an instant on his face, little practiced at expressing
happiness. His features hardened. Winiktón saw himself as the
hollow stem, the stubble that is burned away after the harvest.
He compared himself to ashes. He had no children.

Catalina Díaz Puiljá, barely twenty years old yet already dry
and withered, was given to Pedro from childhood by her parents.
The early times were happy. The lack of offspring was seen as
natural then. But later, when the companions with whom Catalina spun, gathered wood and carried water began to settle their
feet more heavily onto the earth (because they walked for themselves and for the child to come), when their eyes filled with
peace and their bellies swelled like granaries after the harvest,
then Catalina probed her fruitless hips, cursed the lightness of
her step and, turning suddenly to look back, saw that her feet
left no mark behind her. This, she thought with anguish, was
how her name would pass over her people's memory. From that
time on she was inconsolable.

She consulted with the elders, yielded her pulse to the divin-
ers' ears. They questioned the cycles of her blood, investigated
the facts, intoned invocations. Where did your path swerve,
Catalina? Where did your spirit take fright? Catalina sweated,
immersing herself in the smoke of miraculous herbs. She did
not know how to answer. And her moon did not return white
like that of women who have conceived, but stained with
red like the moon of spinsters and widows. Like the whore's
moon.

Then the pilgrimage began. She approached the wandering

peddlers who brought news from far away. She stored the names of the places to be visited in the folds of her mind. There was an old woman in Cancuc who could work harmful magic but was also a healer, depending on what was needed. In Biqu'it Bautisti, a brujo went deep into the night to interpret its designs. An enchanter practiced in Tenejapa. Catalina brought them humble gifts: the first ears of corn, jars of liquor, a young lamb.

In this way the light was gradually hidden from her and she was caught up in a dark world ruled by arbitrary wills. She learned to placate those wills when they were threatening, to excite them when they were auspicious, to transmute their signs. She chanted mind-numbing litanies. She ran through flames, unharmed and delirious. Now she was one of those who dare to gaze on the face of mystery, an ilol, a seer, whose lap is a nest of spells. Those she frowned on trembled and those who saw her smile were reassured. But Catalina's belly was still closed. Sealed like a nut.

As she knelt in front of the metate, grinding a portion of posol, Catalina watched her husband from the corner of her eye. At what moment would he force her to speak the words of repudiation? How much longer would he tolerate the offense of her sterility? Marriages like theirs were not valid. One word from Winiktón would be enough to make Catalina return to her family's hut back in Tzajal-hemel. She would not find her father or her mother there; both of them had been dead for years. There was no one left but Lorenzo, the brother who was called "the innocent" because of his simple nature and the vacuous laugh that split his mouth in two.

Catalina stood up and placed the ball of posol in her husband's bag of provisions. What made him stay with her? Fear? Love? Winiktón's face kept its secret. Without a sign of farewell the man left the hut. The door closed behind him.

An irrevocable decision froze Catalina's features. They would never separate, she would never be left alone, never be humiliated before her people.

Her movements quickened, as if she were about to fight an enemy then and there. She came and went through the hut, guided more by touch than by sight; the only light filtered in through holes in the walls and the room was blackened, impregnated with smoke. Even more than touch, habit steered her, keeping her from stumbling against the objects heaped up randomly in the tiny space. Clay pots, chipped and cracked; the metate, still too new, not yet broken in by the strength and skill of the woman who used it; tree trunks instead of chairs; ancient chests with useless locks. And, leaning against the fragile wall, innumerable crosses. One, made of wood, was so tall it appeared to be holding up the roof; the others, woven from palm fronds, were small and deceptively like butterflies. Hanging from the principal cross were the official insignia of Pedro González Winiktón, judge. And scattered throughout the hut were the professional instruments of Catalina Díaz Puiljá, weaver.

The sound of activity in the other huts, increasingly clear and urgent, made Catalina shake her head as if to chase away the painful dream that was tormenting her. Hurriedly she prepared for the day, carefully placing in a mesh bag the eggs she had gathered the night before, wrapped in leaves to keep them from cracking. When the bag was full, Catalina lifted it to her shoulders. The strap digging into her forehead looked like a deep scar.

Around the hut a group of women had gathered, waiting in silence for Catalina to appear. One by one they filed past her, bowing to show their respect. They did not lift their heads until Catalina had quickly brushed them with her fingers while reciting the courteous, automatic phrase of greeting.

When this ceremony had been completed, they set off. Though all of them knew the way, none dared take a step that was not led by the ilol. Their watchful gestures, rapidly obedient, anxiously solicitous, showed that these women looked to her as a superior. Not because of her husband's position, since they were all the wives of officials and some were married to men whose prestige was greater than Winiktón's, but because of the reputation that transfigured Catalina in the eyes of those whose souls were fearful and unfortunate, those who were avid to ingratiate themselves with the supernatural.

Catalina accepted their respect with the calm assurance of one receiving her due. The other women's submissiveness neither annoyed her nor made her proud. Her conduct was moderate and sensible, in keeping with the tribute she was accorded. Her gift to them was an approving smile, a glance of complicity, a well-timed word of advice, an opportune reminder. And in her left hand she held threats, the possibility of doing harm. Though she kept careful watch on her power. She had seen too many left hands chopped off by vengeful machetes.

Catalina led the procession of Tzotzil women, all uniformly wrapped in thick, dark serapes. All bent beneath the weight they carried (the goods they brought to sell, the small child sleeping against its mother). All going toward Ciudad Real.

The path, made by years of walking feet, coils around the hills. The earth is yellow and loose, easily blown away by the wind. The vegetation is hostile: weeds, curving thorns. Here and there are young bushes or peach trees in their festive garb, peach trees blushing pink from sweetness, from smiling, blushing pink from happiness.

The distance between San Juan Chamula and Ciudad Real (or Jobel, as it is called in Tzotzil) is long. But these women crossed it, untiring and wordless, their attention fixed on the careful placement of their feet and the work spread between their hands, the coils of pichulej that their busy fingers made longer and longer as they walked.

The mass of mountains flowed into a wide valley. Here and there, as if fallen by chance from the sky, were houses. Shingled shacks, inhabited by Ladinos who looked after fields or miserable flocks, precarious shelter against bad weather. Now and then a stately home rose up in all the insolence of its isolation, solidly built but with the sinister look of a fortress or a jail rather than a place meant to lodge the refined softness of the wealthy.

The outskirts; the banks of the river. From here the domes of the churches could be seen reverberating in the humid light.

Catalina Díaz Puiljá stopped and crossed herself. Her followers imitated her. Then, with whispers and quick, skillful movements, they redistributed the goods they were carrying. Some women were given all the weight they could bear. Others pretended to stagger under an excessive load, and they went to the front of the line.

Silent, as if they neither saw nor heard, as if they were not expecting anything to happen, the Tzotzil women moved forward.

As they came around the first corner it happened, and although it was expected, habitual, it was never any less fearsome or repellent. Five Ladinas of the poorest class, barefoot, dressed in rags, threw themselves onto Catalina and her companions. Without saying a single threatening word, without working themselves up with insults or excusing themselves with reasons, the Ladinas fought for possession of the bags full of eggs, the clay pots, the fabrics that the Indian women defended in brave, mute furor. But in the flurry of their gestures, both parties to the struggle took care not to damage or break the objects they were contending over.

In the confusion of the first moments, several of the Indian women managed to slip away and hurried toward the center of Ciudad Real. Meanwhile, those left behind opened their bleeding hands, leaving the goods to the attackers who snatched up their booty in triumph. Then, to give an appearance of legality to her violence, the enemy threw down a handful of copper coins that the other woman picked from the dust, weeping.

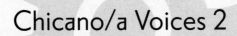

Chicano/a Voices 2

Daddy with Chesterfields in a
Rolled Up Sleeve

The school principal was a white lady
who came to class one day
to say a man claiming to be
my father
was in her office.

Later at tío Manuel's flat
Daddy said Mami was
on her way. (*It must be serious,*
I thought, Mami never misses work.)

All Manuel's tribe gathered:
rotten toothed daughters with children
of varying
hair textures and surnames;
Davíd, a junkie,
mean face of an Apache;
Daniel, smiled nice, did nothing

with his life;
Abel and his boy Cain;
Juanita my madrina, the eldest,
never married.
Twelve children my uncle raised,
his wife died with the 13th.

But this guy across the table
is young with acne,
hair greased back. He smokes cigarettes,
doesn't ask permission, speaks English
with a crooked smile: charm personified.
Hangs out with the boys,
who call him Brodock (they all have
names: Ash Can, Monskis, El Conde,
Joe the Boss, Ming)—this man, who Mami says
doesn't like to work,
plays bongos and mambos loud all day
while Abuelita keeps me out the way
of boys jamming, drinking beer,
while wives work the assembly line.

At tío Manuel's where Daddy took me on the bus,
the Spanish radio has announced
the death of Doña Jovita.
The curandera from Guanajuato—
with jars of herbs
grown in coffee cans—
had raised the Toltec long
after her sons had grown,
her only daughter murdered by her husband.
The boy, the story goes,
was brought forth by the curandera,

or, if you please,
Doña Jovita, herself,
gave birth to him at 60.

And Daddy, who never looks at me
and talks to me at the same time
says "Granny died," and begins to cry.
Daddy is the only one
who calls her Granny.
And i, most delicate of her offspring:
Ana María. Ana María learns English in school,
wears gold loop earrings in mother-pierced ears,
brings flowers to the Virgin every spring.

Anita knows yerba buena, yerba santa, epazote,
manzanilla, ruda, addresses spirits
with Abuelita, touches soreness of those
who come, little hands under
shriveled ones, that heal.

"Granny died," he said, and cried.

Daddy's white foreman
who doesn't believe his mother died,
comes to watch Daddy cry at the coffin.

Every year Mami makes enchiladas for Daddy's birthday,
never as good as the memory of his mother's.
Mami takes her place now,
tells his daughter to her face:
"You're like your father,
don't like to work,
a daydreamer,

think someday you'll be rich and famous,
an artist, who wastes her time
travelling,
wearing finery she can't afford,
neglecting her children and her home!"
The father lowers his eyes.

Had i been 19 not 9
i'd have pulled my hair,
screamed her name, "Don't leave!
Don't leave me behind with this mami
who goes off to work before light
leaves me a key, a quarter for lunch,
crackers for breakfast on my pillow
that rats get before i wake!
Don't leave me
with this mami who will empty out all
your jars, the trunks of your defunct
husband's moth-eaten suits,
the Toltec's wind-up toys,
to move bunkbeds into your
room where you stuck crucifixes
with chewing gum on an old iron headboard!
(A testimony to your faith—
yet the Church did not grant you a Mass
upon your death.)
Don't leave me with this daddy,
smooth talkin', marijuana smokin',
mambo dancin', jumpin' jitterbug!"

The only woman who meant anything in his life.

—No creo que fue tu mamá,—your wife whispers.
"I don't care!" you reply.

—Que ni eres mexicano,—
"I don't care!" you say for
doña Jovita,
la madre sagrada
su comal y molcajete,
la revolución de Benito Juárez y Pancho Villa,
Guanajuato, paper cuts, onyx, papier-mâché,
bullfighters' pictures, and Aztec calendars.

i speak English with a crooked smile,
say "man," smoke cigarettes,
drink tequila, grab your eyes that dart
from me to tell you of my
trips to México.
i play down the elegant fingers,
hair that falls over an eye,
the silk dress accentuating breasts—
and fit the street jargon to my full lips,
try to catch those evasive eyes,
tell you of jive artists
where we heard hot salsa
at a local dive.
And so, i exist . . .

At 15,
Mami scorned me for not forgiving you
when she caught you
with your girlfriend. Had i been 25,
I'd have slapped you, walked out the door,
searched for doña Jovita who loved for no reason
than that we were her children.

Men try to catch my eye. i talk to them
of politics, religion, the ghosts i've seen,

the king of timbales, México and Chicago.
And they go away.
But women stay. Women like stories.
They like thin arms around their shoulders,
the smell of perfumed hair,
a flamboyant scarf around the neck
the reassuring voice that confirms their
cynicism about politics, religion and the glorious
history that slaughtered thousands of slaves.

Because of the seductive aroma of mole
in my kitchen, and the mysterious preparation
of herbs, women tolerate *my* cigarette
and cognac breath, unmade bed,
and my inability to keep a budget—
in exchange for a promise,
an exotic trip,
a tango lesson,
an anecdote of the gypsy who stole
me away in Madrid.

Oh Daddy, with the Chesterfields
rolled up in a sleeve,
you got a woman for a son.

Never Marry a Mexican

Never marry a Mexican, my ma said once and always. She said this because of my father. She said this though she was Mexican too. But she was born here in the U.S., and he was born there, and it's *not* the same, you know.

I'll *never* marry. Not any man. I've known men too intimately. I've witnessed their infidelities, and I've helped them to it. Unzipped and unhooked and agreed to clandestine maneuvers. I've been accomplice, committed premeditated crimes. I'm guilty of having caused deliberate pain to other women. I'm vindictive and cruel, and I'm capable of anything.

I admit, there was a time when all I wanted was to belong to a man. To wear that gold band on my left hand and be worn on his arm like an expensive jewel brilliant in the light of day. Not the sneaking around I did in different bars that all looked the same, red carpets with a black grillwork design, flocked wallpaper, wooden wagon-wheel light fixtures with hurricane lampshades a sick amber color like the drinking glasses you get for free at gas stations.

Dark bars, dark restaurants then. And if not—my apartment, with his toothbrush firmly planted in the toothbrush holder like a flag on the North Pole. The bed so big because he never stayed the whole night. Of course not.

Borrowed. That's how I've had my men. Just the cream skimmed off the top. Just the sweetest part of the fruit, without the bitter skin that daily living with a spouse can rend. They've come to me when they wanted the sweet meat then.

So, no. I've never married and never will. Not because I couldn't, but because I'm too romantic for marriage. Marriage has failed me, you could say. Not a man exists who hasn't disappointed me, whom I could trust to love the way I've loved. It's because I believe too much in marriage that I don't. Better to not marry than live a lie.

Mexican men, forget it. For a long time the men clearing off the tables or chopping meat behind the butcher counter or driving the bus I rode to school every day, those weren't men. Not men I considered as potential lovers. Mexican, Puerto Rican, Cuban, Chilean, Colombian, Panamanian, Salvadorean, Bolivian, Honduran, Argentine, Dominican, Venezuelan, Guatemalan, Ecuadorean, Nicaraguan, Peruvian, Costa Rican, Paraguayan, Uruguayan, I don't care. I never saw them. My mother did this to me.

I guess she did it to spare me and Ximena the pain she went through. Having married a Mexican man at seventeen. Having had to put up with all the grief a Mexican family can put on a girl because she was from *el otro lado,* the other side, and my father had married down by marrying her. If he had married a white woman from *el otro lado,* that would've been different. That would've been marrying up, even if the white girl was poor. But what could be more ridiculous than a Mexican girl who couldn't even speak Spanish, who didn't know enough to set a separate plate for each course at dinner, nor how to fold cloth napkins, nor how to set the silverware.

In my ma's house the plates were always stacked in the center of the table, the knives and forks and spoons standing in a jar, help yourself. All the dishes chipped or cracked and nothing matched. And no tablecloth, ever. And newspapers set on the table whenever my grandpa sliced watermelons, and how embarrassed she would be when her boyfriend, my father, would come over and there were newspapers all over the kitchen floor and table. And my grandpa, big hardworking Mexican man, saying Come, come and eat, and slicing a big wedge of those dark green watermelons, a big slice, he wasn't stingy with food. Never, even during the Depression. Come, come and eat, to whoever came knocking on the back door. Hobos sitting at the dinner table and the children staring and staring. Because my grandfather always made sure they never went without. Flour and rice, by the barrel and by the sack. Potatoes. Big bags of pinto beans. And watermelons, bought three or four at a time, rolled under his bed and brought out when you least expected. My grandpa had survived three wars, one Mexican, two American, and he knew what living without meant. He knew.

My father, on the other hand, did not. True, when he first came to this country he had worked shelling clams, washing dishes, planting hedges, sat on the back of the bus in Little Rock and had the bus driver shout, You—sit up here, and my father had shrugged sheepishly and said, No speak English.

But he was no economic refugee, no immigrant fleeing a war. My father ran away from home because he was afraid of facing his father after his first-year grades at the university proved he'd spent more time fooling around than studying. He left behind a house in Mexico City that was neither poor nor rich, but thought itself better than both. A boy who would get off a bus when he saw a girl he knew board if he didn't have the money to pay her fare. That was the world my father left behind.

I imagine my father in his *fanfarrón* clothes, because that's what

he was, a *fanfarrón*. That's what my mother thought the moment
she turned around to the voice that was asking her to dance. A
big show-off, she'd say years later. Nothing but a big show-off.
But she never said why she married him. My father in his shark-
blue suits with the starched handkerchief in the breast pocket,
his felt fedora, his tweed topcoat with the big shoulders, and
heavy British wing tips with the pin-hole design on the heel and
toe. Clothes that cost a lot. Expensive. That's what my father's
things said. *Calidad.* Quality.

My father must've found the U.S. Mexicans very strange, so
foreign from what he knew at home in Mexico City where the
servant served watermelon on a plate with silverware and a cloth
napkin, or mangos with their own special prongs. Not like this,
eating with your legs wide open in the yard, or in the kitchen
hunkered over newspapers. *Come, come and eat.* No, never like this.

How I make my living depends. Sometimes I work as a translator. Sometimes I get paid by the word and sometimes by the
hour, depending on the job. I do this in the day, and at night I
paint. I'd do anything in the day just so I can keep on painting.

I work as a substitute teacher, too, for the San Antonio Independent School District. And that's worse than translating those
travel brochures with their tiny print, believe me. I can't stand
kids. Not any age. But it pays the rent.

Any way you look at it, what I do to make a living is a form
of prostitution. People say, "A painter? How nice," and want to
invite me to their parties, have me decorate the lawn like an
exotic orchid for hire. But do they buy art?

I'm amphibious. I'm a person who doesn't belong to any class.
The rich like to have me around because they envy my crea-
tivity; they know they can't buy *that.* The poor don't mind if I
live in their neighborhood because they know I'm poor like

they are, even if my education and the way I dress keeps us worlds apart. I don't belong to any class. Not to the poor, whose neighborhood I share. Not to the rich, who come to my exhibitions and buy my work. Not to the middle class from which my sister Ximena and I fled.

When I was young, when I first left home and rented that apartment with my sister and her kids right after her husband left, I thought it would be glamorous to be an artist. I wanted to be like Frida or Tina. I was ready to suffer with my camera and my paint brushes in that awful apartment we rented for $150 each because it had high ceilings and those wonderful glass skylights that convinced us we had to have it. Never mind there was no sink in the bathroom, and a tub that looked like a sarcophagus, and floorboards that didn't meet, and a hallway to scare away the dead. But fourteen-foot ceilings was enough for us to write a check for the deposit right then and there. We thought it all romantic. You know the place, the one on Zarzamora on top of the barber shop with the Casasola prints of the Mexican Revolution. Neon BIRRIA TEPATITLÁN sign round the corner, two goats knocking their heads together, and all those Mexican bakeries, Las Brisas for *huevos rancheros* and *carnitas* and *barbacoa* on Sundays, and fresh fruit milk shakes, and mango *paletas,* and more signs in Spanish than in English. We thought it was great, great. The barrio looked cute in the daytime, like Sesame Street. Kids hopscotching on the sidewalk, blessed little boogers. And hardware stores that still sold ostrich-feather dusters, and whole families marching out of Our Lady of Guadalupe Church on Sundays, girls in their swirly-whirly dresses and patent-leather shoes, boys in their dress Stacys and shiny shirts.

But nights, that was nothing like what we knew up on the north side. Pistols going off like the wild, wild West, and me and Ximena and the kids huddled in one bed with the lights off listening to it all, saying, Go to sleep, babies, it's just fire-crackers. But we knew better. Ximena would say, Clemencia, maybe we should go home. And I'd say, Shit! Because she knew as well as I did there was no home to go home to. Not with our mother. Not with that man she married. After Daddy died, it was like we didn't matter. Like Ma was so busy feeling sorry for herself, I don't know. I'm not like Ximena. I still haven't worked it out after all this time, even though our mother's dead now. My half brothers living in that house that should've been ours, me and Ximena's. But that's—how do you say it?—water under the damn? I can't ever get the sayings right even though I was born in this country. We didn't say shit like that in our house.

Once Daddy was gone, it was like my ma didn't exist, like if she died, too. I used to have a little finch, twisted one of its tiny red legs between the bars of the cage once, who knows how. The leg just dried up and fell off. My bird lived a long time without it, just a little red stump of a leg. He was fine, really. My mother's memory is like that, like if something already dead dried up and fell off, and I stopped missing where she used to be. Like if I never had a mother. And I'm not ashamed to say it either. When she married that white man, and he and his boys moved into my father's house, it was as if she stopped being my mother. Like I never even had one.

Ma always sick and too busy worrying about her own life, she would've sold us to the Devil if she could. "Because I married so young, *mi'ja*," she'd say. "Because your father, he was so much older than me, and I never had a chance to be young. Honey, try to understand . . ." Then I'd stop listening.

That man she met at work, Owen Lambert, the foreman at the photo-finishing plant, who she was seeing even while my father was sick. Even then. That's what I can't forgive.

When my father was coughing up blood and phlegm in the

hospital, half his face frozen, and his tongue so fat he couldn't talk, he looked so small with all those tubes and plastic sacks dangling around him. But what I remember most is the smell, like death was already sitting on his chest. And I remember the doctor scraping the phlegm out of my father's mouth with a white washcloth, and my daddy gagging and I wanted to yell, Stop, you stop that, he's my daddy. Goddamn you. Make him live. Daddy, don't. Not yet, not yet, not yet. And how I couldn't hold myself up, I couldn't hold myself up. Like if they'd beaten me, or pulled my insides out through my nostrils, like if they'd stuffed me with cinnamon and cloves, and I just stood there dry-eyed next to Ximena and my mother, Ximena between us because I wouldn't let her stand next to me. Everyone repeating over and over the Ave Marías and Padre Nuestros. The priest sprinkling holy water, *mundo sin fin, amén.*

Drew, remember when you used to call me your Malinalli? It was a joke, a private game between us, because you looked like a Cortez with that beard of yours. My skin dark against yours. Beautiful, you said. You said I was beautiful, and when you said it, Drew, I was.

My Malinalli, Malinche, my courtesan, you said, and yanked my head back by the braid. Calling me that name in between little gulps of breath and the raw kisses you gave, laughing from that black beard of yours.

Before daybreak, you'd be gone, same as always, before I even knew it. And it was as if I'd imagined you, only the teeth marks on my belly and nipples proving me wrong.

Your skin pale, but your hair blacker than a pirate's. Malinalli, you called me, remember? *Mi doradita.* I liked when you spoke to me in my language. I could love myself and think myself worth loving.

Your son. Does he know how much I had to do with his birth? I was the one who convinced you to let him be born. Did you tell him, while his mother lay on her back laboring his birth, I lay in his mother's bed making love to you.

You're nothing without me. I created you from spit and red dust. And I can snuff you between my finger and thumb if I want to. Blow you to kingdom come. You're just a smudge of paint I chose to birth on canvas. And when I made you over, you were no longer a part of her, you were all mine. The landscape of your body taut as a drum. The heart beneath that hide thrumming and thrumming. Not an inch did I give back.

I paint and repaint you the way I see fit, even now. After all these years. Did you know that? Little fool. You think I went hobbling along with my life, whimpering and whining like some twangy country-and-western when you went back to her. But I've been waiting. Making the world look at you from my eyes. And if that's not power, what is?

Nights I light all the candles in the house, the ones to La Virgen de Guadalupe, the ones to El Niño Fidencio, Don Pedrito Jaramillo, Santo Niño de Atocha, Nuestra Señora de San Juan de los Lagos, and especially, Santa Lucía, with her beautiful eyes on a plate.

Your eyes are beautiful, you said. You said they were the darkest eyes you'd ever seen and kissed each one as if they were capable of miracles. And after you left, I wanted to scoop them out with a spoon, place them on a plate under these blue blue skies, food for the blackbirds.

The boy, your son. The one with the face of that redheaded woman who is your wife. The boy red-freckled like fish food floating on the skin of water. That boy.

I've been waiting patient as a spider all these years, since I was nineteen and he was just an idea hovering in his mother's head, and I'm the one that gave him permission and made it happen, see.

Because your father wanted to leave your mother and live with me. Your mother whining for a child, at least *that*. And he kept saying, Later, we'll see, later. But all along it was me he wanted to be with, it was me, he said.

I want to tell you this evenings when you come to see me. When you're full of talk about what kind of clothes you're going to buy, and what you used to be like when you started high school and what you're like now that you're almost finished. And how everyone knows you as a rocker, and your band, and your new red guitar that you just got because your mother gave you a choice, a guitar or a car, but you don't need a car, do you, because I drive you everywhere. You could be my son if you weren't so light-skinned.

This happened. A long time ago. Before you were born. When you were a moth inside your mother's heart, I was your father's student, yes, just like you're mine now. And your father painted and painted me, because he said, I was his *doradita*, all golden and sun-baked, and that's the kind of woman he likes best, the ones brown as river sand, yes. And he took me under his wing and in his bed, this man, this teacher, your father. I was honored that he'd done me the favor. I was that young.

All I know is I was sleeping with your father the night you were born. In the same bed where you were conceived. I was sleeping with your father and didn't give a damn about that woman, your mother. If she was a brown woman like me, I might've had a harder time living with myself, but since she's not, I don't care. I was there first, always. I've always been there, in the mirror, under his skin, in the blood, before you were born. And he's been here in my heart before I even knew him. Understand? He's always been here. Always. Dissolving like a hibiscus flower, exploding like a rope into dust. I don't care what's right anymore. I don't care about his wife. She's not *my* sister.

And it's not the last time I've slept with a man the night his wife is birthing a baby. Why do I do that, I wonder? Sleep with a man when his wife is giving life, being suckled by a thing with its eyes still shut. Why do that? It's always given me a bit of crazy joy to be able to kill those women like that, without their knowing it. To know I've had their husbands when they were anchored in blue hospital rooms, their guts yanked inside out, the baby sucking their breasts while their husband sucked mine. All this while their ass stitches were still hurting.

Once, drunk on margaritas, I telephoned your father at four in the morning, woke the bitch up. Hello, she chirped. I want to talk to Drew. Just a moment, she said in her most polite drawing-room English. Just a moment. I laughed about that for weeks. What a stupid ass to pass the phone over to the lug asleep beside her. Excuse me, honey, it's for you. When Drew mumbled hello I was laughing so hard I could hardly talk. Drew? That dumb bitch of a wife of yours, I said, and that's all I could manage. That stupid stupid stupid. No Mexican woman would react like that. Excuse me, honey. It cracked me up.

He's got the same kind of skin, the boy. All the blue veins pale and clear just like his mama. Skin like roses in December. Pretty boy. Little clone. Little cells split into you and you and you. Tell me, baby, which part of you is your mother. I try to imagine her lips, her jaw, her long long legs that wrapped themselves around this father who took me to his bed.

. . .

This happened. I'm asleep. Or pretend to be. You're watching me, Drew. I feel your weight when you sit on the corner of the bed, dressed and ready to go, but now you're just watching me sleep. Nothing. Not a word. Not a kiss. Just sitting. You're taking me in, under inspection. What do you think already?

I haven't stopped dreaming you. Did you know that? Do you think it's strange? I never tell, though. I keep it to myself like I do all the thoughts I think of you.

After all these years.

I don't want you looking at me. I don't want you taking me in while I'm asleep. I'll open my eyes and frighten you away.

There. What did I tell you? *Drew? What is it?* Nothing. I knew you'd say that.

Let's not talk. We're no good at it. With you I'm useless with words. As if somehow I had to learn to speak all over again, as if the words I needed haven't been invented yet. We're cowards. Come back to bed. At least there I feel I have you for a little. For a moment. For a catch of the breath. You let go. You ache and tug. You rip my skin.

You're almost not a man without your clothes. How do I explain it? You're so much a child in my bed. Nothing but a big boy who needs to be held. I won't let anyone hurt you. My pirate. My slender boy of a man.

After all these years.

I didn't imagine it, did I? A Ganges, an eye of the storm. For a little. When we forgot ourselves, you tugged me, I leapt inside you and split you like an apple. Opened for the other to look and not give back. Something wrenched itself loose. Your body doesn't lie. It's not silent like you.

You're nude as a pearl. You've lost your train of smoke. You're tender as rain. If I'd put you in my mouth you'd dissolve like snow.

You were ashamed to be so naked. Pulled back. But I saw you

for what you are, when you opened yourself for me. When you were careless and let yourself through. I caught that catch of the breath. I'm not crazy.

When you slept, you tugged me toward you. You sought me in the dark. I didn't sleep. Every cell, every follicle, every nerve, alert. Watching you sigh and roll and turn and hug me closer to you. I didn't sleep. I was taking *you* in that time.

Your mother? Only once. Years after your father and I stopped seeing each other. At an art exhibition. A show on the photographs of Eugène Atget. Those images, I could look at them for hours. I'd taken a group of students with me.

It was your father I saw first. And in that instant I felt as if everyone in the room, all the sepia-toned photographs, my students, the men in business suits, the high-heeled women, the security guards, everyone, could see me for what I was. I had to scurry out, lead my kids to another gallery, but some things destiny has cut out for you.

He caught up with us in the coat-check area, arm in arm with a redheaded Barbie doll in a fur coat. One of those scary Dallas types, hair yanked into a ponytail, big shiny face like the women behind the cosmetic counters at Neiman's. That's what I remember. She must've been with him all along, only I swear I never saw her until that second.

You could tell from a slight hesitancy, only slight because he's too suave to hesitate, that he was nervous. Then he's walking toward me, and I didn't know what to do, just stood there dazed like those animals crossing the road at night when the headlights stun them.

And I don't know why, but all of a sudden I looked at my shoes and felt ashamed at how old they looked. And he comes up to me, my love, your father, in that way of his with that grin that makes me want to beat him, makes me want to make love to him, and he says in the most sincere voice you ever heard, "Ah, Clemencia! *This* is Megan." No introduction could've been meaner. *This* is Megan. Just like that.

I grinned like an idiot and held out my paw—"Hello, Megan"—and smiled too much the way you do when you can't stand someone. Then I got the hell out of there, chattering like a monkey all the ride back with my kids. When I got home I had to lie down with a cold washcloth on my forehead and the TV on. All I could hear throbbing under the washcloth in that deep part behind my eyes: *This* is Megan.

And that's how I fell asleep, with the TV on and every light in the house burning. When I woke up it was something like three in the morning. I shut the lights and TV and went to get some aspirin, and the cats, who'd been asleep with me on the couch, got up too and followed me into the bathroom as if they knew what's what. And then they followed me into bed, where they aren't allowed, but this time I just let them, fleas and all.

This happened, too. I swear I'm not making this up. It's all true. It was the last time I was going to be with your father. We had agreed. All for the best. Surely I could see that, couldn't I? My own good. A good sport. A young girl like me. Hadn't I understood . . . responsibilities. Besides, he could *never* marry *me.* You didn't think . . . ? *Never marry a Mexican. Never marry a Mexican . . .* No, of course not. I see. I see.

We had the house to ourselves for a few days, who knows how. You and your mother had gone somewhere. Was it Christmas? I don't remember.

I remember the leaded-glass lamp with the milk glass above the dining-room table. I made a mental inventory of everything. The Egyptian lotus design on the hinges of the doors. The narrow, dark hall where your father and I had made love once. The four-clawed tub where he had washed my hair and rinsed it with a tin bowl. This window. That counter. The bedroom with its light in the morning, incredibly soft, like the light from a polished dime.

The house was immaculate, as always, not a stray hair anywhere, not a flake of dandruff or a crumpled towel. Even the roses on the dining-room table held their breath. A kind of airless cleanliness that always made me want to sneeze.

Why was I so curious about this woman he lived with? Every time I went to the bathroom, I found myself opening the medicine cabinet, looking at all the things that were hers. Her Estée Lauder lipsticks. Corals and pinks, of course. Her nail polishes—mauve was as brave as she could wear. Her cotton balls and blond hairpins. A pair of bone-colored sheepskin slippers, as clean as the day she'd bought them. On the door hook—a white robe with a MADE IN ITALY label, and a silky nightshirt with pearl buttons. I touched the fabrics. *Calidad.* Quality.

I don't know how to explain what I did next. While your father was busy in the kitchen, I went over to where I'd left my backpack, and took out a bag of gummy bears I'd bought. And while he was banging pots, I went around the house and left a trail of them in places I was sure *she* would find them. One in her lucite makeup organizer. One stuffed inside each bottle of nail polish. I untwisted the expensive lipsticks to their full length and smushed a bear on the top before recapping them. I even put a gummy bear in her diaphragm case in the very center of that luminescent rubber moon.

Why bother? Drew could take the blame. Or he could say it was the cleaning woman's Mexican voodoo. I knew that, too. It didn't matter. I got a strange satisfaction wandering about the house leaving them in places only she would look.

And just as Drew was shouting, "Dinner!" I saw it on the desk. One of those wooden babushka dolls Drew had brought her from his trip to Russia. I know. He'd bought one just like it for me.

I just did what I did, uncapped the doll inside a doll inside a doll, until I got to the very center, the tiniest baby inside all the others, and this I replaced with a gummy bear. And then I put the dolls back, just like I'd found them, one inside the other, inside the other. Except for the baby, which I put inside my pocket. All through dinner I kept reaching in the pocket of my jean jacket. When I touched it, it made me feel good.

On the way home, on the bridge over the *arroyo* on Guadalupe Street, I stopped the car, switched on the emergency blinkers, got out, and dropped the wooden toy into that muddy creek where winos piss and rats swim. The Barbie doll's toy stewing there in that muck. It gave me a feeling like nothing before and since.

Then I drove home and slept like the dead.

These mornings, I fix coffee for me, milk for the boy. I think of that woman, and I can't see a trace of my lover in this boy, as if she conceived him by immaculate conception.

I sleep with this boy, their son. To make the boy love me the way I love his father. To make him want me, hunger, twist in his sleep, as if he'd swallowed glass. I put him in my mouth. Here, little piece of my *corazón*. Boy with hard thighs and just a bit of down and a small hard downy ass like his father's, and that back like a valentine. Come here, *mi cariñito*. Come to *mamita*. Here's a bit of toast.

I can tell from the way he looks at me, I have him in my power. Come, sparrow. I have the patience of eternity. Come to *mamita*. My stupid little bird. I don't move. I don't startle him. I let him nibble. All, all for you. Rub his belly. Stroke him. Before I snap my teeth.

What is it inside me that makes me so crazy at 2 A.M.? I can't blame it on alcohol in my blood when there isn't any. It's something worse. Something that poisons the blood and tips me when the night swells and I feel as if the whole sky were leaning against my brain.

And if I killed someone on a night like this? And if it was *me* I killed instead, I'd be guilty of getting in the line of crossfire, innocent bystander, isn't it a shame. I'd be walking with my head full of images and my back to the guilty. Suicide? I couldn't say. I didn't see it.

Except it's not me who I want to kill. When the gravity of the planets is just right, it all tilts and upsets the visible balance. And that's when it wants out from my eyes. That's when I get on the telephone, dangerous as a terrorist. There's nothing to do but let it come.

So. What do you think? Are you convinced now I'm as crazy as a tulip or a taxi? As vagrant as a cloud?

Sometimes the sky is so big and I feel so little at night. That's the problem with being a cloud. The sky is so terribly big. Why is it worse at night, when I have such an urge to communicate and no language with which to form the words? Only colors. Pictures. And you know what I have to say isn't always pleasant.

Oh, love, there. I've gone and done it. What good is it? Good or bad, I've done what I had to do and needed to. And you've answered the phone, and startled me away like a bird. And now you're probably swearing under your breath and going back to sleep, with that wife beside you, warm, radiating her own heat, alive under the flannel and down and smelling a bit like milk and hand cream, and that smell familiar and dear to you, oh.

Human beings pass me on the street, and I want to reach out and strum them as if they were guitars. Sometimes all humanity strikes me as lovely. I just want to reach out and stroke someone, and say There, there, it's all right, honey. There, there, there.

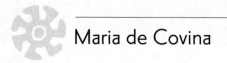

Maria de Covina

I've got two sports coats, about six ties, three dressy pants, Flor-sheims I polish *a la madre,* and three weeks ago I bought a suit, with silk lining, at Lemonde for Men. It came with a matching vest. That's what made it for me. I love getting all duded up, looking fine, I really do. This is the thing: I like women. No, wait. I *love* women. I know that don't sound like anything new, nothing every guy wouldn't tell you. I mean it though, and it's that I can't say so better. It's not like I do anything different when I'm around them. I'm not like aggressive, going after them, hustling. I don't play that. I don't do anything except have a weakness for them. I don't ask anybody out. I already have my girlfriend Diana. Still, it's like I feel drunk around them. Like they make me so *pedo* I can't move away. See what I'm saying? So yeah, of course I love working nights at The Broadway. Women's perfume is everywhere, and I'm dizzy while I'm there.

Even if what I'm about to say might not sound right, I'm say-ing it: It's not just me, it's them too, it's them *back,* maybe even first. Okay, I realize this sounds bad, so I won't talk about it. But why else did they put me in the Gifts department? I didn't know *ni nada* about that stuff, and I noticed right away that most customers were women. And I'm not meaning to brag, but the truth is I sell, they buy. They're older women almost always, rich I see now, because the things we have on the racks—*cositas como* vases and statues and baskets and bowls, from Russia, Germany, Africa, Denmark, France, Argentina, everywhere—are originals and they're expensive. These ladies, maybe they're older, but a lot really look good for being older, they come in and they ask my opinion. They're smiling when they ask me what I'd like if it was for me. I try to be honest. I smile a lot. I smile because I'm happy.

You know what? Even if I'm wrong, *no le hace,* I don't care. Because when I go down the escalator, right at the bottom is Cindy in Cosmetics. She says, "Is your mommy coming for you tonight?" Cindy's almost blond, very pretty, and way out there. She leans over the glass to get close to me. She wears her blouses a little low-cut. She's big for being such *a flaquita.*

"Maybe," I say. "Maybe not."

"Don't marry her yet." That bedroom voice of hers.

"What difference will it make?"

"None to me," she says.

"You talk big," I say, "but do you walk the walk?"

"You know where I am. What're we waiting for?"

She's not wrong. I'm the one who only talks the talk. I don't lie to myself. For instance, I'm about to be nineteen, but I pretend I'm twenty. I do get away with it. I pass for older. I'm not sure why that's true—since I'm thirteen I've had a job—or why I want it to be. I feel older when I say I am. For the same reason I let them think I know so much about sex. *Ya sabes,* pretend that I'm all experienced, like I'm all bad. Lots of girls, and that I know what they like. I feel like it's true when I'm around them. It's what Cindy thinks. And I want her to, I like it that she does,

but at the same time it makes me scared of her. She's not pre-
tending, and I'm afraid she'll find out about me: The truth is
that my only experience is with Diana. I'm too embarrassed to
admit it, and I don't, even to her.

It's not just Cindy though, and this isn't talk, and though it
might sound like it, honest, I'm not trying to brag. Over in
Women's Fashions is Ana, a *morena* with green eyes, and strong,
pretty legs. She's shy. Not that shy. She wants to be in love,
wants a wedding, wants a baby. In Housewares is Brigit. Brigit is
Russian, and sometimes she's hard to understand. You should
see her. She's got the bones of a black girl, but her skin is snow.
I think she's older than she looks. She'll go out with me, I know
it. I don't know how she'd be, and I wonder. Over there, down
the mall, at Lemonde for Men, is where Liz works. That's who
I bought my suit from. Liz is fun. Likes to laugh. The Saturday
I picked up my suit we had lunch together, and then one night,
when I knew she was working, just before we closed, I called her.
I told her I was hungry and would she want to go somewhere
after. She said yeah. We only kissed good-bye. The next time she
was letting me feel her. She likes it, and she's not embarrassed
that she does. I think about her a lot. Touching her. But I don't
want this to sound so *gacho,* porno or something. I like her, that's
what I mean. I like everything about her. I don't know how to
say it better.

"You're such a liar," Maria says. She's my boss. The assistant
manager of Gifts and Luggage, Silverware and China. I worry
that she knows how old I really am, and she's going by that.
Or that she knows I'm not really going to college in the day. I
don't know why I can't be honest about having that other job.
I work for A-Tron Monday through Friday during the day. A
shipping clerk. It's a good job too. But it's better to say you're
studying for something better. I am going to go to college next
year, after I save some money.

"What're you saying?"

"You just want to get them," Maria de Covina says. "You're no different than any other man."

I have told her a lot, I'm not sure why. Probably because she catches me all the time talking to them. The first times I thought she was getting mad and going around checking up on me because I'd be on a break and taking too long. But she's cool. We just seemed to run into each other a lot, and she would like shake her head at me, so now I tell her how I'm thinking. I told her about Liz after she saw us on that first Saturday, eating lunch in the mall.

"It's not true," I say.

"It's not *true*," she whines. She often repeats what I say in a mocking voice. Sometimes she gets close to me, and this time she gets real close, close enough to reach her hand around and grab one of my *nalgas*. "It's not *true*."

"Watch it, Covina," I say. "You Italians think everything you squeeze is a soft *tomate*, but Mexicans got *chiles* that burn."

I call her Maria de Covina because she lives in West Covina and drives in. I call her Italian because she doesn't know a word of Spanish, and Italians can be named Maria. I can't let up. She really is Mexican American, just the spoiled, *pocha* princess type. But I don't let on. She tells me her last name over and over. What do you think Mata is? she asks. Does *Mata* sound Italian to you? I say maybe, yeah. Like a first name like Maria, I say. Like a last name like Corona. Probably it's that, I tell her, and you're messing with me. I don't understand yet what you're up to. Why is it you want everyone to think you're a Mexican when you're not? In my family, everybody always wished they weren't. So she calls me names and means them because this really upsets her. Stupid, she calls me. Buttbreath. Say those in Spanish, I suggest to her, and we'll see what you know. She says, *Estúpido*. One wrong, I tell her. What about the other? No reply. You don't know, do you?

Not a clue, right? This is a game we play, and though there is part of me that can't believe she takes it seriously, another part sees how my teasing bothers her too much.

"Besides, no Chicanos live in West Covina."

"Yes they do."

It cracks me up how serious she sounds. She's too easy. "I never met any from there, ever. It's probably too rich or something."

"You've never even been there, and I bet you don't even know where it is."

"Me and nobody like me."

"My parents just never taught me any Spanish."

"Did they talk it at home?"

"Not really."

"You see? What'd I tell you?"

"Asshole." She whispers that in my ear because we're on the floor and customers are around.

"When they were talking something, if they did, it probably was Italian and you didn't even know it."

I never tell my girlfriend Diana anything about these other girls. Though she's been mad at me anyway. We used to go out more often than we do now, but with my two jobs, and her school, it's almost only been weekends. After we go to a movie, we head back to her place because her parents go to sleep so early. I take her to the door and we kiss and then I leave. I park on the busy street around the corner and I walk back and crawl through her window. It's a big bedroom because she used to share with her sister, who went away to be a nurse. She's very sheltered in a certain way, in that Catholic way, but I'm not Diana's first boyfriend, though I am the first one she's made love to. She let me the second time we went out because she thought I expected it. Because I was so experienced. She's sixteen. She doesn't look it, but she acts it. She worries. She's scared of every-thing she likes. The first time she orgasmed, she told me a couple of months ago, she didn't really know what it was, and it felt too good, so she called her sister's best friend, who can talk about any subject and especially sex, and asked if she was all right. She'll let me do certain things to her, and now she'll be on top sometimes. But she worries that one of us will get too loud. She has been a couple of times. I feel her pulsate in there real hard. She worries that we'll fall asleep after and her mom or dad will be up before we know it. That happened once, and I got out of there, but she's been really worried ever since about everything, every little noise, like they're listening.

The only thing in the room that isn't just for a girl is a statue I gave her of *The Thinker*. It came from Gifts. It had a chip in the wood base and was being sold at 20 percent discount. I kept looking at it, trying to decide if I should buy it. It's big, heavy. He looks smart. I imagined having it in my own place when I got one. I guess that Maria and Joan, the manager of our department, saw how often I stared at it, and so one day they gave it to me, all gift wrapped, a ribbon and bow. I was surprised, embarrassed even, that they bought me a present, and one so expensive, and I didn't think I should accept it, until they explained how it only cost a dollar—they'd marked it down as damaged and, being the manager and assistant manager, signed off on it. This was one of those nights that Diana came to the store to pick me up after work. She was suspicious of Maria, which seemed crazy to me since she was twenty-six and my boss, and then, as we were going down the escalator, of Cindy, who made a sexy wink at me, which didn't seem crazy. So right there in the parking lot I gave *The Thinker* to Diana, and it's been on her bedstand since.

"They got these pretty glass flowers," I say, "and I keep thinking of ways to get them for you. You know, cheap."

"They're not for me," she says. "Those are gifts for grandmothers or mothers."

"Well, then I could give them to your mom."

"A gift from you would be a good idea."

I'm not sure I want that yet. "I could give them to my mom, too. You know, for Mother's Day."

"You better not," she says. "It's stealing."

"Joan sells marked-down things all the time."

"I think you should stop thinking like this."

"But it's easy," I tell her. "I'm good at it."

"How do you know if you're good at it?"

"I know what I'm good at."

"You know I don't like that kind of talk."

"You *know* I don't *like* that kind of *talk*." Lately I've been imitating Maria de Covina.

"You better go," she says.

"Would you stop it," I say. "I'm playing, I'm only teasing."

"You really should go anyway," she says. She's naked, looking for her underwear in the bedsheets, in the dark. "I'm afraid. We're taking too many chances."

I don't take too many chances. One time I did sell something to a friend, for example, for a much lower price than was on the tag. But that was instead of, say, just giving it to him in the bag when he buys something else for a normal price. Which is stealing. I wouldn't do that. Another way is, a customer comes and buys an item, but instead of making a normal receipt, I ring it out on our long form, the one in three-colored triplicate, that one we use when the item has to be delivered. I wait for an expensive purchase. I give the customer the white copy, put the green copy in the register, then fill out the pink copy later—in blue pencil so it looks right, like it's from the stencil. I can stick whatever I want in a box, put that pink copy with a name and address on it, and mail it out of the store. The truth is I think of everything and do nothing. It's only a little game I play in my mind. There's nothing here I want. Well, one time I wanted a ship, a pirate ship to me, with masts and sails and rope the width of string. It was going off the floor because it never sold in over a year, and some items like this are smashed up and thrown away instead of sent back—written off as a loss. I thought I should just take it home instead of destroying it, but Maria insisted on writing me out a slip and selling it to me for three dollars. I gave it to my mom.

"If you really want the valise," I tell Mrs. Huffy, "I'll sell it to you marked down as damaged." Mrs. Huffy sells the luggage. She and I often work the same shift. Sometimes she comes over and sells gifts, and sometimes I sell luggage, but mostly we keep to our separate areas. Maria takes care of the silverware and china. The valise that Mrs. Huffy likes is going to be ripped up and trashed because it's not made anymore and can't be returned to the supplier for a refund.

"It seems like such a waste to throw it away." Mrs. Huffy fidgets with her glasses all the time. She has a chain on them so she doesn't put them down and forget them. You can't tell most of the time if she sees better with them off or with them on. Sometimes the glasses go nervously onto the top of her hair, which is silver gray, the same color as the chain and the frames.

"It is a waste if you ask me."

"You'd think they'd call the Salvation Army instead." Glasses hanging like a necklace.

Mrs. Huffy makes me think of what Diana will be like when she's old. Still worried. "But they're not. They're throwing it away."

"It's terrible," she says.

"I could just sell it to you."

She takes the glasses up to her nose and stares at me. "You can't do that. I wouldn't. Security looks at the receipt." When we leave the building at night, guards examine our belongings, and if we've bought anything from the store, they check the receipt to make sure it matches.

"We'll get it marked down. I'll ask Maria." Everything's okay if a manager or assistant manager says so.

"It wouldn't be right." Glasses on the head.

"Okay then, but I think it's no big deal."

"Do you think she'd do it?"

"I'm sure she would."

"I can't." Glasses on the nose. Holding the valise, snapping it open, snapping it closed. "I can't ask."

"I told you already I'd ask. I know she won't care."

"I don't know."

"*Como quieras*, whatever you decide." I'm walking back to Gifts because I see a customer.

"I don't know," Mrs. Huffy says. "Are you sure Maria would?"

Maria saw me the other night in the parking lot with Cindy, and she wouldn't stop asking me about it. So? she'd say, so? I didn't think I should talk about it. Come on, did you get some or not? I didn't think it was right to talk about it. But she kept insisting and, finally, it seemed okay. I told her how Cindy and I were parked near each other and she said something about a good-night kiss. She started pressing against me hard, and I just put my hand on a *chiche* and then she wrapped her leg around me even harder and rubbed up against me until she put her hand on me. She was physically hot, like sweating. She put her hand down there, I put my hand down there, and then we went into her car. I didn't want to tell Covina the rest, I didn't think I should. But still she says, So? Whadaya mean, *so*? I'm delaying because I feel her close behind me, and I'm not sure. Did you or not? she says. The store's just closed, and I'm at my register, clearing it while we're talking, about to take my tray out to count money, and she's behind me very close. Why don't you want to tell me? she says. She's got her *chiches* against me, moving just a little, and, I don't know, I don't mind but I'm embarrassed too.

In case someone sees. But I don't say anything. I'm also surprised. I don't know why it hadn't crossed my mind. She had her register to clear, and she left.

"I don't like it." Diana's worrying. She's in pajamas.

"It's no big deal," I say. We're whispering to each other in the dark. I'm not sure why it's so dark this night but it is. I surprised her when I came to the window. I had to say her name a few times to wake her up.

"You better stop," she says. Even though I can't see them, the glass flowers I bought damaged are in a vase next to *The Thinker*. I told her I didn't want them for either her mom or mine, and once she saw them, how beautiful they were, she wanted them. "You're gonna get caught."

"You're gonna get *caught*," I say.

"Why would Maria be doing this?" she asks. "I don't trust her."

I feel like Diana is really sensing Cindy, or Liz. I told her I had to work Saturday night, and that's why we couldn't go out. I feel like it's because I'm talking too much about all this to Covina, and it's in the air, that I'm not being smart, talking *esas cosas* out loud. "Come on, it's crazy," I tell Diana. "She's a lot older than me, and she's the assistant manager of the department. She knows what she's doing."

Suddenly she starts crying.

"What's the matter?" I ask.

She's sobbing into her pillow.

"You're making too much noise," I'm whispering. "You're gonna wake up your parents."

"You have to go," she says. She's talking in a normal voice, which is really loud at this time of night. Her face is all wet. I try to kiss her, but she pushes me away. "You have to go," she says.

"Can't we make love?" I'm being quiet at the open window,

and though my eyes have adjusted, it's so dark, and I can barely see her in the bed. "Don't you want to make love?"

I feel sick. I love women, but I realize I don't want to lose Diana. I love her.

Covina shakes her head as I tell her how Diana was acting. Mexican men, she says.

I do like it that she thinks of me as a man. I like being a man, even if it makes me feel too old for Diana. It's confusing. I'm not sure what to do. I wonder if she'd say the same if she didn't think I was almost twenty-one.

I go to the stockroom, and I sit on the edge of the gray desk. "Mrs. Huffy wants this valise real bad. You think you could sign this?" I've already made out a receipt. Instead of forty-five dollars, I made it for forty-five cents, damaged.

Covina gets up, and without kissing me, *ni nada*, she pushes her breast into my face. She has one hand under it, and another on my neck. Pretty quick she opens her blouse and she pulls up her bra and we're both excited and she reaches over and slams the stockroom door and she gets on her knees between mine. I wouldn't tell her, but nobody's ever done that to me before. It was exciting, and I was scared—it *was* right there in our stockroom—and I guess I am a little shocked too, but I don't want her to know it. You know. I follow her to her apartment because she told me to. Before I didn't even think about whether she had her own apartment. I didn't really want to go. And I didn't do very well. She probably saw how inexperienced I am really, and then I made the mistake of telling her how I'm in love with Diana, and how bad I'm feeling.

So I'm tired when I clock in because I stayed with her. I was late in the morning getting to A-Tron, and I wouldn't have gone in if I already didn't know there were a lot of orders we had to fill. Mrs. Huffy is already in Silverware and China when I get to the floor, so worried she can't even take her glasses off when she sees me, and Joan stops me in the middle of Gifts. Joan never works at night.

When Mrs. Huffy checked out with the valise, a security guard opened her package, and asked for the receipt, and the guard said he was going to keep it and make sure it was on the up and up the next day. Instead of, like, scratching the valise when she got home so it really did look damaged, instead of waiting for Joan to deal with it so she could tell us to never do anything like this again, Mrs. Huffy panicked and brought the valise back in the morning.

"Ms. Mata told me everything," Stemp says. Stemp works for the LAPD, or used to, or something like that. I already know who he is, but I'd never talked to him before. He never talks to anybody. He might be chief of security at The Broadway. He wears cheap black slacks and a cheap white shirt and a cheap, plain blue tie. He looks like he might rock in his swivel chair, but he doesn't. He just has it tilted back, his hands folded onto his *panza*. The office has no decorations, no photos or paintings or mirrors on the walls. On his gray desk is the cheapest lamp they sell in Furniture, which is across from Gifts, and one of those heavy black phones. He has a sheet of paper and a pen in front of him. "She told me about how you used triplicate forms and used our courtesy mailing service and how you sold goods to your friends." He stares at me for a very long time, satisfied like he just ate a big meal.

"I never did anything like that," I say. I couldn't believe Maria told him my ideas. "It's not true," I say.

"It's not true," he repeats. He shakes his head with only his eyes. "Do you realize that Ms. Mata was building a career here?"

"She didn't do anything. I know she never did anything."

He really shakes his head. "I don't have time for this. I already have it all." He slides the paper over to me. "Just sign it and get outta here."

I read his form. It lists all these ways I took things from the store, and how Maria cooperated.

"No," I say. "Maria didn't cooperate, she didn't do anything. I didn't do anything either."

"I can call the police right now if you'd prefer. We can deal with this in that manner."

"I guess. I have to think."

He sends me off after I sign a form admitting that I sold a forty-five-dollar valise to Mrs. Huffy for forty-five cents. I loved this job so much. I really loved being here at The Broadway, and I can't think of what I'll do now. I head to the parking lot, and I'm in my car, and I'm trying to decide whether I should go over to Diana's or to Maria's, if either of them would want to see me, when I see Liz waving at me. I get out of the car. How come you haven't called me? she wants to know. I'm wearing the suit I bought from her store. The vest is buttoned but the jacket isn't. I do always feel good in it.

Excerpt from Crossing Over:
A Mexican Family
on the Migrant Trail

Years ago, I wrote several dispatches from the border at Tijuana, easily the most famous crossing point along the two-thousand-mile-long line. On many occasions, I hung out at the *cancha*, a soccer field that runs along the border just a mile from downtown. All there was back then was a scraggly fence, perforated in too many places to count. On a bluff a hundred yards north, Border Patrol jeeps were perched day and night.

Through the dusty heat of day, the *cancha* was empty. But as soon as the sun set, it turned into a veritable migrant fiesta. A great crowd gathered at the fence and began organizing the evening's expeditions. The migrants came from all over Mexico and Central America and from as far away as China, Iran, Pakistan. Packs of lone men, unshaven, dusty-haired, carrying only the clothes on their backs or small, cheap vinyl bags filled with just a handful of belongings. And families, entire families, from grandmothers with crinkled faces and braided white hair to wide-eyed tots in arms.

The crowd gave rise to a mini-economy of vendors exploiting the migrants' last-minute shopping needs. Hawkers pushed everything from booze and running shoes to girlie magazines and sheets of plastic for that unforeseen thunderstorm. Matronly women stood over coal-fired stoves stirring great steaming pots of *pozole*, hominy stew, or sizzling *carne asada*, grilled beef. Prostitutes offered farewell trysts.

Music blared from boom boxes connected through a few dozen extension cords to a socket in someone's living room a couple of hundred yards away or hooked up directly to the fraying, sparking wires hanging above our heads. And there were the soccer matches, intense battles between rival regions throughout the republic: Zacatecas versus San Luis Potosí, Michoacán versus Saltillo, Durango versus Tamaulipas.

Gooooaaallll!

It was a fiesta back then, like a Fourth of July barbecue; everyone was celebrating in anticipation of crossing. Back then, chances were better than fifty-fifty that you would get across on your first attempt. And even if you were nabbed by the *migra*, you'd surely make it on your second try, probably that same night.

Later, after people had eaten, scored a few goals or a blow job in the nearby bushes, the coyotes would gather crews of twenty-five or more migrants, sometimes many more. The coyotes would huddle among themselves, drawing straws to see which route each team would take. There are hundreds of ancient footpaths in the hills above Tijuana, deep ruts carved over the decades by a million migrant footsteps.

All at once, the crews would move out, hundreds of men, women, and children streaming across the chaparral-dotted hills. The Border Patrol would spring into action, but the gringos would quickly be overwhelmed by the massive tide.

Gooooaaallll!

Sure, it was dangerous sometimes, especially along the line in

Texas, where migrants had to ford the trickster currents of the muddy Bravo. But back then migrants were more likely to get robbed or beaten by border bandits than to die of exposure in the middle of the desert.

The border wasn't a border. The line was broken. It was an idea, not a thing.

And then the idea became a reality. In the early nineties, California was in a deep recession. A lot of union jobs had been lost. The Firestone and Goodyear tire plants shut down, as did the last of the old iron and steel works, and aerospace companies laid off tens of thousands of workers. People were angry, and then-governor Pete Wilson looked back in time for inspiration. To the Great Depression and the "repatriation" of hundreds of thousands of Mexican workers. To the postwar recession and Operation Wetback, which deported hundreds of thousands more. And then *la crisis* sent a fresh flood of refugees north. Suddenly Wilson, a Republican who'd always sold himself as friendly to Mexico and Mexicans, a man who in fact once had an undocumented woman clean his house, pointed his finger southward.

"They keep coming!" he declared.

He hated the migrants now. Narco-satanic hordes were at the gates. He swore that he would draw a line in the sand that no wetback would ever cross.

American politicos have paid lip service to "holding the line" at the southern border for the better part of the twentieth century, beginning in the days of the massive migration spawned by the Mexican Revolution of 1910–17. But in 1994, the rhetoric took the form of concrete, steel, arc lamps, infrared cameras and goggles, seismic and laser sensors, and even U.S. soldiers with M-16s offering "tactical support" to a greatly expanded Border Patrol. Operation Gatekeeper sought to block the decades-old illegal crossing at San Diego–Tijuana with a twelve-foot-high steel wall that runs inland twelve miles from the coast. At night, it is lit a harsh amber. The glow that falls from the gigantic light towers straddles the line for several hundred yards in each direction, meaning that the gringo light actually falls on Mexican territory—illegal light, as it were, but the Mexican government has never complained about it or about the constant noise pollution from the helicopters on patrol.

The migrants have complained, though. They called the governor "Pito" Wilson, *pito* for "whistle," but also, in Mexico, for "penis." During the 1994 World Cup, Wilson was on hand to inaugurate a match at the Rose Bowl in Los Angeles. Among the 100,000 people in the stands, there were at least 60,000 Mexicans, Salvadorans, Guatemalans, Nicaraguans, Hondurans, Colombians, Chileans, Uruguayans, Brazilians—migrants each and every one. Wilson stepped up to the microphone. But no one heard a single word he said over the boos, whistles, and chorus of "Pito! Pito!" in great rhythmic waves.

Gooooaaaallll!

Pete Wilson has gone, but one thing remains of his nativist legacy.

After years of being lobbied to help the Golden State beat back the illegals, the federal government obliged with a new fence at Tijuana. To cross into California today, you have to go east of the fence. You have to hike in total darkness, through mountains that block out the beacon of city light from San Diego. You take a long walk in the dark.

East of Nogales, Arizona, my Blazer clatters down the rutted dirt of Duquense Road. At this point, the line consists of little more than a few strands of barbed wire about four feet high. Somewhere close by, Rosa Chávez crossed over with Mr. Charlie.

The sky is a deep Arizona blue, dotted with brilliant white cumuli. In California, the pale light tends to minimize contrasts; here, shadows stand out in stark relief. I am in the Coronado National Monument, named for Francisco Vásquez de Coronado, a sixteenth-century Spanish explorer who searched in vain for the fabled streets paved with gold, the Seven Cities of Cibola. His expedition of 339 soldiers, 4 Franciscan priests, 1,100 Indians, and 1,500 head of livestock set out from Compostela, 750 miles to the south. Indians all along the route confirmed Cibola's existence. It's farther north, the expedition was told again and again. There is some conjecture that the Indians were lying, hoping to push the white men and their horses into a no-man's-land from which they would never return.

Vásquez died without finding Cibola, but he did explore this brutal land of intolerable heat and deadly cold, tracing a crucial overland trade route to the northern territories of the Spanish Crown.

Today, Mexican migrants follow in the footsteps of a conquering Spanish explorer, seeking their own version of the Seven Cities. This is breathtaking and treacherous country, a landscape of eerie, lunarlike beauty, the perfect backdrop for a new Western noir. Here border bandits lie in wait for the vulnerable migrants, and of course there are the Border Patrol, corrupt Mexican police, narcotics smugglers, and DEA agents.

The most recent additions to the tableau are the vigilantes. Dozens of ranchers in the area whose lands are regularly trespassed by border crossers have taken up arms—literally. Like the *migra*, whom they consider inefficient at best, they have availed themselves of such technology as night-vision goggles, but they have also laid in heavier weaponry—some even have assault rifles. The president of the Concerned Citizens of Cochise County has even built a twenty-foot-high lookout station to better patrol his property.

Everywhere I look, there is evidence of migrant journeys. In the brush I come across dozens of discarded bottles of Mexican purified water. Shreds of newspaper lined with shit. A tattered Mexican comic book. A crumpled tube of Mexican Colgate. Along the barbed-wire fence, tiny flags of torn clothing flutter in the breeze. The Coronado National Monument has become a shrine to the migrant. The park rangers might as well have put up exhibit placards.

There are no tourists here. As far as I can tell, I am the only moving thing, the Blazer kicking up a cloud of yellow dust along a road that goes ever higher into the Huachuca Mountains. I look down on the border: a million scrub brushes dot the valley for dozens and dozens of miles southward. The fence is down there somewhere, but it's too small to see from five thousand feet.

I come around a bend and hit the brakes: there is a van stopped by the side of the road, a seventies Dodge Sportsman. I stare at the vehicle as if it were road kill that might come back to life. There is only the sound of my car's motor idling; the Blazer's cloud of dust now flows forward over me.

The van sits off-kilter, its left rear wheel missing, the brake disc half buried in sand. I spot the tire about ten yards ahead. There is a deep rut through the dirt for over fifty yards up to where the van sits; either it took the driver that long to stop or he actually tried to keep moving forward. Probably the latter— all the van's windows have been blasted in with football-sized rocks.

I turn paranoid, wondering if the perpetrators of this vio-lence are still close by. The incident appears to have occurred just a few hours or even a few minutes ago—no dust has settled on the van yet.

Inside the van a thousand glass shards are sprinkled amid the rocks that crashed through the windows. A pair of navy blue men's bikini briefs. An embroidered Indian sash. A flyer

announcing a gig by Banda la Judicial, a third-string outfit pic-
tured in red suits with white tassels, snakeskin boots, and white
Stetsons. Santa María water bottle, empty. Unopened package
of Alka-Seltzer. A cheap vinyl backpack, the classic migrant's
luggage, the logo a poorly stenciled map of the world. A Puré-
pecha rebozo, spread on the floor with a canteloupe-sized rock
sitting on it.

Arizona license plates. The gas cap is missing; the driver stuck
in a red rag. On the exterior right-side panel, there is a splatter
that has dried a dark brown. It looks like blood.

The interior side panels have been ripped open, as has much
of the floor carpet. The bandits were looking for something,
probably drugs. It is impossible to tell if they found anything.

I crest the ridge at the top of the Coronado Pass, leaving the
crime scene behind. To the south, the massive, craggy San Jose
peak; to the east the savannalike beauty of the San Juan River
Valley, promising a temperate respite from the Arizona bad-
lands. Somewhere between the mountains and the flats stands
the border, invisible and implacable.

INS agent Laura Privette is a small, sinewy woman with coarse
Indian hair cut stylishly short. She is dark—*prieta,* as they say in
Spanish—the descendant of immigrants. She is an Indian who's
assumed the role of cowboy; tonight, she is field supervisor for
Border Patrol operations in the Nogales sector. She has left her
silver BMW Z3 convertible behind at the station parking lot
and boarded a Ford Explorer BP cruiser to show me how the
United States holds the line.

The radio crackles. The dispatcher talks in code: "Five-
seventy, activity." Marijuana. Every couple of minutes we are
apprised of "hits" from the motion detectors buried in the
desert along the line.

I like Privette. No woman rises through the ranks of a paramilitary agency—the most macho of environments—without proving her mettle. She grew up Mexican in southern Arizona, where there are lots of Mexicans but precious little space for them in the middle class. As a child, she saw the BP at work on the nightly news, as well as on the streets. The job struck her as heroic; just like a kid in the suburbs who dreams of being a fireman or astronaut, she dreamed of working the line, applying the righteous force of the law against unscrupulous smugglers of human and narcotic cargo. Like many other BP agents, especially Hispanics, Privette professes empathy for the migrants. She believes that there are legal ways to get into this country and illegal ones, safe passage and dangerous crossings. It is pointless to argue with her.

"Things are going pretty good right now," Privette says. With a budget that has tripled in the last five years, the INS's interdiction force has seen its ranks swell by thousands. Its logistical equipment is state of the art.

Privette guides the climate-controlled Explorer, still reeking new-car smell, toward the line—represented in Nogales by a replica of the twelve-foot-high steel wall that blocked migrants from crossing in Tijuana. After claiming success with Operation Gatekeeper in California, the INS proceeded with Operation Safeguard along the Arizona border in 1995, doubling the number of Border Patrol agents, upgrading surveillance technology, and building the wall.

It is late afternoon on a searing late-spring day. There's not much to see yet; the real action starts after dusk. We ride down the avenue that leads to the port of entry, pulling over next to a concrete-lined channel. A Church's Chicken stands nearby, along with a McDonald's, a Jack in the Box, and a taco truck advertising itself as "Parikutín," a Michoacán family enterprise named after Mexico's youngest volcano and a source of endless pride for the Michoacanos.

Back in the days before the massive BP buildup, when a hand-ful of agents battled the mighty stream of migrants who easily cut the chain-link fence, Church's was a kind of migrant drive-through. While the BP was kept busy at the fence, smugglers would bring migrants through the drainage tunnels that traverse the line, hop up to street level, grab a snack, and phone contacts to pick up the cargo. Today, only a trickle comes via the tunnels. It is, however, a popular route for migrants returning to Mexico, a way for them to avoid corrupt Mexican customs officials.

The walls of the tunnel feature generations of graffiti, most of it put here by Barrio Libre, a gang of homeless illegal kids who call the border tunnels home. As Privette sweeps a hand over the scene in explanation, we catch sight of a group of eigh-teen men double-timing through the wash, headed south. When they notice us, most of them pull up their shirts to cover their faces, but there's no need to worry. The BP rarely bothers to apprehend migrants heading back to Mexico.

Despite laws and technology and the dangers of the road, the border can still be breached dozens of ways. Enterprising smug-glers have concocted a scheme that allows an illegal to cross right under the nose of the *migra*. At the San Diego–Tijuana port of entry, a considerable number of crossings take the form of foot traffic through a simple turnstile past a lone cus-toms agent, who often doesn't press for identification from "American-looking" types. "Nationality?" the guard asks. If you say, "American," in good ole Americanese, you're in like Flynn.

For up to $2,000, the smuggler serves more like an acting coach than a coyote. First off, the wardrobe. He gets rid of the invariable polyester threads of your provincial home in favor of 100 percent American cotton. Then he works on your accent and your story, which includes the city, neighborhood, streets, high school, sports teams, and so on of your supposed home-town in the States. If the customs official suspects something, you're merely herded back across the line to try again. And again. The odds, in the long run, are in your favor.

There are still other ways. It is increasingly difficult and expensive to forge the so-called green card (which actually hasn't been green in ages) that denotes legal residency in the United States. Currently, the holographic, "forgery-proof" model looks more like a credit card than a proof of residency. Therefore, there is a brisk business in buying and selling other bona fide documents, including passports, birth certificates, and Social Security cards, which can be conveniently "lost," giving smugglers a window of opportunity of weeks or months to use them until the owner reports them missing.

One day there might indeed be a truly forgery-proof method of admitting people into the country, perhaps the sci-fi scenario of a scanner that identifies on the basis of the uniqueness of the human iris. Such proposals are being seriously considered these days. But for the moment, there is a smuggler's response to every measure the INS introduces.

The Explorer winds into the hills east of Nogales. The border evolves—the towering steel wall becomes a chain-link fence and, a short while later, hip-high barbed wire, the strands cut in many places. We get out of the truck and Agent Privette squats down on one knee, examining hoof marks and the tire tracks that crisscross the line. This examination is called "sign cutting."

"Horses, drugs," Privette says in law enforcement minimalese. "Car. Probably a big old Buick or Impala. Illegals, ten, maybe fifteen."

Sunset. The long, thin fingers of ocotillo bushes stretch into the orange-gold, reaching for the wisps of feathery, gilded cirrus in the darkening sky. Down below, we can see the wall cutting straight across the two Nogaleses. Streets on one side of the line continue on the other. It looks like one huge barrio, artificially divided.

Nothing much is happening in the hills, so we head back toward town.

Suddenly, the radio comes to life. "Hits in sector I–5." We speed through the barrios on the outskirts of Nogales, past humble homes with front doors ajar in the balmy evening, elders swaying in rockers and kids dashing about the street. No one bats an eye at our Border Patrol truck. In this landscape, the Explorers are as omnipresent as the ocotillos.

We pull up next to a drainage tunnel scant yards from the border, where there is another BP truck, commanded by another Indian agent. His bronze face shines with sweat under the amber streetlight. "I lost sight of 'em. I think they came through here. About twenty of 'em."

Privette commands her subaltern: "I'll go above ground, you go under." The green-suited agent, walkie-talkie tacked to his shoulder, runs off, his black flashlight bouncing madly in the dark.

I run after him. I've purchased a flashlight myself—a rubber-coated, impact-resistant field model—for just such an occasion. But, of course, I've forgotten it back in the Explorer. The BP agent is about fifty yards ahead of me in the tunnel, running east. I can see only the distant, wavering beacon of his flash-light. Around me, it is pitch-black. My footsteps echo strangely, expanding concentric circles of sound with a metallic ring. I kick at unseen garbage at my feet. Now puddles of dank water. Deep puddles.

The flashlight up ahead slows its frantic dance. In a few seconds, I am at the agent's side, at an opening in the tunnel. Above us, there is traffic, American traffic. "Lost 'em," he says into his walkie-talkie "Stay where you are," Privette's voice crackles in response. We hear running steps approaching above us. Privette looks down at us from street level. For several moments there is only the sound of panting all around.

The two agents try more sign cutting.

"It doesn't look like they came this way," says the male agent. "They might have jumped up to the road. Maybe they backtracked."

Privette: "No, they definitely came this way. I've got tennis shoes going through here. Adidas."

The migrants have disappeared into the night. The BP's billion-dollar high-tech arsenal has failed, at least on this occasion.

The border is not in a war zone, to be sure. But the battle at the line has all the trappings of a low-intensity conflict between two sides, one armed with state-of-the-art surveillance equipment and the other with the kind of ingenuity inspired only by poverty and desire.

It is a tribute to the political furor over drugs and immigration that between them the two Nogaleses host one of the most impressive arrays of public safety infrastructure in the Northern Hemisphere. Consider the battery of forces amassed here, for towns whose combined population is under 200,000: the U.S. Border Patrol and Customs Police, the Arizona National Guard (which assists the Border Patrol in "intelligence gathering"), the Santa Cruz County sheriff's department and the local Nogales Police Department, mirrored on the Mexican side by the Sonora State Police (*judiciales*), the Mexican Federal Police (*federales*, akin to the American FBI), the Grupo Beta (a special force under federal control that deals with border crime), the local police, and, finally, the quixotically named Talón de Aquiles (Achilles' Heel), whose basic charge is to keep the streets of Nogales clear of unseemly characters for the important tourist industry (which includes such border mainstays as greyhound races, bookie joints, countless curios shops, and plenty of bars that won't card American teens).

Sometimes the Border Patrol can almost convince you it's winning the war. Late in the evening, Privette takes me downtown, where, she has been apprised, a large crew of illegals has been detained. When we pull up, they are seated on the benches under the shade trees of the plaza. A brazen smuggler brought them straight across the wall, maybe with a ladder, apparently convinced they would make it precisely because the BP wouldn't expect a crossing right under its nose.

Several agents, with their broken Spanish, interview the illegals, jotting information into their notebooks.

Nombre? Edad? Domicilio? Firme aquí, por favor.

"I don't know how to write," says an elder in a cowboy hat.

"Then just put an X."

Eighteen men, two women. No kids. From Michoacán, from Guanajuato, from Sinaloa, from Zacatecas and Puebla. There are looks of fear, of quiet resignation, of lackadaisical boredom. A teenager with a baby mustache winks at me. *We'll be back.*

Privette, perhaps aware that she hasn't shown her department at its best tonight, takes me to the station, where narcotics are being registered after a bust. The agent on duty is a young, chipper African American woman named Eealey. In the evidence room, she empties two burlap sacks, each containing several plastic-wrapped bundles of marijuana. They come to 41.25 pounds on the scale, but she wasn't able to arrest the "mules," the drug runners.

Quite a scene out there, Eealey says. She and another agent arrived after receiving word from a video surveillance officer of a probable narcotics crossing. They caught sight of two kids who, with nowhere else to run, hightailed it back toward the line, hastily dumping their loads on American soil. (There'll be hell to pay on the other side.) Eealey got to one of them just as he was diving down to crawl underneath the fence. She grabbed him by the leg, and the kid actually dragged her halfway into Mexico before she realized this was an international incident in the making and let go.

In Nogales, Sonora, that night, I hang out at a dive called

Palas—that's Mexican Spanish for Palace. On the stage, women from every corner of Mexico writhe, women who came to the border thinking of the States but somehow got stuck in limbo. A lot of people got stuck at the line, deferring their American dreams, because there's all kinds of underground business for provincial kids to get caught up in. Many people realized you could make more money playing the black market on the Mexican side than picking fruit on the American side. But then came the wall.

"Isis," from Puerto Vallarta, golden-skinned and Asian-eyed—Egyptian-looking, come to think of it—tells me that business was good until that damn *muro* went up a few months back. Coyotes and narcos used to party here at Palas all night, though they were often scary types with big mustaches, big paunches, big guns, and, often as not, big badges, in the true Mexican corrupt fashion.

"But it's dead now with the wall," says Isis. "Don't the Americans realize that it's bad for business?"

At night, as one looks down from the American side into Mexico, the wall is merely an amber-lit smudge in a swath of small-town light stretching across the valley to the south. Because Nogales, Arizona, is not exactly a model of American affluence and Nogales, Sonora—buoyed in recent years by the *maquiladora* industry of giants like Sony and General Electric—is not the poorest of the Mexican border towns, the Mexican side doesn't necessarily seem Third Worldish.

The two Nogaleses are one, at least geographically, but also in terms of key urban infrastructure—such as the drainage canals and tunnels that traverse the cities north and south. Without this shared drainage system, the sudden summer thunderstorms that toss down a couple of inches of rain within an hour would flood both sides. If there are two cities at this border crossing, they are the Nogales aboveground and the Nogales below.

The city beneath the city is thriving, too. The drainage tunnels are home to all the characters you'd expect at a crossing as contested as this: alien smugglers and narcotics traffickers, down-and-out dope fiends and various other outlaw types. Down below, all these, along with the coyotes and illegals, face off against law enforcement from both sides of the line.

The other player in this border drama is Barrio Libre, whose members range in age from five to their late teens. Barrio Libre is family to a pregnant sixteen-year-old girl, a nine-year-old boy who's been on the streets since he was four, and a few dozen others who pass the time scrounging up meals and occasionally assaulting vulnerable illegals as they cross through the tunnel. For the tunnel kids, as they're called, the battle for the border is simply one of survival.

Some are runaways escaping abusive family situations. Others were separated from their parents in the chaos of a Border Patrol bust. Still others are just plain dirt-poor, restless, and rebellious. Unable to make it aboveground—not with the *migra* and the Mexican police after them—they've descended below, just a few feet under the steps of gringo tourists, Mexican border executives, and squeaky-clean kids their age in blue and white school uniforms.

The only other place these kids call home is a drop-in center on the Mexican side called Mi Nueva Casa, and it is here that I first meet a few members of Barrio Libre. Mi Nueva Casa, funded largely by liberal American foundations, is a humble stucco house just a hundred yards from the border wall.

A typical day begins at about nine in the morning. But Ramona Encinas, the benevolent matriarch of the center, starts brewing coffee and boiling pots of beans and rice much earlier.

The kids straggle in one by one or in twos and threes, their faces pale and puffy—a telltale sign they've slept in the tunnel. They are received with a gushy *"¡Buenos días!"* from Ramona, a counselor named Loida Molina and her twenty-something son Isaac (who's known, in the center's lingo, as the "older-brother type"), and Cecilia Guzmán, a schoolteacher. There are hugs and kisses for the girls, street handshakes for the boys, although a couple of them are in a foul mood and plop themselves down on one of the well-worn couches in the living room without uttering a word to anyone.

Mi Nueva Casa lives up to its billing as a *casa:* besides the living room with its TV and couches, there is a dining room with fold-up tables and about a dozen chairs, which doubles as the computer room (three terminals featuring race car and ancient Pac-Man–type games); a bathroom where the kids can shower if they want (or are forced to by staffers); the small kitchen where Ramona holds court; an outdoor patio in back where washing machines are constantly sloshing the kids' clothes clean. The remaining space is taken up by a Foosball center, a dressing room (hung with dozens of donated shirts, pants, sweaters, and jackets), and a classroom.

After a light breakfast of juice or milk with cookies, some of the kids join Cecilia for the day's school session. Through a screen door in the classroom, one can look straight across the street at the grounds of a local public elementary school, hear the shrieks of "regular" kids.

On this particular morning, several kids arrive late, after ten. They were detained by the *migra* on the American side of the tunnel—the place they currently call home. In comes Pablo, a thirteen-year-old wearing a T-shirt featuring Chupacabras (the blood-sucking bogeyman of northern rural Mexico), and his friend Jesús, about ten years old, in an oversize Raiders shirt. They both sport cholo buzz cuts with thin braided ponytails trailing down the backs of their necks. Their shoes are caked with mud. Within seconds of their entrance, the room begins to smell like unbathed kid.

"The *chiles verdes* got us," says Jesús, using the kids' nickname for the *migra* officers, who wear green uniforms. He tells how Border Patrol agents confiscated the only belongings he had to his name: his flashlight and his aftershave—he doesn't have facial hair yet, but it comes in handy to cover up body odor. Now Toño, at nine the youngest in the group, walks in and promptly pulls up his shirt to show off pinkish scar tissue on his side and abdomen, the result, he says, of bites from a *migra* patrol dog.

Officials on both sides of the border agree that incidents of crime perpetrated by the tunnel kids have diminished since Mi Nueva Casa opened. What they don't say is that the law enforcement agencies on both sides have hit the kids hard—with lessons not soon to be forgotten. They are regularly run down, as this morning, by armed Border Patrol agents in four-wheel-drive vehicles. They are chased by Grupo Beta police whose shouts and threats echo terrifyingly along the concrete walls of the tunnel; several kids say they receive regular beatings from the Beta. There is also an unconfirmed report of a youngster sodomized by a Mexican agent.

But at Mi Nueva Casa the horrors of the tunnel are a world away, even though one popular entrance to the underground is barely a block and a half down the street. There are also incentives to behave well. If the kids don't swear, smoke, do drugs, or carry beepers while they're here—and if they attend Cecilia's classes regularly—they can earn "benefits," all written on a sign hanging in the dining room above the computers: "love and tenderness," "food," "clothes," "respect," "bath," "computer games," "television," "videos," "guitars," and "much, much more!"

Cecilia has her hands full, even though there are only six kids in school today. She dissipates a bit of her own nervous energy by chewing gum as she tries to get Jesús to concentrate on math tables. The kids are distracted by me, of course, but also plainly nervous after the morning's encounter with the *migra*. They flip pencils over and over on the desk, bounce their knees up and down.

In walks Gilberto, the coolest of the bunch, dressed all in black, his hair perfectly combed. A ceramic medallion of a classical European baby Jesus floating amid cherubs hangs on his chest. Heavy with attitude, he scoffs when Cecilia asks him if he wants milk and cookies. Says he wants coffee.

Responding to a question about drugs in the tunnel he says, "You can get crack whenever you want." And pot and pills, and if there's nothing else, well, there's always the poor kid's high—paint thinner inhaled straight from the can or spray paint sniffed from a soaked bandanna.

"If you're from Barrio Libre, you can get anything, anywhere," says Gilberto. Barrio Libre, the Free Barrio. With cliques in Phoenix, Chicago, Las Vegas, L.A., and Nogales, Gilberto claims.

Jesús talks of the war between the coyotes and the Barrio Libre kids. "They think we're bad for their business," he says. And they are. When the kids assault the migrants, word gets back quickly to the other side, causing prospective border crossers to eschew the tunnels for coyote crews that breach the line elsewhere. Jesús recounts a recent incident in which a coyote shot at him with what he says was a 9-millimeter pistol.

Gilberto justifies the assaults: he's following the adults' example. "We're just asking for our *mordida* [bribe], a little something to buy a soda with," he says. But there is plenty of evidence that when some Barrio Libre kids don't get what they want from the *chúntaros* ("hayseeds," a nickname for the illegals), they are capable of viciously beating their victims.

It's nearly noon. Cecilia has done her best for the morning. As lunchtime approaches, the kids begin to drift in and out of the classroom. Some head off for a Foosball game, others to wash their clothes. Gilberto is at the chalkboard, tagging it up with BARRIO LIBRE. Jesús scratches his arms, which are covered with tiny red lumps, a rash he picked up down in the tunnel. Now Gilberto is twirling about the room, blowing up a paper bag he picked up in the trash and pantomiming the inhaling of fumes.

But one student is still intent on doing class work, practicing his handwriting in his notebook. Cecilia tells me that up until a couple of months ago, José, one of the quieter of the group, was practically illiterate, but today his handwriting is precise. Carefully he draws the curving os and as in Spanish, copying down an exercise in alliteration and assonance:

Dolor, dulce dolor. Pain, sweet pain.

Mi mamá me ama. My mother loves me.

He repeats the lines over and over again, filling the entire page.

Homeless youth would seem to be almost an oxymoron in Mexico, where virtually every mother or grandmother is considered a saint and the family unit is by turns loving, claustrophobic, and dictatorial—all-powerful. Unmarried children typically stay at home well past their teens; many stay at home even after they marry. But something's happening to the Mexican family, and it is not just the economic crisis that's chipping away at the institution; migration has a lot to do with it as well. Hundreds of thousands of households, perhaps millions (no one knows how many) are now single-parent or parentless—Mami and Papi are working in the fields of the San Joaquin Valley or cleaning hotel rooms in Dallas; the kids remain in Mexico until there's enough money to bring them across.

Sometimes the kids themselves leave to try their luck in the north as well. Occasionally they run away; often they're encouraged by their parents. (Wense Cortéz made his first trip to the States at age thirteen; his parents did nothing to stop him.) The family separations are always thought of as temporary, but increasingly (and in proportion to the greater difficulty of crossing back and forth at will) they last for years.

Or forever. Papi, gone for two years, suddenly has a new girlfriend in Illinois or even a new family in Illinois. Or maybe Mami isn't coming back because she's sick of her small town's suffocating morality. In all the hustle and bustle and back-breaking effort to provide for the family—and amid the cultural changes that accompany the migrants' journeys—the kids are getting lost. Mexican family values, ironically, are being undone by the very effort to support family in Mexico by working in the United States.

Mi Nueva Casa does not offer a complete, twenty-four-hour shelter. It can't—funding for the program is chronically anemic. While up to twenty-two young people might hang out here during the day, the doors close at five in the afternoon Monday through Saturday and the staffers go home to their families. The kids, meanwhile, go back to their own "family" in the tunnels.

Despite the clear binational nature of homeless children accumulating on the border, binational policies, free-trade agreement or no, have not made fund-raising or even donating materials easy. Mi Nueva Casa was recently awarded a major grant from the Kellogg Foundation, but the money came with the stipulation that it could be spent only for research and staff training on the American side of the border. On more than one occasion, staffers have had to sneak donated clothes into Mexico from the United States in the trunk of a car because if the items were declared before Mexican customs the red tape would be endless. (A Ping-Pong table given to Mi Nueva Casa by an American benefactor remained in a Mexican customs warehouse for over a year.)

"There've always been problems at the border," says a member of Mi Nueva Casa's board. "But the thing is, the number of people coming up, including the kids, keeps on increasing. The Mexican authorities have been overwhelmed."

But according to American law enforcement agencies, the problem has been taken care of, all because of Mi Nueva Casa. The Santa Cruz Juvenile Detention Center says there has been a dramatic decrease in youthful-offender apprehensions on the border. So does the Border Patrol. "As recently as 1994, we had our hands full," says a BP spokesperson. "But Mi Nueva Casa's made a hell of a difference. Plus, we have the tunnels effectively monitored now."

Which is not to say that the tunnels have been closed or that there aren't kids living in them. There is no way to close the tunnels. They are for drainage, after all. "Effectively monitoring" means that the Border Patrol dispatches a team down into the tunnel two or three times a week to weld shut the steel gate that serves as the barrier between the American and Mexican sides. According to Border Patrol officials, the weld can stand four hundred pounds of pressure per square inch, which means that a dozen or so kids can break it easily. And, in fact, the gate is busted open two or three times a week by the kids, or anyone else who wants to get across.

Romel is one of Barrio Libre's *veteranos*. At seventeen, he's already an old man. He's beaten others and been beaten, robbed and been robbed, known the life of the tunnel for almost four years. Now he is caught between that life and a growing desire to find a straight job. For the moment, he's leaning toward the job.

Romel sits in the living room of Mi Nueva Casa, watching

the original Batman and Robin dubbed in Spanish. His father was a drug dealer who was nabbed by the FBI; he lived with his stepmother in Washington State for a few years, but eventually the stepfamily sent him back to the border like a piece of unclaimed luggage. There he fell into the tunnel, into Barrio Libre. He freely admits to *tumbando*, assaulting people in the tunnel for money. But something in the back of his head has been nagging at him lately.

"I'm tired of it and . . ."—he searches for the words—"they're my own people, after all."

Romel's friend Iram shows up, a tall, lithe, good-looking teenager who still lives "down below." He teases Romel about his new life. Ultimately, he goads him into going down for a visit.

We zigzag along the tourist streets of downtown Nogales, looking out for Beta agents, who, Romel says, are after him for a tunnel rape that he swears he had nothing to do with. We head south along Avenida Obregón, Nogales's main drag. A strip joint announces *"chicas sexis."* A blind accordionist sits on the sidewalk playing for change. A middle-aged gringo tourist in shorts, white socks, and huaraches marvels at a wrought-iron design.

About half a mile from the border on Obregón, we veer left and drop down into a weedy abandoned lot. The kids turn left again around the corner of an apartment building, looking over their shoulders. Now we're underneath the building, in a four-foot crawl space. Knees and backs bent uncomfortably, we walk along a trickle of a river running down the middle of the tunnel. It's not so bad, I think to myself.

But the real tunnel begins only about two hundred yards later, and the space there is barely over three feet high. As if someone had snapped off a switch, suddenly all light is gone. Romel flicks on the only flashlight we have—one equipped with rapidly dying batteries. The light barely cuts through the dark. Staggering along sideways, I can barely keep up with the kids.

The stench hits me: this is not supposed to be a sewage line, but there is obviously leakage from homes and businesses above. The river widens. What appear to be puddles are actually two-foot-deep mini-lakes of stagnant shit and piss. We hear the drip of more sewage coming down. The air is at once too thick and too thin. I breathe heavily and sweat profusely, although it's a few degrees cooler down here than outside.

I manage to stammer a concerned question about battery life. "Don't worry," Romel says. "Even if it goes out, I can tell you exactly where we are and how to get out of here. I can walk in and out of here without a flashlight." I wonder if he's boasting or serious; there are hundreds of yards of pitch-black tunnel left before we reach the line. *Watch out for the electrical wire—might be live or it might not, you don't want to find out. Careful of this beam. Ouch!*

Concrete dividers are encrusted with surreal collections of goo and trash—baseball caps and egg cartons, underwear and hairbrushes—that rush through here when it rains. My left leg gives way into a shit lake and I fall forward, striking my knee on something sharp. Fetid water splashes up in my face. Giggles from Tram and Romel. My jeans are torn and my knee feels like there's a knife stuck in the socket.

It's deathly quiet down here, no breeze, nothing to see, only the feeling that there are a dozen things that you could knock yourself out cold on.

We approach an ever-so-dim source of light. It's a man-hole cover. Through two half-dollar-size holes, the light comes down gray-white in perfect tubes, two tiny spotlights hitting the sandy-muddy floor of the tunnel. Beyond, darkness again. I stand below the iron lid. Directly above us, I see and hear pedestrians along Obregón. A Mexican vendor is earnestly trying to get a tourist to put on a sombrero and pose with his wife next to a burro.

After a while, we come to a stop before another tunnel, running perpendicular to the first. The international line. We clamber over a three-foot-thick black sewage pipe. Iram points east with the flashlight. About twenty-five yards away is the mouth of the north-south tunnel that takes you up to Church's Chicken—where Romel once lived and where Iram and many other Barrio Libre kids still live.

Suddenly bright lights flash ahead. Unintelligible whispers ripple along the dead air, reverberating off the concrete. Iram gets nervous. "Romel—there's somebody up there!" he says. The lights disappear. A few seconds later there is a tremendous metallic bang, loud enough to be felt in the pit of your stomach. Silence again.

"That was the sound of the tunnel opening," Romel says.

But by whom? Other members of Barrio Libre? *Polleros* eager to teach the kids a lesson? Or is it the Border Patrol on one of their strolls into the tunnel, eager to swoop up the day's quota of illegals?

Romel and Iram wait in silence. To the west, a hundred yards away, a veil of gray light—an opening to street level that is part of a construction project on the Mexican side, just a block and a half from Mi Nueva Casa.

Into the darkness or toward the light?

The kids make a run for it, scared out of their wits.

A minute later, alone, I'm climbing up through chunks of concrete and iron reinforcement rods.

The light of the sun glinting off car fenders and house windows is blinding. Above, the deep blue Sonoran sky. And then a man wearing a red beret and aviator glasses is asking me where I am going. Romel and Iram are pushed against the wall, legs spread. I have the presence of mind to show my journalist's credential and the Beta agent calls off the dogs.

"If you hadn't been there," says Romel later, "they would've beat the shit out of us."

The next day, another trip down into the tunnel, this time led by Toño, the nine-year-old I'd met in Mi Nueva Casa—the one with the dog bites. We take the same route, and this time there are no strangers flashing lights.

We turn toward the steel gate the Border Patrol welds shut a few times a week. As we approach, we hear whispers on the other side. Toño slows down, shines his flashlight directly at the gate. It creaks open; the BP hasn't welded it yet. Squinting into the light are a pair of glassy eyes set in a twelve-year-old's face.

"Where you from?" the kid asks.

"Barrio Libre!" Toño responds quickly, and then the door opens fully, revealing half a dozen more kids. Handshakes all around.

The boys show me the weld—it looks like nothing more than a Radio Shack soldering job—that they break open whenever they want. I get a tour of the immediate surroundings, the graffiti-scarred walls. BARRIO LIBRE! on one side, BETA! on the other—the Mexican border agents, not to be outdone by the kids, do their own tagging.

We are advised by the older Barrio Libre members not to go farther into the tunnel; there is something going down deep inside. They close the door and scamper back to the Mexican side, maneuvering quickly with their dimming flashlights.

The last time I visited the tunnel, all hell broke loose. I was standing with the kids on the American side, at the mouth of the tunnel, just below Church's Chicken. There were several kids present whom I didn't know. And the ones I did know were high—very high. There was a spray can being passed around with a rag. Gold-fleck paint was everywhere, on the kids' noses and mouths, on their hands, on my tape recorder. The kids were stumbling, twirling, kicking at puddles of water, shouting themselves hoarse.

I was surprised to find Romel among the crew, although perhaps I shouldn't have been. Once you've gone underground, it's hard to stay away. I try to imagine Romel as a mature man in his thirties. I cannot.

Something was about to happen—the combination of the paint and the large number of kids, about twenty in all, was volatile. All they needed was the spark.

There was much drugged banter. Romel announced that he was going to steal a TV set from someone's house on the American side.

"Yeah, we could have cable TV, and beds, and a stove . . ." Jesús enthused. Romel thought there should be a library, too, with comic books and Nintendo games.

The reverie was cut short by the sudden appearance of a man in his thirties coming up from the tunnel. He was dressed in a white shirt opened several buttons down his chest, white pants, smart boots. He was definitely not *migra*, but he wasn't a typical *chúntaro*, either. The kids surrounded him instantly. It was a strange sight: a well-built, mature man mobbed by scrawny preteens and malnourished adolescents, not unlike a bear set upon by coyotes. One of the kids had noticed him stuffing something into his mouth just as he'd come within sight.

"Spit it out!" someone shouted. One kid pried the man's jaws open and took out a wadded-up ten-dollar bill.

"He's with Beta, I recognize him!" someone else yelled. The man remained quiet, amazingly calm considering the circumstances. He was fully patted down, but the kids found nothing else on him. Was he a narco? An illegal? A coyote?

"Are you alone?" a kid demanded.

"No, there are others behind me," he said, his voice devoid of emotion.

I was beginning to think he was bullshitting, stalling for time, but then we heard noises from deep inside the tunnel and saw the flashing of lights. The kids ran into the darkness, and the man in white slowly walked away, jumping up to street level without looking back. There were no Border Patrol agents or Nogales policemen anywhere to be seen. The kids could do what they wanted. From the tunnel I heard them shout "Barrio Libre!" and there were the sounds of scuffling. A few moments later, the kids reappeared, laughing, hoisting the spoils high: a gold necklace, a silver crucifix, diamond earrings in the shape of bunny rabbits, all the real thing. Unlucky *chúntaros.* Romel pulled me aside, breathing hard. He said the victims were about a dozen women. He suspected that the man in white was their coyote. He'd probably told them to wait inside while he checked out the scene at the mouth of the tunnel. There was nowhere for the women to run in the darkness. They sat huddled together, vulnerable as lambs, and then the kids were upon them. "There was nothing I could do to stop it," Romel told me.

As I left, the kids were still sniffing, and there was talk of a big party in the tunnel that night. When I clambered up to street level, I saw a Border Patrol Explorer pull into Church's parking lot. I looked back down. The kids were running back into the tunnel, deep into the darkness.

Naco, Arizona, is a minor port of entry some fifty miles east of Nogales. My father was stationed at the nearby army base back in the fifties. "Wasn't much in Naco," he told me. Nevertheless, I imagine him knocking back several cold ones in a cantina on the other side with his army buddies, he the Mexican in GI greens, a Mexican with papers, a Mexican with an American passport. Mexican only, in the end, for his brown skin and the memory of his parents' struggle to make it in America.

Second generation on my father's side and first on my mother's, I have come back to the line, swimming against the tide, drawn by memory, drawn by the present and by the future. I see the Mexicans pour into Los Angeles, I see them on the banks of the Mississippi in St. Louis. I see their brownness, I see my own. I suppose my sympathy can be summed up simply as this: when they are denied their Americanness by U.S. immigration policy, I feel that my own is denied as well. They are doing exactly what my father's parents and my mother did. They are doing exactly what all Americans' forebears did.

Here in Naco, the border is merely a few broken strands of barbed wire. There is an obelisk marking the boundary established in 1848, in English on the north-facing side, in Spanish on the south. I become giddy. No wall! Just open range, and that's exactly what it is, open range for cross-border cattle. West of here, on the O'odham Reservation, there is no wall or fence either. The O'odham people have been caught in the middle of a transnational caper that has nothing to do with them. They aren't Mexican, they aren't American, they are O'odham. For most of the last century and a half, the tribe has moved freely back and forth across the line, along with their livestock. The Border Patrol never bothers them; the territory is so far removed from major highways that smugglers rarely think of crossing there.

The O'odham have homes on both sides of the line. "There are no sides here," an elder tells me. Except that in recent years the Mexican migrant tide has begun coming across O'odham land because of the new wall in Nogales. And so the Border Patrol has arrived on the res with its Explorers and helicopters. O'odham people have found dessicated migrant bodies in the middle of their desert.

I leap over to one side; I am Mexican!

I leap back to the other side; I am American!

I dance a jig back and forth across the line, laughing at it, damning it, and recognizing the mighty power of the very idea of a line that cannot, does not exist in nature but that exists, nevertheless, in political, that is, human terms.

And just as I am marveling at the absurdity, an Explorer pulls up and two BP agents, one Asian, one Caucasian, saunter over.

The Asian asks, in fairly good Spanish, *"Qué hace usted aquí?"* What are you doing here?

I answer, of course, in English.

I am informed that I am in violation of the United States Immigration Code. I flash my credentials, and after a bit of radio repartee between the agents and their supervisors, all is fine and dandy. I can keep walking along the line as much as I want, as long as I stay on this side—right here happens to be public land so I'm free to engage in whatever lawful activity I please. But I'm also advised that I might have many such encounters with BP officers because I will be tripping seismic sensors all along the way, which is why I was detained by the BP outside of Naco in the first place.

"We get a lot of 'em in through here," one agent says. "Most of 'em are from Mitch-oh-ah-cahn."

And so I get in the Blazer, point it east, and drive toward Douglas, Arizona, another embattled border village on the forlorn frontier. Hundreds of coyotes and tens of thousands of migrants wait on the other side in Agua Prieta, and a beefed-up Border Patrol waits on this one, not to mention mad-as-hell gringo ranchers whose land is being trampled by the migrant stampede.

In Douglas and Naco and Sonoita and El Paso and Laredo, all along the two-thousand-mile line, it's the same thing each and every day. Helicopters toss down ladders of light, and the *migra* put their night-vision goggles and laser grids and seismic sensors and video cameras to work. Mexican teenagers with slingshots target the BP trucks, so much so that the Explorers now have iron window grilles. The vigilantes patrol their properties, fingering the triggers of their assault rifles. A handful of activists protest human rights abuses on both sides of the line, and a few compassionate preachers liken the crossing to wading across the Jordan into Canaan.

It's like this all along the border, and it's a matter of politics, of money, of ideas, desire, death, life.

New Departures

to survive the scimitars of the Tuaregs. But the warning went unheeded in the mind of the would-be hermit. Convinced that his rotting soul would one way or other attract evil spirits, Brother Degard reminded the abbot that his hands were already stained with blood, so that the pardon of God or of men counted for little with him. What he was seeking was oblivion, and oblivion, he added, was something he could attain, not with the force that God had denied him when he was most in need, but by attempting the utter surrender of his will. And he ended by saying, as he made a bundle out of his few belongings, that out there, where they could put up with a murderer, there had to be a devil.

Once installed in his cave, Degard settled down to wait for the devils to appear. Months passed unnoticed, days and nights of fasting in which the ascetic began to fear that the devil might have in fact forgotten that state in which someone will summon him without being sufficiently sinful to deserve him. Degard sensed the passing of the hours as his eyes wandered over the landscape, calling on the devil by each of his known names, or by others that he himself had invented from a mishmash of Latin and Arabic, tracing arcane circles in the sand and burning incense until he had used up his store of matches. His pale Breton peasant's skin took on a deep tan from his exposure to the open air, waiting for the peckings of nonexistent succubi, and his worm-eaten spirit broke out on his skin in the form of blisters that gushed blood, a liquid discharge that he in his madness took to be only a physical manifestation of the unsheddable memory of his crime. Meanwhile, the desert remained impervious, and Degard decided then that the devil's most fiendish twist lay in his utter indifference toward those who cried out to him. Not to be present to anyone or for anyone, not even to relish a perdition long anticipated. That was what most vexed the hermit; and that was why he went on abasing himself just as fiercely as he cursed the devil's absence.

On a certain night Degard mistook the torches of a caravan
for the manifestation of a spirit from another world, come in
search of him, and he left the cave in a gesture of welcome. His
appearance, his cries, his drooling and cursing had the opposite
effect on the Tuaregs, for, taking him for a devil, they fled the
place, invoking the protection of their god. It was then that
Degard, once more immersed in his solitude, saw that the indifference of the desert should be understood rather as a message
in code, an invitation to him to find in the stretches of his dev-
astated spirit the ingredients necessary to create the devil. From
his sins, from his sins alone, a monstrous creature would have to
emerge, formed from pieces of his live flesh blended with a
steady flow of remorse. In short, he would be the father and
creator of evil, for only so could he confront the devil and recognize himself in that face.

At first the hermit imagined that bringing the devil into being
would be fairly easy, but in fact his invocation alone took much
more time and effort than he had expected. To summon the
Dark One was no longer a matter of plural names and charts of
the stars. He had to give himself up to remembering his own
wrongdoings, to that excremental stench that Degard at times
confused with the disquieting odor of sanctity. Perhaps in
this way, with a measure of patience, he would rescue himself
from his own affliction and cause its darkness to lift from his
spirit.

Finally, one day, the hermit's fits stopped being mystical experiences and turned into epilepsy. The devil then frothed at the
lips and settled himself expectantly in the depths of the cave.
His creator spent hours gazing at him, wondering why his guest
remained as still as a statue. Mean and hunchbacked, wrapped in
a djellaba that to Degard looked altogether too like the one his
onetime victim had worn, the devil did no more than return his
gaze, all the time gnawing on a goldfinch wing. His replies to
the hermit were so laconic that it was not even possible to make

out which language he was speaking, and Degard was at his wits'
end looking for a way to startle his creature out of its apathy.

One afternoon, almost at the point of giving up and asking
for pardon, Degard decided that the only way to challenge his
devil was in the persona of a saint. Where before he had invoked
evil, now he had to conjure up a saint to rouse the anger of the
other and allow himself to tangle with him on the sand floor
muddied by their own urine.

Creating a saint was for Degard much more arduous than his
previous task—his invocation of the devil had almost drained
him of the remains of his virtue. So he had to relive the times
of his childhood, and from there progress in his memory to
the monastery of La Clochette. Thus, slowly and in pain, he
brought it about that one day the devil stopped gnawing on his
goldfinch wing and inclined his head toward a reawakened man
whose sanctity had finally summoned him out of his lethargy.

With the creation of the saint, things changed dramatically.
Before any physical confrontation, there first arose a more dev-
astating intellectual one between the two of them. Materializing
in the cave, the saint decided to confront the devil using his own
logic, and drive him to a combat in which Degard's spirit would
devour itself. He began one night by posing questions to the
devil that at first seemed inoffensive and somewhat byzantine,
which the devil answered sometimes with simple tricks of language, sometimes with tedious sophisms. Satisfied that he had
understood the rules of the game, the saint then began to com-
plicate the questions with the pleasure a chess player takes in
playing a game against himself, trying to play fair and to cheat
at the same time for the game to count. Very soon the rules and
the trials of the game had so clarified themselves that saint and
devil both worked out in the end a tacit agreement that each had
to observe for their mutual convenience. From a position of
moral objectivity, the hermit first formulated a theological ques-

tion that he, playing the saint, would try to answer with the help of a truth; and then, immediately assuming the role of devil, he would go about destroying that truth with arguments convincing enough to undermine the original logic of the saint.

The nature of evil, the existence of God and his connections to nothingness, the impotence of a Being omnipotent enough to create a rock so huge that its creator could not lift it, predestination, and, above all, the inequity between blame and pardon were only some of the dilemmas that came up in the interminable game of Brother Jean Degard. Sometimes the very nature of the questions caused saint and devil to spend entire weeks without reaching agreement, for the contest was logically balanced, and the truths rationally achieved by the saint could always be countered when the devil's arguments were up to it. They were drawn more always to the theological debates, and if on some occasion the devil tried to pull a trick, introducing in mid-debate a carnal temptation or a reminder of Degard's crime, the game came to a halt, and both players ended up exchanging apologies in order to resume what now took up their entire existences.

With the passing of the months, Brother Degard managed to dissolve all memory of his crime in the ins and outs of the combat. His life and the bloodiest details from his past suddenly moved to the territory of forgetting, where they might well have vanished had not Degard at that moment come up with a question he would later regret. The hermit himself could never understand what drove him to do it, but it is quite possible that it may have indicated a certain wish to put an end to a game that in the end he knew could not last forever. Perhaps that night, betrayed by memory, Degard might have recognized in the face of the devil the features of the man he had murdered, and thought that getting rid of him would succeed in removing the last obstacle to his happiness. However it was, this time the her-

AUNT LEONOR

Aunt Leonor had the world's most perfect belly button: a small dot hidden exactly in the middle of her flat, flat belly. She had a freckled back and round, firm hips, like the pitchers of water she drank from as a child. Her shoulders were raised slightly; she walked slowly, as if on a high wire. Those who saw them tell that her legs were long and golden, that her pubic hair was a tuft of arrogant, reddish down, that it was impossible to look upon her waist without desiring all of her.

At age seventeen she followed her head and married a man who was exactly the kind you would choose, with your head, to accompany you through life. Alberto Palacios, a wealthy, stringent notary public, had fifteen years, thirty centimeters of height, and a proportionate amount of experience over her. He had been the longtime boyfriend of various boring women who became even more tiresome when they discovered that the good notary had only a long-term plan for considering marriage.

Destiny would have it that Aunt Leonor entered the notary's office one afternoon accompanied by her mother to process a supposedly easy inheritance, which for them turned out to be extremely complicated, owing to the fact that Aunt Leonor's recently deceased father had never permitted his wife to think for even half an hour in her lifetime. He did everything for her except go grocery shopping and cook. He summarized the news in the newspaper for her and told her how she should think about it. He gave her an always sufficient allowance, which he never asked to see how she spent; he even told her what was happening in the movies they went to see together: "See, Luisita, this boy fell in love with the young lady. Look how they're gazing at each other—you see? Now he wants to caress her, he's caressing her now. Now he's going to ask her to marry him, and in a little while he will abandon her."

The result of this paternalism was that poor Aunt Luisita found the sudden loss of the exemplary man who was Aunt Leonor's papa not only distressing but also extremely complicated. With this sorrow and this complication they entered the notary's office in search of assistance. They found him to be so solicitous and efficacious that Aunt Leonor, still in mourning, married notary Palacios a year and a half later.

Aunt Leonor's life was never again as easy as it was back then. In the only critical moment, she had followed her mother's advice: Shut your eyes and say a Hail Mary. In truth, many Hail Marys, because at times her immoderate husband could take as long as ten Mysteries of the Rosary before arriving at the series of moans and gasps that culminated in the circus that inevitably began when, for some reason, foreseen or not, he placed his hand on Leonor's short, delicate waist.

Aunt Leonor lacked for nothing a woman under twenty-five should want: hats, veils, French shoes, German tableware, a diamond ring, a necklace of unmatched pearls; turquoise, coral, and filigree earrings. Everything, from underdrawers embroidered by Trinitarian nuns to a tiara like Princess Margaret's. She had whatever she might want, including the devotion of her husband, who little by little began to realize that life without precisely this woman would be intolerable.

From out of the affectionate circus that the notary mounted at least three times a week, first a girl and then two boys materialized in Aunt Leonor's belly. And as happens only in the movies, Aunt Leonor's body inflated and deflated all three times without apparent damage. The notary would have liked to draw up a certificate bearing testimony to such a miracle, but he limited himself to merely enjoying it, helped along as he was by the polite and placid diligence that time and curiosity had bestowed upon his wife. The circus improved so much that Leonor stopped getting through it with her rosary in her hands and even came to thank him for it, falling asleep afterward with a smile that lasted all day.

Life couldn't have been better for this family. People always spoke well of them; they were a model couple. The neighbor women could not find a better example of kindness and companionship than that offered by Señor Palacios to the lucky Leonor, and their men, when they were angriest, evoked the peaceful smile of Señora Palacios while their wives strung together a litany of laments.

Perhaps everything would have gone on in the same way if it hadn't occurred to Aunt Leonor to buy medlars one Sunday. Her Sunday trips to market had become a happy, solitary rite. First she looked the whole place over, without trying to discern exactly from which fruit came which color, mixing the tomato stands with those that sold lemons. She walked without pausing until she reached an immense woman fashioning fat blue tacos, her one hundred years showing on her face. Leonorcita picked out one filled with pot cheese from the clay tortilla plate, carefully put a bit of red sauce on it, and ate it slowly while making her purchases.

Medlars are small fruit with intensely yellow velvety skin. Some are bitter and others are sweet. They grow in jumbled clusters on the branches of a tree with large, dark leaves. Many afternoons when she was a girl with braids and as agile as a cat, Aunt Leonor climbed the medlar tree at her grandparents' house. There she sat to eat quickly: three bitter ones, a sweet one, seven bitter, two sweet—until the search for and mixture of flavors became a delicious game. Girls were prohibited from climbing the tree, but her cousin Sergio, a boy of precocious eyes, thin lips, and a determined voice, induced her into unheard-of, secret adventures. Climbing the tree was among the easiest of them.

She saw the medlars in the market, and they seemed strange, far from the tree yet not completely apart from it, for medlars are cut while still on the most delicate, full-leaved branches.

She took the medlars home, showed them to her children, and sat the kids down to eat, meanwhile telling them stories of her grandfather's strong legs and her grandmother's snub nose. In a little while, her mouth was brimming with slippery pits and velvety peelings. Then suddenly being ten years old came back, his avid hands, her forgotten desire for Sergio, up in the tree, winking at her.

Only then did she realize that something had been torn out of her the day they told her that cousins couldn't marry each other, because God would punish them with children who seemed like drunkards. And then she could no longer return to the days past. The afternoons of her happiness were muted from then on by this unspeakable, sudden nostalgia.

No one else would have dared ask for more: to add to her complete tranquility when her children were floating paper boats in the rain, and to the unhesitating affection of her generous and hardworking husband, the certainty in her entire body that the cousin who had made her perfect navel tremble was not prohibited, and that she deserved him for all reasons and forever. No one, that is, but the outrageous Leonor.

One afternoon she ran into Sergio walking down Cinco de Mayo Street. She was coming out of the Church of Santo Domingo, holding a child by each hand. She'd taken them to make a floral offering, as on every afternoon that month: The girl in a long dress of lace and white organdy, a little garland of straw, and an enormous, impetuous veil. Like a five-year-old bride. The boy with a girlish acolyte's costume that made him even at seven feel embarrassed.

"If you hadn't run away from our grandparents' house that Saturday, this pair would be mine," said Sergio, kissing her.

"I live with that regret," Aunt Leonor answered.

That response startled one of the most eligible bachelors in the city. At twenty-seven, recently returned from Spain, where it was said he had learned the best techniques for cultivating olives, cousin Sergio was heir to a ranch in Veracruz, another in San Martín, and one more in nearby Atzalan.

Aunt Leonor noticed the confusion in his eyes and in the tongue with which he wet his lips, and later she heard him say:

"If everything were like climbing the tree again."

Grandmother's house was on 11 Sur Street. It was huge and full of nooks and crannies. It had a basement with five doors in which Grandfather spent hours doing experiments that often soiled his face and made him forget for a while about the first-floor rooms and occupying himself playing billiards with friends in the salon constructed on the rooftop. Grandmother's house had a breakfast room that gave onto the garden and the ash tree, a jai-alai court that they'd always used for roller-skating, a rose-colored front room with a grand piano and a drained aquarium, a bedroom for Grandfather and one for Grandmother; and the rooms that had once been the children's were various sitting rooms that had come to be known by the colors of their walls. Grandmother, sound of mind but palsied, had settled herself in to paint in the blue room. There Leonor and Sergio found her drawing lines with a pencil on the envelopes of the old wedding invitations she'd always liked to save. She offered them a glass of sweet wine, then fresh cheese, then stale chocolates. Everything was the same at Grandmother's house. After a while, the old woman noticed the only thing that was different:

"I haven't seen you two together in years."

"Not since you told me that cousins who marry each other have idiot children," Aunt Leonor answered.

Grandmother smiled, poised above the paper on which she was sketching an infinite flower, petals upon petals without respite.

"Not since you nearly killed yourself getting down from the medlar tree," said Sergio.

"You two were good at cutting medlars. Now I can't find anyone who can do it right."

"We're still good," said Aunt Leonor, bending her perfect waist.

They left the blue room, almost ready to peel off their clothes, and went down to the garden as if drawn by a spell. They returned three hours later with peace in their bodies and three branches of medlars.

"We've lost our touch," Aunt Leonor said.

"Get it back, get it back, because time is short," advised Grandmother, her mouth full of medlar pits.

AUNT NATALIA

One day Natalia Esparza, she of the short legs and round breasts, fell in love with the sea. She didn't know for sure at what moment that pressing wish to know the remote and legendary ocean came to her, but it came with such force that she had to abandon her piano school and take up the search for the Caribbean, because it was to the Caribbean that her ancestors had come a century before, and it was from there that what she'd named the missing piece of her conscience was calling relentlessly to her.

The call of the sea gave her such strength that her own mother could not convince her to wait even half an hour. It didn't matter how much her mother begged her to calm her craziness until the almonds were ripe for making nougat, until the tablecloth that they were embroidering with cherries for her sister's wedding was finished, until her father understood that it wasn't prostitution, or idleness, or an incurable mental illness that had suddenly made her so determined to leave.

Aunt Natalia grew up in the shadow of the volcanoes, scrutinizing them day and night. She knew by heart the creases in the breast of the Sleeping Woman and the daring slope that capped Popocatépetl.[1] She had always lived in a land of darkness and cold skies, making sweets over a slow fire and cooking meats hidden beneath the colors of overly elaborated sauces. She ate off decorated plates, drank from crystal goblets, and spent hours seated in front of the rain, listening to her mother's prayers and her grandfather's tales of dragons and winged horses. But she learned of the sea on the afternoon when some uncles from Campeche passed through during her snack of bread and chocolate, before resuming their journey to the walled city surrounded by an implacable ocean of colors.

Seven kinds of blue, three greens, one gold—everything fit in the sea. The silver that no one could take out of the country, whole under a cloudy sky. Night challenging the courage of the

[1] The Sleeping Woman (Iztaccíhuatl), a dormant volcano, and Popocatépetl, an active one, are both visible from Puebla.

ships, the tranquil consciences of those who govern them. The morning like a crystal dream, midday brilliant as desire.

There, she thought, even the men must be different. Those who lived near the sea that she'd been imagining without respite since Thursday snack time, would not be factory owners or rice salesmen or millers or plantation owners or anyone who could keep still under the same light his whole life long. Her uncle and father had spoken so much of the pirates of yesteryear and those of today, of Don Lorenzo Patiño, her mother's grandfather, whom they nicknamed Lorencillo between gibes when she told them that he had arrived at Campeche in his own brig. So much had been said of the callused hands and prodigal bodies that required that sun and that breeze, so fed up was she with the tablecloth and the piano, that she took off after the uncles without a single regret. She would live with her uncles, her mother hoped. Alone, like a crazed she-goat, guessed her father.

She didn't even know the way, only that she wanted to go to the sea. And at the sea she arrived, after a long journey to Mérida and a terrible long trek behind the fishermen she met in the market of that famous white city.

They were an old man and a young one. The old man, a talkative marijuana smoker; the youth, who considered everything madness: How would they return to Holbox with this nosy, well-built woman? How could they leave her?

"You like her too," the old man had told the young one, "and she wants to come. Don't you see how she wants to come?"

Aunt Natalia had spent the entire morning seated in the fish stalls of the market, watching the arrival of one man after another who'd accept anything in exchange for his smooth creatures of white flesh and bone, his strange creatures, as smelly and as beautiful as the sea itself must be. Her eyes lingered on the shoulders and gait, the insulted voice of one who didn't want to "just give away" his conch.

"It's this much, or I'll take it back," he had said.

"This much or I'll take it back," and Natalia's eyes followed him.

The first day they walked without stopping, Natalia asking and asking if the sand of the seashore was really as white as sugar, and the nights as hot as alcohol. Sometimes she paused to rub her feet, and the men took advantage of the chance to leave her behind. Then she put on her shoes and set off running, repeating the curses of the old man.

They arrived on the following afternoon. Aunt Natalia couldn't believe it. She ran to the sea, propelled forward by her last remaining strength, and began to add her tears to the salty water. Her feet, her knees, her muscles were aching. Her face and shoulders stung from sunburn. Her wishes, heart, and hair were aching. Why was she crying? Wasn't sinking down here the only thing she wanted?

Slowly it grew dark. Alone on the endless beach, she touched her legs and found that they had not yet become a mermaid's tail. A brisk wind was blowing, pushing the waves to shore. She walked the beach, startling some tiny mosquitoes that feasted on her arms. Close by was the old man, his eyes lost on her.

She threw herself down on the white bed of sand, in her wet clothes, and felt the old man come nearer, put his fingers in her matted hair, and explain to her that if she wanted to stay, it had to be with him because all the others already had women.

"I'll stay with you," she said, and she fell asleep.

No one knew how Aunt Natalia's life was in Holbox. She returned to Puebla six months later and ten years older, calling herself the widow of Uc Yam.

Her skin was brown and wrinkled, her hands callused, and she exuded a strange air of self-confidence. She never married, yet never wanted for a man; she learned to paint, and the blue of her paintings made her famous in Paris and New York.

Nevertheless, her home remained in Puebla, however much, some afternoons while she watched the volcanoes, her dreams would wander out to sea.

"One belongs where one is from," she would say, painting with her old-lady hands and child   ves. "Because like it or not, wherever you go, they send you back home."

Identity Hour or, What Photos Would You Take of the Endless City?

Visually, Mexico City signifies above all else the superabundance of people. You could, of course, turn away from this most palpable of facts towards abstraction, and photograph desolate dawns, or foreground the aesthetic dimension of walls and squares, even rediscover the perfection of solitude. But in the capital, the multitude that accosts the multitude imposes itself like a permanent obsession. It is the unavoidable theme present in the tactics that everyone, whether they admit it or not, adopts to find and ensconce themselves in even the smallest places the city allows. Intimacy is by permission only, the "poetic licence" that allows you momentarily to forget those around you—never more than an inch away—who make of urban vitality a relentless grind.

Turmoil is the repose of the city-dwellers, a whirlwind set in motion by secret harmonies and lack of public resources. How can one describe Mexico City today? Mass overcrowding and the shame at feeling no shame; the unmeasurable space, where almost everything is possible, because everything works thanks only to what we call a "miracle"—which is no more than the meeting-place of work, technology and chance. These are the most frequent images of the capital city:

- multitudes on the Underground (where almost six million travellers a day are crammed, making space for the very idea of space);
- multitudes taking their entrance exam in the University Football Stadium;
- the "Marías (Mazahua peasant women) selling whatever they can in the streets, resisting police harassment while training their countless kids;
- the underground economy that overflows onto the pavements, making popular marketplaces of the streets. At traffic lights young men and women overwhelm drivers, attempting to sell Kleenex, kitchenware, toys, tricks. The vulnerability is so extreme that it becomes artistic, and a young boy makes fire—swallowing it and throwing it up— the axis of his gastronomy;
- mansions built like safes, with guard dogs and private police;
- masked wrestlers, the tutelary gods of the new Teotihuacán of the ring;
- the *Templo Mayor*: Indian grandeur;
- *"piñatas"* containing all the most important traditional figures: the Devil, the Nahual, Ninja Turtles, Batman, Penguin . . . ;
- the Basilica of Guadalupe;
- the swarm of cars. Suddenly it feels as if all the cars on earth were held up right here, the traffic jam having now become second nature to the species hoping to arrive late at the Last Judgement. Between four and six o'clock in the morning there is some respite, the species seems drowsy . . . but suddenly everything moves on again, the advance cannot be

stopped. And in the traffic jam, the automobile becomes a prison on wheels, the cubicle where you can study Radio in the University of Tranquillity;

• the flat rooftops, which are the continuation of agrarian life by other means, the natural extension of the farm, the redoubt of Agrarian Reform. Evocations and needs are concentrated on the rooftops. There are goats and hens, and people shout at the helicopters because they frighten the cows and the farmers milking them. Clothes hang there like harvested maize. There are rooms containing families who reproduce and never quite seem to fit. Sons and grandsons come and go, while godparents stay for months, and the room grows, so to speak, eventually to contain the whole village from which its first migrant came;

• the contrasts between rich and poor, the constant antagonism between the shadow of opulence and the formalities of misery;

• the street gangs, less violent than elsewhere, seduced by their own appearance, but somewhat uncomfortable because no one really notices them in the crowd. The street gangs use an international alphabet picked up in the streets of Los Angeles, fence off their territories with graffiti, and show off the aerial prowess of punk hairstyles secure in the knowledge that they are also ancestral, because they really copied them off Emperor Cuauhtemoc. They listen to heavy metal, use drugs, thinner and cement, destroy themselves, let themselves be photographed in poses they wish were menacing, accept parts as extras in apocalyptic films, feel regret for their street-gang life, and spend the rest of their lives evoking it with secret and public pleasure.

The images are few. One could add the Museum of Anthropology, the Zócalo at any time (day or night), the Cathedral and, perhaps (risking the photographer), a scene of violence in which police beat up street vendors, or arrest youngsters, pick them up by the hair, or swear that they have not beaten anyone. The typical repertoire is now complete, and if I do not include the *mariachis* of Plaza Garibaldi, it is because this text does not come with musical accompaniment. Mexico: another great Latin American city, with its seemingly uncontrollable growth, its irresponsible love of modernity made visible in skyscrapers, malls, fashion shows, spectacles, exclusive restaurants, motorways, cellular phones. Chaos displays its aesthetic offerings, and next to the pyramids of Teotihuacán, the baroque altars, and the more wealthy and elegant districts, the popular city offers its rituals.

ON THE CAUSES FOR PRIDE THAT (SHOULD) MAKE ONE SHIVER

It was written I should be loyal to the nightmare of my choice.
—JOSEPH CONRAD, *Heart of Darkness*

Where has that chauvinism of old gone for which, as the saying goes, "There is nowhere like Mexico"? Not far, of course: it has returned as a chauvinism expressed in the language of catastrophe and demography. I will now enumerate the points of pride (psychological compensation):

- Mexico City is the most populated city in the world (the Super-Calcutta!);
- Mexico City is the most polluted city on the planet, whose population, however, does not seem to want to move (the laboratory of the extinction of the species);
- Mexico City is the place where it would be impossible for anything to fail due to a lack of audience. There is public aplenty. In the capital, to counterbalance the lack of clear

skies, there are more than enough inhabitants, spectators,
car-owners, pedestrians;
• Mexico City is the place where the unlivable has its rewards,
the first of which has been to endow survival with a new
status.

What makes for an apocalyptic turn of mind? As far as I can
see, the opposite of what may be found in Mexico City. Few
people actually leave this place whose vital statistics (which tend,
for the most part, to be short of the mark) everyone invents at
their pleasure. This is because, since it is a secular city after all,
very few take seriously the predicted end of the world—at least,
of *this* world. So what are the retentive powers of a megalopolis
which, without a doubt, has reached its historic limit? And
how do we reconcile this sense of having reached a limit with
the medium- and long-term plans of every city-dweller? Is it
only centralist anxiety that determines the intensity of the city's
hold? For many, Mexico City's major charm is precisely its (true
and false) "apocalyptic" condition. Here is the first megalopolis to fall victim to its own excess. And how fascinating are all
the biblical prophecies, the dismal statistics and the personal
experiences chosen for catastrophic effect! The main topic of
conversation at gatherings is whether we are actually living the
disaster to come or among its ruins; and when collective humour
describes cityscapes it does so with all the enthusiasm of a witness sitting in the front row at the Last Judgement: "How awful,
three hours in the car just to go two kilometres!" "Did you hear
about those people who collapsed in the street because of the
pollution?" "In some places there is no more water left." "Three
million homes must be built, just for a start. . . ."
    The same grandiose explanation is always offered: despite
the disasters, twenty million people *cannot leave Mexico City or the
Valley of Mexico, because there is nowhere else they want to go; there is nowhere*

else, really, that they can go. Such resignation engenders the "aesthetic of multitudes." Centralism lies at the origins of this phenomenon as does the supreme concentration of powers—which, nevertheless, has certain advantages, the first of which is the identification of liberty and tolerance: "I don't feel like making moral judgements because then I'd have to deal with my neighbours." Tradition is destroyed by the squeeze, the replacement of the extended family by the nuclear family, the wish for extreme individualization that accompanies anomie, the degree of cultural development, the lack of democratic values that would oblige people to—at least minimally—democratize their lives. "What should be abolished" gradually becomes "what I don't like."

To stay in Mexico City is to confront the risks of pollution, ozone, thermic inversion, lead poisoning, violence, the rat race, and the lack of individual meaning. To leave it is to lose the formative and informative advantages of extreme concentration, the experiences of modernity (or postmodernity) that growth and the ungovernability of certain zones due to massification bring. The majority of people, although they may deny it with their complaints and promises to flee, are happy to stay, and stand by the only reasons offered them by hope: "It will get better somehow." "The worst never comes." "We'll have time to leave before the disaster strikes." Indeed, the excuses eventually become one: outside the city it's all the same, or worse. Can there now really be any escape from urban violence, overpopulation, industrial waste, the greenhouse effect?

Writers are among the most sceptical. There are no antiutopias; the city does not represent a great oppressive weight (this is still located in the provinces) but, rather, possible liberty, and in practice, nothing could be further from the spirit of the capital city than the prophecies contained in Carlos Fuentes's novel *Christopher Unborn* and his short story "Andrés Aparicio" in

Burnt Water. According to Fuentes, the city has reached its limits.
One of his characters reflects:

> He was ashamed that a nation of churches and pyramids
> built for all eternity ended up becoming one with the card-
> board, shitty city. They boxed him in, suffocated him, took
> his sun and air away, his senses of vision and smell.

Even the world of *Christopher Unborn* (one of ecological,
political, social and linguistic desolation) is invaded by fun
("relajo"). In the end, although the catastrophe may be very real,
catastrophism is the celebration of the incredulous in which
irresponsibility mixes with resignation and hope, and where—
not such a secret doctrine in Mexico City—the sensations asso-
ciated with the end of the world spread: the overcrowding
is hell, and the apotheosis is crowds that consume all the
air and water, and are so numerous that they seem to float
on the earth. Confidence becomes one with resignation, cynicism and patience: the apocalyptic city is populated with radical
optimists.

In practice, optimism wins out. In the last instance, the
advantages seem greater than the horrors. And the result is: *Mexico, the post-apocalyptic city.* The worst has already happened (and
the worst is the monstrous population whose growth nothing
can stop); nevertheless, the city functions in a way the majority
cannot explain, while everyone takes from the resulting chaos
the visual and vital rewards they need and which, in a way, com-
pensate for whatever makes life unlivable. Love and hate come
together in the vitality of a city that produces spectacles as it
goes along: the commerce that invades the pavements, the infin-
ity of architectonic styles, the "street theatre" of the ten million
people a day who move about the city, through the Underground system, on buses, motorbikes, bicycles, in lorries and

cars. However, the all-star performance is given by the loss of fear at being ridiculed in a society which, not too long ago, was so subjugated by what "others might think." Never-ending mixture also has its aesthetic dimension, and next to the pyramids of Teotihuacán, the baroque altars and the more wealthy and elegant districts, the popular city projects the most favoured—and the most brutally massified—version of the century that is to come.

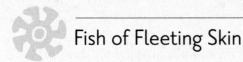

Fish of Fleeting Skin

Its edge is a very fine mouth, a sharp and brilliant division—
the black like a form of light that marks shores, befuddled
spaces bordering fires. As I advance the water changes.

The fiesta was impregnated with little inapproachable
monkeys. Some grafted onto the mud a structure of hollow
branches intersecting in squares and it was like opening a
mirror to the anxieties of swimming.

Everything scatters in yellows. The monkeys leap.

Before, when I looked at how time gently touches a piece of
silk, how little fish are gulped down. The sun disengaged from
the air bunches of dust.

It's an abrupt but precise space; where the trees begin.
Downward uncontrollable longings.

The monkeys, as everyone said, were savage: taut and yellowish little bodies. Their play was prodigious, uprooted, their hands filled with mud.

The water shines, slow and sleepy fish; in their eyes night is vague and oscillating, outlined—a thin mouth—by a dark slice.

But to begin here with the consolation of seeing them all inflamed, and to look suddenly at their hybrid, childish fingers.

Piping boiling voices that burst deserted.

On the border an abyss of tones, of sharp clarity, of forms. One should enter lightly, darkly that instant of dance.

There's a crack here, in this lapse. In the cave roots stick with fanatic cunning, branches bend gracefully.

Instead of biting the recent thickness, or pushing aside the foamy light shadows with a faun's disdainful gesture. Nearby, it rains.

Behind, the umbrellas stretch over the waves. Their colors are slow and their forms piercing. The hours whirl. And I have faith, because that's how they speak of the pools.

Small ivy iridescent fish.

Cats, insects, tigers: when they tried to open the doors, all, from the temple, were immediately concentrated in two lines: two bazaar fragments.

They dance on the shores.

They hold back, because peering over is attraction without docks. Where to lean one's calm looking from afar without risking touch.

The outcome is allusive. Shadows open sometimes slowly. Threshold region of softened nostalgias, of clean and dry words.

But it's the land of salt. Nobody returns or measures. Water that drains in certainty and in oblivion brief sea backwaters.

Remaining distant, then. And their tiny slender cold hands like a sharp agility emerge from impregnable spaces.

From here, the tree trunks and underbrush shine their intact clarity. Virgin exhaling a warm, self-absorbed cadence. The fish leap.

The monkeys leap. At the bottom the light narrows and bodies grow small. Then asphyxia is released: a full albuminous thirst.

They drink leisurely sips of tea.

And if you lower your face to look closer.

They also dragged the tents. The circus: the whole shore was like a fire, the animals trickled in trenches and on platforms.

To hold themselves up, perhaps. The difficult part. Sometimes their irruptions open an orange space.

It's beautiful to touch the waters then. The sky gathers in deep blues. The greens grow till they touch the waters.

He stretches his elastic little arms in a relieving whirl.

The roots inhale. It's enough to slide one's fingers slowly but surely over the rocks to know that they are smooth and uninhabited. Glass trees.

And it's the moment to estrange the boat from its keel and to set limits to the edge. Long and slender fingers.

Those limpid eyes.

This silken languor that spills over. But to begin here.

Slow—thin mouth—fiesta. From the cave their voices are released like gentle clusters. Juicy stones. Seeping from the circus.

And it's the moment; but to begin here. Those avid, unfathomable eyes. On their thick edges, the voices, the waters change: fish of fleeting skin.

NOTES ABOUT THE AUTHORS

Rudolfo Anaya (b. 1937) was born in Pastura, New Mexico, and is the author of numerous novels and plays, as well as collections of short stories, poetry, and criticism. He received his B.A. and M.A. from the University of New Mexico, where he is professor emeritus of English. His novel *Bless Me, Ultima*, published in 1972, is considered a landmark in Latino fiction and is still widely read today.

Gloria Anzaldúa (1942–2004) was raised in Hargill, Texas, which she has described as having "one signal light and thirteen bars and thirteen churches and maybe two mini-marts." A critic and poet with a strong feminist, lesbian, and mestizo agenda, Anzaldúa was completing her doctorate at the University of California, Santa Cruz before her untimely death. Her best-known work, *Borderlands/La Frontera: The New Mestiza* (1987), is a bilingual tour de force aimed at dismantling cultural and linguistic patriarchy.

Jimmy Santiago Baca (b. 1952) is the author of numerous books of poetry, including *Immigrants in Our Own Land, Martín & Meditations on the South Valley*, and *Black Mesa Poems*, and a memoir. He writes with a lyrical intensity about the magnetic isolation of the Southwest's deserts and the people who live there, by choice or necessity. Denise Levertov has said that Baca's poetry "perceives the mythic and archetypal significance of life events."

Coral Bracho (b. 1951) has published six books of poems, including *Peces de piel fugaz, Tierra de entraña ardiente*, and *La voluntad del ámbar.* She is considered one of Mexico's premier contemporary poets and has won the Aguas Calientes National Poetry Prize and a Guggenheim Fellowship, among other awards. She is a professor of language and literature at the Universidad Autónoma de México.

Rosario Castellanos (1925–74) grew up on a ranch in the southern Mexican state of Chiapas. At sixteen, her family left for Mexico City after land reforms diminished their holdings. A poet, critic, playwright, and novelist, Castellanos explored feminism and its connection to the culture of identity in Mexico. Poet José Emilio Pacheco wrote: "Nobody in her time had as clear a consciousness of the twofold condition of being a woman and a Mexican." Castellanos died in a freak accident while ambassador to Israel.

Ana Castillo (b. 1953) has written novels, short stories, poetry, and criticism including, *So Far from God, The Mixquiahuala Letters, Loverboys, My Father Was a Toltec*, and *Massacre of the Dreamers*, a series of essays on Chicana feminism, which she calls Xicanisma. Castillo has received the American Book Award and two fellowships from the National Endowment for the Arts. She lives in Chicago.

Sandra Cisneros (b. 1954) was born in Chicago of a Mexican father and Mexican-American mother and studied at the Iowa Writers' Workshop. Her first novel, *The House on Mango Street*, a coming-of-age story of a Mexican-American girl told in winsome vignettes, has become a standard multicultural text. Cisneros has also written short stories, poetry, and another novel, *Caramelo.*

Carlos Fuentes (b. 1928) is the son of a Mexican diplomat and grew up in various cities, including Washington, D.C. He is a prolific novelist, playwright, critic, political essayist, and short story writer. Among his best-known works are *Where the Air Is Clear, The Death of Artemio Cruz, Terra Nostra, The Old Gringo,* and *Christopher Unborn.* Fuentes served as Mexico's ambassador to France from 1974 to 1977 and has taught at Harvard, Cambridge, and other universities.

Dagoberto Gilb (b. 1950) is a novelist, short story writer, and essayist whose works include *The Magic of Blood, The Last Known Residence of Mickey Acuña, Woodcuts of Women,* and *Gritos.* He has received the PEN/Hemingway Award and a Guggenheim Fellowship. He teaches at Southwest Texas State University.

Ramón López Velarde (1888–1921) was born in Zacatecas and moved to Mexico City after the Mexican Revolution. It was in the capital that he "discovered women, loneliness, doubt, and the devil," according to Octavio Paz. López Velarde also discovered his own highly personal language to describe quotidian Mexico. His books of poetry include *La sangre devota, Zozobra,* and *El minutero.*

Rubén Martínez (b. 1962) has chronicled the diverse lives of Mexicans and Chicanos in such books as *The Other Side: Notes from the New L.A., Mexico City, and Beyond* and *Crossing Over: A Mexican Family on the Migrant Trail.* He is an editor at Pacific News Service and teaches at the University of Houston.

Ángeles Mastretta (b. 1949) was born in Puebla and has worked as a journalist for many years. She is the author of two novels, *Tear This Heart Out* and *Lovesick,* which won the Rómulo Gallegos Prize, a collection of short stories, *Women with Big Eyes,* and other works.

Carlos Monsiváis (b. 1938) is the most prolific and respected social commentator in Mexico today. He has tackled such widely diverse subjects as Juan Rulfo, Dolores del Río, and Latino hip-hop with a sardonic wit and humorous style. His works include *Amor perdido*, *Entrada libre*, and *Los rituales del caos*.

Ignacio Padilla (b. 1968) was born in Mexico City and studied literature and communications in Mexico, South Africa, and Scotland. He began publishing at an early age and his works include novels, short story collections, and essays, among these *Subterráneos*, *La catedral de los abogados*, and *Amphitryon*. The multilingual Padilla is a former cultural attaché for the Mexican embassy in London.

Octavio Paz (1914–98) grew up reading voraciously in his novelist grandfather's decaying mansion in Mexico City. He was in Spain during the Civil War, an experience that marked him for life and fueled his interest in social causes. As a poet, essayist, diplomat (he was Mexico's ambassador to India), and cultural historian, Paz attempted to reconcile opposites in a complex world. He was awarded the Nobel Prize in 1990.

Elena Poniatowska (b. 1932) was born in Paris but moved to Mexico when she was eight years old. She is the author of more than forty works of fiction and nonfiction, including such contemporary classics as *Massacre in Mexico* and *Here's to You, Jesusa!* As a journalist, feminist, and artist, she has been at the cultural forefront of Mexican literature for over forty years.

Samuel Ramos (1897–1959) studied medicine before moving to Mexico City and immersing himself in the capital's intellectual life. He grew interested in European-style existentialism and wrote numerous influential works, most notably *Profile of Man and Culture in Mexico*, a psychoanalytic look at Mexican identity.

Alfonso Reyes (1889–1959) was a prolific poet, fiction writer, and essayist and one of Mexico's most respected men of letters as well as a longtime diplomat. His prose works alone number more than a hundred volumes and include studies on the classics. His most important poetic works include *Huellas, Pausa, Yerbas de Tarahumara, Golfo de México,* and *Romances.*

Richard Rodriguez (b. 1946) grew up in Sacramento and is considered one of the foremost essayists in the United States. His first book, *Hunger of Memory: The Education of Richard Rodriguez,* set off a firestorm of debate on bilingual education, affirmative action, and ethnocentrism when it was published in 1982. His subsequent works include *Days of Obligation: Conversations with My Mexican Father.*

Juan Rulfo (1917–86) was born in a village in the state of Jalisco and lost both parents at an early age. At fifteen, he left an orphanage for Mexico City, where he earned a living in nonliterary ways, including a stint as a tire salesman. Rulfo is the author of two highly acclaimed and influential books, *El llano en llamas,* a collection of short stories, and the classic novel *Pedro Páramo.*

Xavier Villaurrutia (1903–50) founded the first experimental theater group in Mexico City and is best known in his country for the play *Invitación a la muerte.* But those familiar with his one book of poetry, *Nostalgia for Death,* cherish its dark, complex poems. Octavio Paz has written that Villaurrutia's poetry occupies "a place beyond geography and history, beyond myth and legend."

PERMISSIONS ACKNOWLEDGMENTS

Rudolfo Anaya: "B. Traven Is Alive and Well in Cuernavaca" from *The Man Who Could Fly and Other Stories* by Rudolfo Anaya, copyright © 1979 by Rudolfo Anaya (originally published in Escolios, Vol. IV, # 1–2, published by Warner Books and subsequently in 2006 by the University of Oklahoma Press). All rights reserved. Reprinted by permission of Susan Bergholz Literary Services, New York.

Gloria Anzaldúa: "How to Tame a Wild Tongue" from *Borderlands / La Frontera: The New Mestiza* by Gloria Anzaldúa, copyright © 1987, 1999 by Gloria Anzaldúa. Reprinted by permission of Aunt Lute Books.

Jimmy Santiago Baca: "Meditations on the South Valley, Poem IX" from *Martín & Meditations on the South Valley* by Jimmy Santiago Baca, copyright © 1987 by Jimmy Santiago Baca. Reprinted by permission of New Directions Publishing Corp.

Coral Bracho: "Fish of Fleeting Skin" from *Reversible Monuments: Contemporary Mexican Poetry*, edited by Mónica de la Torre and Michael Wiegers (Copper Canyon Press, Port Townsend, Wash., 2002). Reprinted by permission of Copper Canyon Press.

Carlos Monsiváis: "Identity Hour or, What Photos Would You Take of the Endless City?" from *Mexican Postcards* by Carlos Monsiváis, translated by John Kraniauskas (Verso, London, 1997). Reprinted by permission of Verso, London.

Octavio Paz: "The Day of the Dead" from *The Labyrinth of Solitude* by Octavio Paz, translated by Lysander Kemp, copyright © 1962 by Grove Press, Inc. Reprinted by permission of Grove/Atlantic, Inc.

"I Speak of the City" from *Collected Poems 1957–1987*, by Octavio Paz, translated by Eliot Weinberger, copyright © 1986 by Octavio Paz and Eliot Weinberger. Reprinted by permission of New Directions Publishing Corp.

Ignacio Padilla: "Hagiography of the Apostate" from *Antipodes* by Ignacio Padilla, translated by Alastair Reid, translation copyright © 2004 by Alastair Reid. Reprinted by permission of Farrar, Straus and Giroux, LLC.

Elena Poniatowska: Introduction from *Here's to You, Jesusa!* by Elena Poniatowska, translated by Deanna Heikkinen, copyright © 1969 by Elena Poniatowska, translation copyright © 2001 by Farrar, Straus and Giroux, LLC. Reprinted by permission of Farrar, Straus and Giroux, LLC.

Samuel Ramos: Excerpt from "The Use of Thought" from *Profile of Man and Culture in Mexico* by Samuel Ramos, translated by Peter G. Earle, copyright © 1962 by University of Texas Press. Reprinted by permission of University of Texas Press, Austin, Texas.

Richard Rodriguez: "India" from *Days of Obligation: An Argument with My Mexican Father* by Richard Rodriguez, copyright © 1992 by Richard Rodriguez. Reprinted by permission of Viking Penguin, a division of Penguin Group (USA) Inc.

Juan Rulfo: Excerpt from *Pedro Páramo* by Juan Rulfo, translated by Margaret Sayers Peden, copyright © 1994 by Northwestern University Press. Reprinted by permission of Grove/Atlantic, Inc.

Ramón López Velarde: "My Cousin Agueda" and "In the Wet Shadows" by Ramón López Velarde from *Mexican Poetry: An Anthology,* translated by Samuel Beckett. Reprinted by permission of Indiana University Press.

Xavier Villaurrutia: "L. A. Nocturne: The Angels" from *Nostalgia for Death: Poetry by Xavier Villaurrutia & Hieroglyphs of Desire: A Critical Study of Villarrutia by Octavio Paz,* translated by Eliot Weinberger for *Nostalgia for Death,* and Esther Allen for *Hieroglyphs of Desire* (Port Townsend, Wash.: Copper Canyon Press, 1992). Reprinted by permission of Copper Canyon Press.